Praise for *Boys of Alabama*

"A stunner, with prose that is always imaginative and sensual. *Boys of Alabama* feels like a luscious expansion of the voice that characterizes the prose of [Genevieve] Hudson's short fiction: crystallized, vivid, tactile, and totally hypnotic. . . . It is at this meeting of bodies that a love story unfolds. And like all love stories, this one is not tidy, but beautiful."   —Sarah Neilson, *Believer*

"*Boys of Alabama* is a shapeshifting story of queer witchy love in the American deep south. This book is creeping vines, verdant desire; it's a study of belief systems both true and terrifying. Genevieve Hudson dismantles and spins a new category of fairy tale for us, one that's equal parts dirt and splendor. A glinting, dark beauty. An incantation."

—T Kira Madden, author of *Long Live the Tribe of Fatherless Girls*

"A capturing and sensitive novel. . . . Hudson unpicks the themes of boyhood, masculinity, mystery, love, immigration and religion with such strong imagery that I hope it's one day adapted for the screen."

—Ugonna-Ora Owoh, *Stylist*

"*Boys of Alabama* brilliantly reinvents the Southern Gothic, mapping queer love in a land where God, guns, and football are king. I adore Hudson's bewitching characters and the mesmerizing sentences that bring alive their pain and joy. An absolutely magical novel."

—Leni Zumas, author of *Red Clocks*

"With prose that consistently delights and a grasp of character and story that's never less than engrossing, *Boys of Alabama* is one of the finest—and weirdest!—first novels I've read in quite some long time."

—Tom Bissell, author of *Apostle* and coauthor of *The Disaster Artist*

"With *Boys of Alabama*, Genevieve Hudson mixes magic and faith, small-town politics and high school mayhem, to depict a brand of Southern-fried masculinity that is immediately recognizable and startlingly fresh. This is an exquisite book."   —Nick White, author of *How to Survive a Summer*

"Genevieve Hudson's American South is by turns wondrous and menacing, oppressive and sweet. Hudson is a stunning talent, and this novel is a spellbinding exploration of what it means to be a stranger in a strange place."

—Kimberly King Parsons, author of *Black Light*

"*Boys of Alabama* is full of magic surprise. A gripping, uncanny, and queer exploration of being a boy in America, told with detail that dazzles and disturbs. I really love this book." —Michelle Tea, author of *Against Memoir*

"This novel is a love song to outsiders of all kinds, a queer love story about the ways we find to heal ourselves and each other, and proof that there can be magic amid the burdens of masculinity. Hudson's prose is perfect and I will remember her *Boys of Alabama* for a long, long time."

—Melissa Febos, author of *Whip Smart* and *Abandon Me*

"A magical, deeply felt novel that breathes new life into an old genre."

—*Kirkus Reviews*

"In *Boys of Alabama*, Genevieve Hudson creates a new American erotics of longing and belonging, flush with want and desire, hope and home, translation and transformation. A fantastic debut by one of my favorite new writers."

—Matt Bell, author of *Scrapper*

"Hudson writes tenderly about cultural displacement, toxic masculinity, and friendship. This complex tale achieves a startling variation on the theme of teenage rebellion." —*Publishers Weekly*

"*Boys of Alabama* reminds us that behind so many of America's most rigid beliefs lies the lonely human heart: twitchy, slippery, alive."

—Mikkel Rosengaard, author of *The Invention of Ana*

"Hudson goes right to a place where violence comes from—uncomfortably close to desire for magic, God, sex, whatever might actually heal us—and doesn't turn away. A gorgeous, smart debut from an uncannily talented writer." —Kristin Dombek, author of *The Selfishness of Others*

BOYS OF ALABAMA

GENEVIEVE HUDSON

LIVERIGHT PUBLISHING CORPORATION

A DIVISION OF W. W. NORTON & COMPANY

Independent Publishers Since 1923

Copyright © 2020 by Genevieve Hudson

For information about special discounts for bulk purchases, please contact W. W. Norton Special Sales at specialsales@wwnorton.com or 800-233-4830

Manufacturing by LSC Communications, Harrisonburg
Book design by Lovedog Studio
Production manager: Lauren Abbate

Library of Congress Cataloging-in-Publication Data

Names: Hudson, Genevieve (Genevieve Katherine), 1986– author.
Title: Boys of Alabama : a novel / Genevieve Hudson.
Description: First edition. | New York : Liveright Publishing Corporation,
a division of W. W. Norton & Company, [2020]
Identifiers: LCCN 2019051376 | ISBN 9781631496295 (hardcover) |
ISBN 9781631496301 (epub)
Subjects: GSAFD: Bildungsromans. | Occult fiction.
Classification: LCC PS3608.U3455 B69 2020 | DDC 813/.6—dc23
LC record available at https://lccn.loc.gov/2019051376

ISBN 978-1-63149-902-9 pbk.

Liveright Publishing Corporation, 500 Fifth Avenue, New York, N.Y. 10110
www.wwnorton.com

W. W. Norton & Company Ltd., 15 Carlisle Street, London W1D 3BS

1 2 3 4 5 6 7 8 9 0

For my parents

She believed in angels, and, because she believed, they existed.

—Clarice Lispector, *Hour of the Star*

BOYS OF ALABAMA

THE BOYS ARE ALABAMA. They are red dirt and caked mud. They are grass stains on knee pads, names on the backs of jerseys, field goals and fullbacks, Heisman trophies and touchdowns, a fat lip and a happy concussion. They are pine trees ripped up to make room for gas stations, stadium lights, drive-thrus, gridirons, and steel mills. Alabama wasn't built by them, but the boys swell with pride, a rabid and real thing like peanuts planted in the fields that they can harvest. Their trucks roll over roots and through dry creek beds and their bellies bulge with the surplus of it: the grain and corn culled from the ground that God watered for them. Their muscles remember the past. They know how to gut a deer, how to slice a fish, how to tear cotton from the stem, how to tighten a fist in the middle of a hot house and lie.

Rivers run fast in Alabama and sometimes as slow and sleepy as one of those rocking chairs abandoned on a porch where women used to sip sweet tea and wait. Wait for something that isn't coming, because nothing comes to Alabama anymore except for you.

PART 1

From the plane, Alabama unfurled in green fields and thick forests. Wilder than Max had pictured. Trees went in all directions and houses were hidden among them. He touched his nose to the glass window. The aerial engines whirred. The plane banked against a shelf of sky. The landing gear slammed into place, and his mother, the fearful flier, gripped the hand rest between them. She slid her fingers over the back of Max's wrist. They descended over a neighborhood of slanted clapboard shacks that leaned toward one another, strewn junk going rotten in the yards.

You've got the good seat, said his father. The plane lowered and lowered. Front row to the action.

In the airport, Max's family bought sweet teas served in Styrofoam cups so big he had to hold his with both hands. He drank half of it and felt high. Sugar soared through him. He bought a disposable camera in the terminal kiosk from a man with marble eyes and a baseball cap with an Alabama A. Max had attended an exhibition in Berlin the previous month where an artist made collages out of pictures developed from a disposable camera and construction paper. The fuzzy, low-res images had created a nostalgic quality out of dried toast and lonely mandarins. Max held the green plastic camera in his hand. Its picture quality would pale in comparison to the power of his phone, and that was the point. Max wanted to document the drive to his new home. He wanted the pictures he took to look sentimental and unsettled.

Outside the air hung in sheets. It was heavy when he swallowed it and left a taste in his mouth he didn't know how to identify yet. His nose started to run, his legs to sweat, and his breathing moved up into his throat. As they waited for their rental car, his family stood beside a group of men whose skin shone a porkish pink.

On the drive to their new town, Max's mother mumbled, Oh, it's actually quite beautiful, and Max agreed.

He thought the landscape was exotic, all those red rivers they drove past, rushing like arteries cut open across the earth. The sky was burnt blue and the trees were jagged things that huddled together. Forests fattened along the sleepy highway. Max tried to look through the trees to see what was back there, but he only saw rows of more pines pointing upward, reaching. Some had signs stapled to their trunks that warned KEEP OUT and NO TRESPASSING and SMILE YOU ON CAMERA. Others had fallen horizontal, their roots severed like veins, as if a storm or some terrible force of nature tore them from the soil, and no one had cared enough to clear them away.

They passed a billboard advertising BBQ ribs. Then a billboard advertising the Bible. A truck with monster wheels boomed past. It flew a Confederate flag from its bed. Max knew the flag from the movies, but here it was in real life. The line on a bumper sticker: GOD BLESS OUR MILITARY, BUT ESPECIALLY OUR SNIPERS. The family drove for almost an hour with their chests tipped forward. The rental car smelled like Hawaiian Aloha, a scent his father had chosen. A football-shaped air freshener swung from the rearview mirror. This is where the Hawaiian Aloha smell originated.

His mother flicked it and said, Aloha headache.

His mother lit a cigarette and blew a line of smoke at it.

The sunset was enough to make them pull over and step onto the shoulder of the road. Max brought out his camera and his father snapped a picture of him flexing his muscles in front of I-20. A glow stretched across the horizon and electric purple clouds pulled apart like sweet taffy. In Alabama, the sunset held an extra charge, everything did, because everything was new. The pink particles of light wielded their strange power. The sky appeared bigger. Maybe it was.

When the car plant came into view on the left, Max's father jabbed a thumb at it. That's where he would be stationed. The main building was German-looking, white, and clean, with a sleek roof made to mimic a series of coastal hills. The sterile campus and its familiar design relieved Max. He turned his head and stared as the buildings shrunk into the distance.

His father took the exit into town—WELCOME TO DELILAH—and began to laugh. Max wondered if he should laugh, too. Something about the scene did seem funny. It was funny that they had arrived. This was *it*. The car slowed to an inch in front of a series of traffic lights. In the truck next to them, a hard-jawed man in a cowboy hat hung an arm out the window and ashed a cigarette. They were home, if you could call it that yet. On both sides of the street, neon signs pulsed with life. They beckoned with taco burgers, catfish platters, frozen yogurt parfaits, and paper cones of popcorn chicken. There was so much brightness, Max could have forgotten it was night.

They drove down a road named after a legendary college football coach who'd led the team to many national championships decades ago. His father had heard of him. All the way in Germany he knew of the man whose street they drove down. His father seemed impressed by his proximity to the dead man's legacy, pleased with himself for knowing.

If you want to understand this place, you need to understand the pride they have for this man, his father said. He gave them hope. And hope is a remarkable thing to give.

They passed the high school Max would attend, a prisonlike sprawl of low buildings flanked by green fields, named God's Way. The school was a private evangelical school, and although Max's family was not religious, the school had been recommended to them by his father's new colleagues.

The public schools here are full of violent kids.
There's at least one stabbing in the cafeteria each year.
Everyone's daddy's got a gun.
All the boys know where to find the gun.
He'll get a better education in private.
The teachers are more invested.
We aren't going to be able to provide housing in a good school district.
Whether it was true that the schools were as violent as they'd been told, the word *gun* scared Max's parents into obedience.

The houses in the neighborhood frowned at Max from their

perches. The space between the yards excited him. The suburbs. American largeness. The homes looked like they had fallen asleep, their curtains drawn, their interior lights a drowsy blue. Inside the rooms of the houses they passed, Americans did American things.

Max felt television-famous when his father pulled their rental car into the circular driveway of their new house. Houses like this existed only in the sitcoms that came careening into his TV. Ivy climbed and curled up the redbrick face, past two stories of shuttered windows. In Germany, houses this big were reserved for the rich. A stone settled in his stomach when he thought of Germany, all those hours behind him now. He remembered the two Americans he had seen on a bus in Hamburg just days before and how he hadn't been able to stop watching them: their too big pants and the confident grins affixed to their boyish faces. They had seemed assured there in a foreign city, as if it, too, were theirs. Now Max was in America, but he did not feel that it was his.

In his new backyard, blond slates of wood formed a perfect square fence. It reminded Max of a story he had read about an American boy called Tom Sawyer and how Tom's evil aunt forced him to whitewash a fence as punishment for skipping school. But Tom made the work seem like an honor and fooled boys into painting the fence for him. *American boys are clever,* thought Max. *And they want to trick you.* Max visualized himself washing this fence white, making friends from it. *Friends.* He could not imagine. His parents reeled through the rooms inside. They called out for him, but Max stayed in the backyard, taking in the purple night that seemed to glitter with kicked-up dust. He bent down and stared at a blade of rotten grass.

He still spotted dead things right away. Dead grass looked the same here. He plucked the blade. In his fingers, the brown grass turned green. The taste of peppermint filled his mouth. He swallowed the sweetness down, pinched the blade of grass to the wind, and let it go. He almost expected the chlorophyll to stain his hand green as punishment. Shame washed through him. He thought of Nils in his coffin. Cold dead body, cold stretched skin. *No,* he told himself, smoothing the front of his khakis with his palms. He formed a fist with his entire body and clenched it tight. He wouldn't do that here.

MAX'S HOUSE STOOD AGAINST THE back edge of the neighborhood. A highway bent close to it, hidden by sight, but not sound. Max couldn't picture where the cars went, but he wanted to know. They might lead to parties with American boys. To 24-hour diners. To anywhere he didn't know yet. All night Max turned and twisted to the sounds of engines, the occasional hot shriek of a horn, the skid of tires over black pavement. He stared at the plaster ceiling. In Germany, their street had been quiet. He had heard his father cough down the hall, the squeak of his mother's feet on the stairs, nothing more. He had heard neighbor voices, Nils's mother, moving through their open windows into his.

On his first morning in Alabama, birds cried in the trees outside Max's window. Their song was neither happy nor sad. He ran his hand along the sheets. They smelled like eucalyptus, like a detergent called Sunshine. He tried to miss something about Germany.

He walked downstairs, through the cool, open living room. The house seemed breakable, almost flimsy in its construction. Nothing like the solid brick home his family had in Hamburg. Their new rental had come furnished, but the house looked somehow familiar to him in the daylight. It was every house he'd ever seen in an American movie. The words *Sweet Home Alabama* had been cross-stitched in crimson and hung above a fireplace made from river rock tiles. He touched the birch of the frame and thought *home*. But it sounded more like *home?* in his head. The couch held large pillows upholstered in blue stripes. He imagined the nap he would take on it later. He rubbed his temples. The ache was back. Claws gripped the corners of his eyes. He held up his hand to study its subtle tremor. Still there.

The couch faced a flat-screen television. The walls around him had been painted daffodil. Cheery like outside. An antique bowl sat on the coffee table. Grapes spilled over its sides. Max pinched one grape and watched it ooze. He thought of an eyeball plucked from a face. He picked another grape and placed it inside his mouth. Sweet burst of green on the tongue. A distraction in the body. He craved sugar again. All it took was one blade of grass and the symptoms rose up in him. He almost missed the comedowns, the hollow of exhaustion that overtook him, the headaches that sent him to sleep. No amount of sugar or exercise or afternoons spent in dreams could serve as enough balm to distract him from his most base desire. Max sunk his bare toes into the thick carpet. Carpet. The tacky, bandage-colored material covered all the floors.

Max walked out of the front door, which was two doors and not one. A wooden door then a screen one. He squinted into the brightness and inhaled the smell of dug soil. He felt eyes press into his back. Someone was watching him. He turned to see a neighbor woman in her garden.

Y'all must be the new Germans, the neighbor woman said.

She stood with her hip cocked to the side, grinning temple to temple. Her voice had a drowsy quality that Max wanted to curl up against.

We wondered when y'all would show up. The old Germans said new Germans would be coming soon. Never could say their names right so I just called them the Germans. Hope you don't take offense to that.

Nine a.m. and the neighbor woman held a diet cola. She walked over to Max and extended five fingers tipped in red talons. Max shook her leathered hand, which went limp at his touch.

Honey, look at you already sweating.

She laughed but not at him.

How to say it, he said. It's very, what is the word, wet.

Humid! she said. Honey, don't I know that.

She had slathered her face in makeup and wore flip-flops bejeweled with rhinestones. Her hair hung in loose, self-imposed curls. Most bizarre to Max was that she wore an oversized red football jersey. The rest of her outfit seemed to call for another kind of shirt, a blouse of some sort, anything besides a sports uniform. Max liked her right away. He hardly understood a thing she said but her eyes sizzled and cracked with life. They seemed to say FUN. Max's mouth twitched, as if he had no choice but to smile, too. Her name, she said, was Miss Jean.

Y'all better come over one Saturday to watch a game. Too much excitement to miss. The season's not too far off now. So y'all mark it on your calendars, you hear?

Please? Max said. Can you say it one more time?

The word *y'all* confused him. The phrase *you hear.*

Miss Jean didn't answer. Something else sat in her mind.

Saddest thing. That's Tammy's house. Was Tammy's house. See it? She pointed toward the cul-de-sac where a police car nested in front of another brick house. Max squinted.

I don't mean to gossip with you, she said. Her voice dipped into conspiratorial tones. But what kind of neighbor would I be if I didn't say something? Aneurysm killed her in the middle of the night.

What? Max said.

Killed?

Now tell me how in the Sam Hill does someone as healthy as Tammy fall down dead out of nowhere? I can't pretend to understand it.

It sounded sad but Miss Jean recounted it in a singsong voice.

Someone died? asked Max. On Sam's Hill?

I wouldn't worry about it, hon, I'm just telling you to keep saying your prayers each night. Keep on praying. We never know what God has in store, now do we?

Max did not mention that he didn't pray, had never once in his life thought to pray.

The screen door hit its hinges.

Max's mother called to him from the porch.

Max, will you to introduce me to your new friend?

It was strange to hear his mother's English, but he guessed he'd get used to it here. She walked up to their neighbor to say hello, and Max marveled again at her command of the language. Her confidence with the American words in her mouth. His mother looked odd beside

Miss Jean. Her cropped black hair and swooping bangs did not flatter her in the morning light. Next to Miss Jean's coin-colored face, smeared in bronze blush and golden eyeshadow, his mother was plain and underdone. Her lips looked sucked of color.

You speak such good English! You sound like you're from Australia. Not Germany!

His mother had studied painting in London for graduate school, and her English arrived in a British accent. His parents had met in an expat bar in North London and lived there for many years before moving to a small studio in Paris's Twelfth Arrondissement, where they would have continued their international life with their international friends if his mother had not gotten pregnant and his father had not taken a practical job offer in his hometown in Germany to support a new family.

I don't know about Australia, his mother said. But thank you.

The old Germans did not speak English this good is all I'm saying.

Miss Jean recommended breakfast at the Touchdown, and that's where they went. Eating out for breakfast! A rare occasion to mark a rare day.

~~~~~~

A WAITRESS with a meringue of yellow hair wearing what appeared to be a cheerleading uniform led Max and his family to a table set with jars of sugar and hot sauce. Photographs of the college football team were tacked from ceiling to floor. Grainy images from the early 1920s showed players in leather helmets and wool sweaters. In more recent pictures, sleek uniforms stuck in sweaty patches to the curves and divots of the players' shoulders and stomachs. Their arms were raised in V's for victory. They had won, won, won. It appeared that they were always winning. Even their grins were winning.

A dozen national championship flags hung from a beam by the kitchen. Max let his eyes linger on the lore affixed to the walls: the stuffed elephant mascots, the old-time ribbons decrying greatness, the lyrics from a fight song scrawled on the back of a famous quarterback's shirt. Portraits of coaches shouting, discourteous, praying beneath a flag. WHO BELIEVE IN 2009???? was scribbled across a large poster board. Under it lived the names of every fan who knew their team would take the championship that year.

The photograph above Max's table showed a bird's-eye view of the college campus. The football stadium reached over the top of even the highest building, like the university's castle. Lights pointed their golden faces toward it, as if to italicize its significance. The campus was in another town about an hour away. But its lore, the storied football team, reached all the way to Delilah and beyond. Pride raced down every red dirt road in Alabama.

Max's father whistled and flicked his fork toward the frame.

His mother said, Well, they certainly are proud.

Reminds me of Rome, Max said. He snapped a picture of the picture with his disposable camera. Like the Colosseum, he said. The size of them. The stadium's huge. People take trips there just to look, right?

His mother snorted.

Max took a picture of his mother drizzling honey over her biscuit like the cheerleading waitress recommended.

I've never tasted something this good, said his mother. She held up her biscuit and stared at its breaded face. They imported you from heaven. I'm sure of it. Almost makes me believe in this God.

Max chewed on something called chicken-fried steak. His craving caused him to pour syrup over his meat. His mouth stung with a sweetness that reached into the roots of his teeth. He took more pictures of the photographs above their table. The players made him think of Florence and the summer he'd seen the David statue, how he'd pushed his way to the front of the crowd to gaze at the Roman body. Here were those same lines chiseled into football players from Alabama as they reached their notched arms out to catch something coming right for them.

MAX HAD NEVER WATCHED an American football game, but when the guidance counselor asked what he was good at, his father cut in and said: Max is a runner. Fastest on his track team.

Max eyed the crucifix on the counselor's wall, the daily devotional that doubled as a calendar on her desk. The guidance counselor smiled at Max with a new warmth.

Oh, she said. You'll be a football boy.

Max's father nodded. He draped his arm around his son's shoulders.

That'll keep you busy, he said as they walked out into the soupy afternoon. Keep those headaches away.

At practice, the boys on the football team towered over him. Their shadows prowled beside them like animals on the freshly sheared field. Their eyes were soft, and their teeth were tinted Coca-Cola brown. The heat did not slow them. It sat in sweaty foreheads and shimmered down their necks. Max had difficulty enduring the weather. Monday was hotter than Sunday and Sunday had been hotter than Saturday. It seemed to continue that way, each day trying to stuff more heat inside itself. Relief happened at the less-hot times, early mornings when the sun was just a promise edging at the sky and in the late afternoon, nearly dusk, when the midday rain had left a layer of cool behind it. Sweat found Max anyway. It slipped out of his body and greased his limbs.

Coach lined the players on the edge of the field. They crouched low. Max heard himself breathe inside his helmet. He'd been tackled with such ferocity he feared his ear was bleeding, but he hadn't had a chance to take off his helmet to check. His elbow throbbed. His knee screamed. His leg made a right angle with the earth.

Ready.

Coach jabbed at the air, and the whistle trilled.

Run!

Running was the only part of the game Max understood. The shape of the ball and the arrangement of the offensive and defensive lines puzzled him. The slow way they moved toward the goalpost. The pain of collision and the courage it took to hit someone bigger than you. But to run, he understood. His body shot forward.

Max pulled out ahead of the pack of boys, revealing his speed like it was a kind of trick. He could hear their grunts behind him, trying to catch up. His legs burned. He lived for that feeling, that burning under his skin like his muscles might melt. He liked to reach through the pain and touch what was on the other end of it. He could run forever. As Max won each round of sprints, he felt himself becoming a prize. Suicide after suicide, he hit the white line first.

Nazi dude sure got a talent for gassers, said a boy named Davis.

Max winced.

Do not please, he said, call me that.

Davis's corn-silk hair was long enough to slip behind his ears. He studied Max. Max hoped he hadn't sounded too formal. He hadn't learned the regional slang yet. He smiled because he knew that Americans liked smiles. This was something his mother had told him. Americans like smiles and they like pleasant, happy things. You should speak as though you are ending your sentences with an exclamation point. Everything should sound cheerful. Awesome and amazing.

All right then, Davis said. He spat at the ground. We'll call you Germany then.

Davis didn't smile, and Max wondered if something had gone wrong. Davis had perfected a scowl of detached evaluation that could sweep over a person and bring them into immediate awareness of their own physical shortcomings. But Max had a feeling Davis wanted to be his friend. He didn't know what he had done to deserve it, but he basked in the promise of it.

This here is Wes, Davis said catching a handsome player by the shoulder and corralling him. He's like a pinch of genuine Miracle-Gro sprinkled upon our dumb, dirty asses.

Max must have looked confused because Davis continued.

What I mean is—he brings the magic to the team. Wes is our quarterback. His arm is a wonder of the world. So, handle him with care.

Pleasure, said Wes. His hand extended from a limb of pure, perfect muscle. Max watched his bicep flex and felt something tighten at the base of his tongue.

A pleasure, Max said back because he didn't understand the context of the word, and what he didn't understand, he repeated.

Max here is from Naziland and we're going to call him Germany.

Cool, said Wes. Sup, Germany?

Wes here is the whitest black boy on earth, said Davis.

It seemed Davis meant this as a compliment, and Wes smiled and shook his head, but Max wasn't sure what Wes was thinking. Max was not skilled at discerning what lived below the surface of a person.

Max here is one fast fucker, said Davis.

I like to run, said Max. Feels freedom.

Davis said, Say what? You feel freedom? That's cute, Germany. I need to remember that one. Running feels freedom.

Davis spread his arms before him like he was visualizing the slogan written in the clouds.

Wes began to laugh. The two of them, Davis and Wes, stood in the sun laughing until Max began to laugh, too. It felt good to laugh with other people.

As Max got in line for the next drill, sweat pouring down his chest and his whole aching torso, he was happy. He'd never played a team sport. Never felt like another person might count on him and come to love him for how well he played a game. Coach patted Max on the back and his spine grew an inch to meet it.

During a Gatorade break by the bleachers, Max looked up toward the parking lot at a line of trucks. He noticed a figure pacing the lot. Max had a moment of déjà vu. The figure smoked in broad daylight on school property. There was something about the angle of the elbow as it lifted the cigarette, something about the way the chin tilted to the sun. The familiarity unsettled him. The figure walked in front of a row of pickups like a kind of dark angel, beautiful and gaunt and hawkish in high heels and lipstick so black Max could see it from where he stood. The figure seemed to be waiting for something. Davis caught Max staring.

Every town got a witch, don't it? said Davis, who was standing in line behind him. Well, that up there is ours. Don't worry. He don't bite.

Break was over. Davis shoved him forward, and Max stumbled toward the orange cone that marked the start of the sprint.

Impress me, Coach yelled as they ran. Show me you're faster than I think you are. Impress yourselves. Show that boy next to you how bad you want it! Show yourself how bad you want it.

When Max finished running, he scanned the parking lot for the witch, but it was gone.

Someone named Knox came up to Max as they walked to the locker room after practice. His eyes wouldn't focus when he talked, a side effect Max attributed to the continual collision of helmet on helmet at high gait. Knox was missing a tooth. Not one of the front ones, but a noticeable one in the back of his mouth.

You fast as a Cheeto, Knox said. A goddamn Cheeto Puff. He sounded pleased. Goddamn, he said. Now we just need to see if you have soft hands.

Max stared at his hands. What did Knox know about his hands?

It's another figure of speech, Max assured himself. *It's about catching a football.*

You all right, Cheeto Puff? You look spooked.

A patch of hair fuzzed above Knox's lip. He licked the sweat from it. The fading light lit up his acne scars, which were driven like craters into his skin. *He cares,* thought Max, *about how I am.* Max glanced again at Knox's missing tooth, at the black nothing between his molars, and Knox snapped his mouth shut. Max felt he'd done something he shouldn't.

A group of boys hollered past them and took off running up the embankment behind the metal backs of the bleachers. Knox jogged ahead to catch them. The boys' butts flexed beneath their dirty football tights as they ran. Max averted his eyes. The scoreboard's bulbs were off, but the presence of the dimmed lights standing sentinel along the field reminded Max of the stakes of each tackle. The gravity of each yard.

MAX WOKE UP WITH HIVES. The headache behind his eyes pulsed white each time he blinked. He took a handful of Skittles from his bedside table and swallowed them. Running helped. He could travel through the pain. It healed him. He took off toward the highway behind his house, but he stayed on the shoulder. Cars yelled their horns at him as if running on the road was so weird, they had to comment on it, scare the impulse out of him. It worked. One truck drove so close he thought the side mirror might clip his arm.

Get off the road! bellowed a man from the truck's open window.

The vehicle careened away, leaving Max in a cough of mean smoke. He jogged from the main road, down the side of the shoulder into a slant of land where something like a sewage drain carried sludge and leaves in a slow trickle. It looked almost like a creek. Beyond the creek, a wooded area thickened with spindly bushes and pine needles and tallish trees.

He sat down on a slab of concrete and caught his breath and stared at the forestlike thing in front of him. Stuff grew everywhere. Really, everywhere. Heat pulled life out of the cracks in the concrete, gashes in tree trunks, putrid planks of wood. A purple bloom grew out of a rubber tire. But a bunch of things were dead, too, burned up and withered. Max moved his gaze over the death uneasily. The wilted azaleas, trampled clovers, a cat with a bouquet of flies buzzing above its mashed brain. People here did not take care of the land or the creatures in it. He popped every knuckle on his hand and tried to push down the urge clawing its way up from some hidden place.

Death had begun calling out to him years ago, when puberty mounted his body. It had come as suddenly as the new creak and boom that thickened his voice. That winter had been lonely and long-shadowed.

Max had been walking behind his house in Hamburg, under the naked arms of the trees when he discovered a dead mouse. Steam had lifted up from the tuft of fur, and bright blood stained the white ground. The year had been filled with sadness, and Max couldn't take another inch of it. Not even the dead mouse. He had knelt before it and let out a sob. Snow had drenched the corduroy of his knees. That's when the feeling had gotten into him. Like a voice whispering in his ear: *Touch the body. Eat the death.* Max could taste it even now in the heat of Alabama, like a flake of snow melting into his gums.

The mouse's life had been hovering somewhere nearby, caught in the air just outside of its body, and Max had known that he could guide the life back into the mouse if he tried. It would be like pointing the way. Max remembered taking off his mitten and directing one finger toward the mouse's belly. He had touched it, slowly, as if to pet it. A warm blue had spilled into the back of Max's throat. The mouse's life had tasted like a slow stroll through a garden at sundown. The tail had twitched, and Max had watched as the guts wiggled back in as if the animal were eating its intestines. Max's tongue had turned into a blueberry. A burst of ice. He had continued to stroke the body, and as he did, it repaired itself.

Max had wanted to tell Nils immediately, to climb through the window of his friend's bedroom and confess what he had discovered, his terrifying new ability, but they had stopped seeing each other by then. Max had been standing in the yard between his house and Nils's. He had looked toward Nils's room half expecting to see the gaunt face, pale as a plate of salt, watching him. But no one had been watching. The window had been empty and the curtains inside were drawn.

Max had wondered at first if the mouse had just been sleeping. But he tested his ability again on a beetle and then a rose. Both burst back to life. Both left stains of sweetness in his mouth. He had felt chosen, but for what, he hadn't known. For days after, he had sought out death and had delighted in what he could do to it. His hands were magic. They could save. The new power thrilled him until it didn't.

The chosen feeling turned to fear. *Where did the power come from and what did it want?*

Max stood up from the log. He shook the memory away and walked toward the dead cat. *Whose cat was this?* Max wondered. He knelt down. It looked so dead. Maybe the cat belonged to a girl, a small girl who buried a shoe box filled with torn paper and no body. The girl must miss her cat. *How evil was he,* Max wondered, *if he did not bring the animal to life for the sake of this catless girl?* He pictured her discovering her pet returned—alive and purring.

No, Max thought. He grabbed his right hand and shoved it into his pocket.

Clips of memory came colliding back.

His mom at Nils's funeral.

His hand a thing he hated.

What happened to your hand, honey?

I saw him punch a window threaded with steel.

That's ridiculous.

Max had told himself: *Be normal in America; watch someone kill a cockroach, walk past roadkill, let the butterfly stay withered between two panes of glass.* The curse could stay in Germany along with the rest of his strangeness and darkness and shame. Max held his right hand down with his left and trudged back up the hill. A dead bush withered before him. He saw this new landscape, and he couldn't help himself.

He ran his hands over his arms like he was cold. He ran his hands over his face and down his neck, trying to keep them busy. *Maybe it was worse to leave the things dead,* Max thought. No cars charged down the road behind him, a lull in traffic. He was alone. It was so quiet now. No one would see him. He walked to the brain-smashed cat. He picked it up and felt a warm body purr in his arms. He tossed it back to the ground. It landed on all fours and meowed. He struck his hand through the dead twist of shrunken, budless branches. It felt so good.

Burst of honey crystal.

Wet raspberries.

Syrupy apples.

Max dragged his fingers through the jasmine bushes. The wilted buds burst into bloom behind him. His mouth a tart cherry. His mouth a rose and an orange. Max never knew how the soul of a dead thing would taste as it traveled into his mouth, through his body, back into form. But death always tasted sweet. Even though the sweetness never lasted. It wore him out. The recovery period required long naps that lasted an entire afternoon. His healings induced bright, burning headaches, sharper than the hiss in his eyes when he stared into the direct sun.

A boy his age shouldn't be sleeping all afternoon.

Shh, he just lost his best friend.

What's with the sling?

He should be playing with other kids.

He's sleeping with a wet cloth across his eyes when it's daylight.

He's just different, that's all.

He's failing his classes.

He falls asleep at his desk.

As Max walked through the Southern death, he used his power on everything in his way: dried-up leaves, a stepped-on spider, crushed clovers.

He stopped, panting, in the middle of the thicket and glared. A fence stood right in front of him. This piece of forest wasn't so big after all. It was just section of land running between the road and part of a neighborhood. His neighborhood. A dog began barking on the other side of the wooden slats. Max's heart pounded in great, thundering blows. The traffic in the distance came charging toward his ears. He'd been careless. He was not alone.

Something back there, Bruno? called a gruff man's voice. What's back there? Who's there?

Max fought the urge to ram his knuckles into the bark of a tree as punishment.

Who's back there, Bruno? the voice graveled again, closer to the fence this time.

Max took off running toward the incline, toward the shoulder of the main road. Running felt good, that familiar fast feeling in his legs. *How could I be so stupid?* His stomach turned and burned. The people in Alabama had been so nice. But would they talk to him so sweetly, he wondered, if they knew what he could do?

DELILAH DID NOT HAVE a town square. Delilah had stores laid out in strips, one real mall, about a dozen churches, and state-famous BBQ restaurants that promised to make you lick your own fingers. It had cotton fields and enormous amounts of land owned by men. Men owned the earth in Delilah, and you weren't allowed on it unless invited. That's what Max's mother explained. In Germany, you could walk anywhere not circled in by a fence, but here a man could own the ground and forbid others from it. If you entered without permission, anything could happen.

In Delilah, you could eat breakfast at gas stations. Max's mother dropped him off at the gas station near school so he could get a biscuit before class. He'd walk the rest of the distance to God's Way alone. Max felt silly standing in line in his uniform. The stitched cross anchored over his left breast. In line in front of him was another student. When Max got closer, he saw it was the witch. The witch's name was Pan.

Pan said, I reckon you as new.

Just have moved here, Max replied.

Daddy's got a job making SUVs? asked Pan.

How do you know this?

Vell, let me vink.

My accent, said Max. Okay.

Max noticed the stick-and-poke tattoos on Pan's hands. REAL read one, LIFE the other. They weren't sentences, but they counted. Pan held his REAL hand out toward Max as if it were something he did every day, as if his fist were anyone's fist, as if Max could shake it and then put it away. The déjà vu feeling rose up again and unfolded around him. He had the sensation he was standing with Pan inside a memory they shared. They had met before. He was sure of it. He almost asked: *Do I know you?*

Pan ordered a biscuit with no chicken. It made Max want to eat no chicken, too.

Gracias for the titillating convo, said Pan. Welcome to the U S of A. See you around. I hope.

Pan brushed past him, touching Max's hip with what seemed like intention.

See you around.

IhopeIhopeIhopeIhope.

Pan in his all-black. Pan with his goth choker and the gel that made his hair go straight up. Pan with the smooth skin he covered in dark brown foundation. Pan with teeth that stayed braceless and crooked as crossed legs. Max stood in line blinking. The cashier had to ask if he wanted butter or bacon with his biscuits twice.

Three times.

Four.

Please yes. Bacon and butter for the biscuit. Please yes.

Max smiled at the cashier.

He arrived late to Physics and found Pan scrawling furiously in an open notebook. The witch had been transferred into his class. Their teacher divined them as lab partners. *A miracle,* Max thought. *No small thing.* Pan looked up from the desk, mesmerized as he seemed to be by the grains of wood, and smiled like he expected him. Max shifted under Pan's gaze, which ran the length of him in one flash. Pan's cheeks were stamped with freckles. Max never realized chapped lips, held open like that, could look exotic.

One with the biscuits, said Pan. I knew we'd meet again.

Pan kept a collection of comics in his backpack. He pulled one out and placed it in his lap and read it as the teacher lectured. Teacher was orange-skinned with buzzed blond hair and breath of burnt coffee. Pan's comics were not the adventures of Tintin but comics about monsters and muscled men. The world was always about to end but it never did. Good always stepped in. The day was saved from evil. Heroes existed. Pan fiddled with the choker on his neck, a clipped piece of panty hose. Twirltwirltwirl. Max glanced down at the comic that covered Pan's crotch but could only make out the word *Ka-Pow.*

Pan giggled as he read the panels. He elbowed Max beside him, as if Max were in on whatever joke he discovered.

Teacher made the class stand up, gather in a ring in front of their desks, grab palms. He showed them how to pass a charge of electricity around the circle by just holding hands. Muscles might spasm when static electricity triggered the nerves. Before class disbanded, an assignment was given. Pan looked at the textbook in front of Max.

Be careful with hot wires.

Pan circled the caution in a paragraph about electricity.

Don't leave batteries connected for more than several seconds at a time.

AFTER PHYSICS, MAX HEADED to his locker to switch his books. A girl stood by as if expecting him. Her nose turned up like in the movies and her hair framed her face in close-cropped braids.

New boy, she said. Allow me to introduce myself.

A different colored bead sat on the end of each braid. Her name was Glory. When she turned her head, the beads tinked.

How do you know I am new boy? asked Max.

Glory picked at her bitten nails. Hands of someone less confident than she presented.

For real? There's like fifty kids in each class. Getting a new kid is like getting a celebrity. We get one or two a year. Most of them just sit in the back of the class and look terrified. You get extra points for being an exotic German. But word on the street is your English is dialed in.

Germany is not exotic, said Max. We are not an island. We eat a lot of sandwiches and potatoes. Here is glamorous. The sun is what you have.

Glory was the only girl he'd seen who wore the uniform of a boy. Girls at God's Way wore skirts or jumpers. Pants were for the boys. Everyone wore a polo with three buttons and the embroidered cross.

Okay, a geography lesson. Word, said Glory. Listen when you need a rundown of shit around here, you come to me. I'll give you intel on whatever you're looking to know.

Can you say it again? asked Max.

You got a question, said Glory. I got an answer.

Max stared at Glory.

You play football? asked Glory.

I'm going to be wide receiver.

Cool, said Glory. I don't know what that means but football is as much religion as religion is around here. Friday nights are all football. You'll meet Davis. Might have already. Best friend status with Davis is like tying yourself to a social life raft. So, you're good.

I'm good? Max asked.

It means you did it right. You're all right. No one is going to mess with you. You decided who you're going to be.

Football makes me a decision?

Sure does, said Glory.

And do you know also Wes? asked Max.

You can't say stuff like that here, said Glory. You can't ask me if I know Wes just because we're both black.

Is that what Max had done? he wondered. Red crept into his face. He had done a racist thing maybe.

Everyone here knows everyone. Wes's my brother but that's beside the point. Just because you don't know any black people doesn't mean all black people know one another.

Max opened his mouth to apologize, to find the sorry word. He wasn't sure if Glory meant Wes was her brother as in biological or brother as in friend. Brother in American could mean both. Glory changed the subject before he could get clarification.

You got a question you want answered. I got an answer. Just remember that. This school is small. I kick it with the public kids mostly. If you ever want to widen your gyre. Let a girl know.

Widen a what?

It's a Yeats reference. Aren't you Europeans supposed to be cultured and shit? I'm saying if you want to expand your circle to nonprivate school, I'm your person. Hey—

A girl with a red pigtail on either shoulder and a bright blue monographed backpack walked past them. The air smelled of a boiled meat sandwich. The girl with the pigtails had a cabbage odor, but Glory waved her down excitedly. The girl drove something into Glory and stole her attention. Max was no longer the center of things.

Adios, Germany, she said. Catch you when I catch you.

WHAT CHURCH YOU GO TO ANYWAY? Davis asked, threading his belt through the loops in his jeans.

The locker room steamed around them. Davis looked solid standing as the vapors rose across his chest.

Religion is fine for people who need that kind of thing.

We're not that sort of family.

Church, said Max. We still look.

Listen, said Davis. If you haven't been to church before or if your family doesn't go or something, it's nothing to be ashamed of. We all start somewhere.

Yes, said Max. Okay.

You don't have to do what your parents do.

Davis sat down on the bench. The locker room's steel corridors stood empty, but Max could hear the spray from a running shower and knew they were not alone.

Davis bit into a protein bar and said, Stuff tastes like a cardboard shoe. You want a bite? You're supposed to eat protein thirty minutes after working out if you want to get swoll.

Max shook his head. He wanted a chocolate bar. The one in his backpack. A dead spider near his shoe. He tried to focus on Davis.

You ever wonder what else there is to all this, Germany? Like you ever wonder what the meaning of it all is?

Yes, Max said. Yes, I wonder.

Davis lifted his face toward Max. Max saw in Davis's squinting that he'd said the right thing. It was good to wonder. To want more.

There's church and then there's God, Davis said. He used a finger, pointed at Max, to hit the end of each word. People get church wrong a lot of the time. But then God comes for you so fast it knocks the wind from you. He sends his spirit to you and you can't help but go blind.

You go blind? Max was confused. Max had always believed that God, in terms of religious people, helped you see better. God did not obscure your sight.

Yeah, I mean it's a speech figure, said Davis. It sounds confusing, but you just feel it. Some things are better understood in the body than the mind. Davis placed his hand over his heart when he said *body*, as if that's where it lived. Right in the chest. The center of the body breathed. God will send his love to you and you'll never be alone again. You just make sure you believe—and God, he'll do the rest.

Max looked down at his hands, which held his chocolate bar, which he hadn't remembered fishing from his bag. Someone opened the door to the parking lot and a brush of hot air whipped through the room. Max bit into the bar and chewed.

MAX STOOD ON HIS PORCH in his football sweatpants, hair still matted, and sleep crusted in the corners of his eyes. A fresh bruise fattened across his chin. Max pushed the bruise and thought of the boy who gave it to him. He stayed outside for a moment, loving how the rays of morning sun struck him as if to cleanse him. It was a Sunday. Church was where the boys were. He thought of what Davis said about going blind for God. Blindness might steal your literal sight, but Max understood how constriction worked. Other senses would expand to take over the deficiency. Without sight, who knew what you would hear, taste, or smell?

Max touched the ivy that lived on the bricks of his house and considered blindness, a kind of gift. The living green vine curled around a dead yellow sprig. He left the dead parts dead. He would need to run today, he told himself, as he left the browned edges as they were.

Max brought in the paper. By the door, a bouquet of tulips shot their heavy heads out of the end of a vase. He noticed his mother had removed the magnet from the refrigerator—BUT FIRST, COFFEE! Max's mother called church a gateway drug, so he knew better than to bring up his curiosity. He slid the paper from its plastic and spread it across the kitchen table.

Again, the Judge. Front page. The Judge, with his square-shouldered stance, looked nothing like his oafish son Lorne, who played football with Max. He looked like an advertisement for a good father or for testosterone supplements. Max spread his hands over the photograph, over his jaw and the smile lines etched into either side of his mouth. The Judge's eyes were clear as a stream. They seemed to look up from the rough paper and straight into Max's soul.

The smell of ground coffee rose through the kitchen. The percolator gurgled and the clink of espresso cups meant breakfast. The table had been set the night before, a routine his mother brought with her to Alabama. Max should have gone to retrieve the yogurt, but the Judge peered up at him. He held eye contact with the Judge as his father filled the table with deli ham, dry sponges of American bread, boiled eggs, and raspberry jam the neighbor had brought to say welcome.

The Judge was running for governor and his campaign announcements were everywhere: taped to restaurant doors, stuffed into mailboxes, pressed into the worn leaves of Bibles that girls clutched to their chests at school. The Judge gazed down over streets from billboards, like he was keeping watch or like he was God or God-sent. Max took a seat and his father picked up the paper to read it.

Look at this, his father said. The man's campaign slogan is *Rise up, Alabama*.

Max leaned closer, so he could read the headline. His mother joined them. She had expressed many times how disappointed she was by the tasteless kitchen, the breakable appliances, the tacky stone-look laminate countertops. Her posture conveyed more disappointment. Slouched shoulders, unlike his mother. She peered at the newspaper, too.

A populist thug, his father said. This article says he's trying to make it mandatory for every resident of Alabama to register with a church or religious organization.

His father whistled as if that was something.

What's next, a Kristallnacht? said his mother.

Says here he can quote the entire Bible by memory. Entire pages with not a word missing, his father said. Says God places the paragraphs right into his brain.

It's called a photographic memory, said his mother. And many people have it. It's not some kind of miracle.

Says here, his father continued, leaning close to the page, he fell from a cliff in his twenties and died. He was left out in the woods wandering around for days as a dead man.

Fell from a cliff? his mother said.

Says he fell the length of seven stories and survived nights out there alone. He ate nothing. On the last day, he drank a can of poison he found in an abandoned shack. After the poison, he saw God and was given new strength and suddenly knew exactly how to leave the woods and find the road to town. God turned the poison into something that healed him.

It's called a hallucination, said his mother. This man is leading the governor's race? People believe the story and vote for him?

From his mother's plate, a piece of unbuttered toast stared at the wooden ceiling. She did not eat it. She looked displaced in the new kitchen and defeated. She had been excited to have more time to paint in Alabama, since she would no longer have her job volunteering at the modern art museum, but Max did not see her easel unpacked or her paintbrushes unrolled on any surface.

Well, it's an impressive story, his father said. Don't you think?

His son plays on your football team, am I right? Max's mother asked, turning to him.

Yes, said Max.

He tried to appear unmoved by the story, but the truth was he found it intriguing. The Judge had cheated death. Death had entered him, and it had not stayed.

I heard him say on the NPR they should teach creationism in schools, said his mother. Creationism. As in God made the world in seven days. Is that what they're teaching you in science class? Are they teaching you intelligent design or are you learning evolution?

I don't know, said Max. We haven't gotten there yet.

You'll probably never get there, said his mother. That's how they'll deal with it. I don't care what they believe. Honestly, I just don't want it to affect your education.

What kind of things do these boys talk about on your team? They say anything that sounds off to you? said his father.

No, Max said. They just talk normal stuff. Boy stuff.

Boy stuff? said his mother.

His mother snorted and whacked the top off her boiled egg with the back of her spoon, splitting the shell. His father took a sip of orange juice and stood up, groped his pockets for something.

Okay, he said. Well. I mean, I've never met the man. But his story is a tall tale if I've ever heard one.

People love a story, said his mother.

His dad shrugged as if he wasn't sure and didn't care.

Max regarded the Rorschach blob of jam smeared across his yogurt. On the face of his breakfast, Max saw a raspberry boy sprinting across an organic, whole-milk field. He saw a seedless red cross rising up behind him as he ran. He saw a risen Judge bleeding life into a white sky.

AT WALMART, MAX FELT SMALL in the huge expanse of space. The shelves were filled with American treats like peanut butter cups, candy corn, and marshmallow squares his mother would never let him eat in Germany. He walked past pyramids of Kit Kat bars and displays of vacuum cleaners and shelves filled with condoms and strawberry-flavored lubricant. He walked past a wall of television sets playing three different football games. The television faces spoke in silent sentences to no one in particular. He stood in the middle of an entire aisle of Bibles. He'd never known there could be so many different kinds of Bibles. Max could have bought guns and two-liter bottles of Coke and lawn chairs in one trip. He could have bought anything at any time, because Walmart only ever closed one day out of the entire year, Christmas, Jesus's birthday. He wasn't in Germany anymore. He knew it for sure as he stood in aisle 7 under the hiss of the bright white lights. He wanted to fit in, Max realized, as he touched a bag of Cheetos.

You fast as a Cheeto, Knox had said. The memory made him smile. A cartoon cheetah with sunglasses stared at Max from the front of an orange foil bag. *Dangerously Cheesy*, promised the cartoon cheetah.

Max used to love going with this mother to the market in town for dark bread. It would still be warm from the oven as they carried it home. He could feel the weight of it in his hand now, heavy as a potted plant. He stood in the Walmart bread aisle, which smelled of nothing, especially not bread. The sterile, plastic-wrapped loaves sat slack on the shelf. There seemed to be more things to buy in Walmart than people in town to buy them. *Who*, he wondered, *would purchase all this bread? All these TVs? All these guns?*

Max asked a Walmart employee where he could find the fried chicken. The salesperson wore a scoutlike vest with many patches of smiling yellow faces pinned all over it. HOW MAY I HELP YOU? was written in bubbly font on his back. He looked too old to be working a service job. To be working at all. He walked with a plastic cane. He kept calling Max *sir*. Like—*Yes, sir. I can show you where the chicken is, sir.* Max felt he should be the one calling him *sir*, since he was younger, but he went along with it. Before he walked away, the man raised a speckled hand and said something that sounded like Haffagoodunnowyahhere. Max nodded and that seemed to be enough. The chicken sizzled and steamed in a paper bag below a row of blistering lights. The bag fumed as he carried it to the checkout line.

His mother drove him to Davis's house. Max could not drive in Alabama. He did not have a license and his parents weren't keen on him getting one anytime soon. The other boys could drive and owned their own vehicles, which they drove to school themselves and let bake on the black asphalt lot. They waited like treaded chariots. That's freedom, thought Max. To be sixteen and own a car.

Davis's house loomed at the end of a cul-de-sac, surrounded by smaller, lesser houses with fewer levels and puny yards. Max counted three stories out loud with his mother in the car. Sunlight hit the clean, white paint and glinted against a wide, screened-in porch where potted ferns and sculptures of rattan elephants guarded a rocking chair. Max readied to knock on the front door but voices beckoned from the backyard.

There he is, said Davis, when Max walked into the barbecue with the exact right thing.

Coach surrounded Max in a hug that contained much slapping. His back stung from the flat hand hitting him.

Walmart's got the best fried chicken in town, Coach assured Max.

Max lifted a chicken thigh to his mouth. The meat was the sweetest flesh his tongue had ever tasted. He gnawed. He chewed at the bones. He pulled barbecue onto his plate. The sauce stained his chin and got under his nails until he was marked like the rest of them. It felt like he signed his name to something important.

Max had never been invited to a party before. In Germany, his classmates had found him incredibly strange. His lonesome runs that stretched on for hours, the way he always needed people to repeat themselves, the time it took to form the right word with his mouth. After Nils died, he had sometimes worn a sling around his arm as a reminder not to touch anything dead in front of other people. He'd cinched down his fingers with ace bandages and said he sprained them. Sometimes he inflicted real harm on them. *Weird boy with the weird bandages. Runner boy always running away.* But in Alabama, no one had a reference for how Max should act or how he should respond. If he stared at someone without talking for whole minutes after they asked him a question, they thought it was an issue with translation. His strangeness was connected to his foreignness. If he didn't know how to say a thing correctly, it was the language he hadn't mastered, not living itself that he couldn't do right. He could learn everything like it was the first time. A second chance.

The boys streamed music from speakers. They walked through the music in their camouflage pants and hats with cursive A's and cartoon elephants holding footballs. It was exactly what Max had seen in the movies: a party in the backyard of a suburban house with cars parked in the driveway and gallons of soda poured into plastic cups and paper napkins to use once and throw away. People brought jars of white sauce and slathered the meat in it. He watched a man open a soda can and pour in a pack of sugar. Max couldn't stop admiring how similar it was to what he expected, even with all the ways it was different. Someone asked him—what you want? Cola? Diet Dew? Grape?

When Max said nothing, they said, Why you smiling goofy like that? Cat got your tongue?

Max blinked at them. His face told them he did not understand.

Aw, he's just messing with you, said Davis, who dug his hand deep into a cooler full of crushed ice. A Coke appeared in his hand. He held it out to Max.

Here you go, buddy, Davis said. Loosen the mind. Soften the spirit. You're wound real tight. I see it in your jaw.

Just messing with you, Max thought in his head. He popped the top of the Coke. He tried to tell his shoulders: unclench the jaw. *Cat got my tongue.*

Thank you, buddy, said Max, trying out the new word.

The boys and their fathers wore clothes a size too big. They seemed to dress intentionally unstylishly, as if to announce their masculinity, but somehow, maybe without meaning to, they'd invented a new style. The dress code was specific and mandatory. Their feet wore strappy sport sandals or cowboy boots or sockless boat shoes. The shirts that hung from their shoulders were pastel polos or rayon casuals or ragged white tees with Confederate aphorisms. DIXIE REPUBLIC. THIS IS OUR HERITAGE. They clasped delicate gold crosses around their thick necks. The songs they played told of tractor trucks, fishing lines, and girls in short skirts who loved them. They sung these songs loudly. They tossed their arms around one another's shoulders and swayed. One song was about Alabama itself and how blue the sky was and how sweet it was to be home and how big the wheels were that would take them there.

Knox's dad slapped Max on the back, startling him back into his body.

That'll put some hair on your chest, son, he said, giving Max's frame a once-over.

He pointed at the Coke perspiring in Max's grip and laughed.

Scrawny, isn't you? said Knox's father.

It was true Max's body appeared smaller than the others who loomed above him, bloated and strong. It was true his chest was without hair. Max gripped his can tighter.

Just don't drink too many.

Knox's father narrowed his red-edged eyes, frowned from behind a slim, drawn face, like he was scolding Max for something he hadn't done yet.

Too many will make you fat. You want to be strong. Not fat.

Okay, said Max. I will not too many.

Not okay, said Knox's dad. *Yes, sir.*

Apologizing, Max said, Yes, sir.

Fellas, said Coach, with his booming voice. Fellas, circle up!

He raised his pitch, so he could be heard above the chatter.

Wes turned down the music and took off his hat.

I want to pray with y'all, Coach said.

The crowd swarmed him. They formed a huddle, almost like it was muscle memory. The warmth of the bodies could have felt smothering, but it had a sedative effect.

Know why? Coach said. Because we got something to lift up to the Lord God right here. Right now.

Max looked around. The boys nodded, peered at their feet, squinted at Coach lit by the sun. Max wondered what they had to lift up, wondered what lifting up even meant. He stepped back into the crowd, almost behind the toe line, trying to blend in.

Fellas, we got a new friend that's come to us from all the way over in Europa.

Max's heart struck the curve of bone around it.

Max, son. C'mon over here. C'mon here, son.

Coach moved his arm in a corralling motion, gesturing for Max to come to him. His voice was lighter than it was at practice, silky at the edges, almost inviting with that peculiar, pleasant twang. Max walked over and stood beside Coach. The sting of being watched spread over him, squared his shoulders. Coach's skin had the charred sheen of someone who'd spent a lifetime outdoors. Max could see Coach's son, Hayes, in his father's hook nose and watery eyes, in the square tips of his fingers that he now slammed together in front of his polo-clad chest. The boys bent their heads in unison. Someone named Graham kept staring at Max and nodding his head with a deranged look, like one of those bobble-head dolls that keeps bobbing forever, eyes painted open.

Father God, started Coach. We know whenever two or three are gathered in your name you're here, too, God. So, we want to take that opportunity to welcome Maximillian today. We ask that you make his heart a fertile ground for your seeds of everlasting love to sprout. We ask you be with him, bless him, and keep him well in his new life here in Alabama. We ask you use *him* as a vessel to do *your* blessing.

Coach's hand rose up and clasped Max's neck. Max felt the Coach's calluses. The hand squeezed. Maximillian was not Max's name, but he said nothing to correct this.

Father God. Coach's voice split down the center. The grasp on Max's neck tightened. Max wanted to step into the crack of his voice. The voice could carry him. He might like where it went. The emotion that clenched Coach's voice raised a response from the crowd, too. Max had never observed emotion in a man like this, in a man like Coach, who preferred crudeness and coarse talk and handshakes that hurt you.

Yes, Lord.

Yes, Lord.

A minute of silence passed. Max heard the traffic in the distance, the breeze thick in the trees.

Lord God. We ask you protect this boy. Show him your love so he might see you as we see you. Let him never lose the faith.

Amen! Coach bellowed to end it.

Amen, Father, said the boys.

Amen?

Amen!

With the final amen, the tension that had seized the backyard eased. Coach's voice returned to its growl. He gave Max a shove.

All right, boy, all right, he said, chuckling to himself.

All right, said Max.

Son, Coach said. Coach leaned in so that their eyes were fixed on each other, at the same level. Max focused on the sty on Coach's left lid. Do you know the love that Jesus Christ has for you?

What? said Max. I mean, he said, catching himself, What, sir?

Coach's brow had a high, skeptical arch. He seemed to want to say something else but thought better of it. He slapped Max on the shoulder. *So much touching,* thought Max.

You'll know soon, son. The Lord's got plans for you. For all of us.

Yes, sir, said Max.

Good boy, Coach said, giving him an uneasy once-over. *Good. Boy.* Then Coach walked off.

Wes turned the music back up. No one else seemed affected by the outburst of prayer. Above them, the sun sizzled. Everyone flushed under a fine layer of sweat. Max's neck was sticky from the meat of Coach's hand. The spot where he had held him while he prayed vibrated and hummed. He didn't want to touch it, for fear that he would wipe the sensation away.

Wes licked his thumb and stuck it into Max's ear. Max laughed. It felt good to laugh. Wes laughed back like they were friends.

They lifted their Cokes to the chemical blue sky and toasted to their luck but also to their God. The can was so thin, Max wanted to crush it in his fist. He wanted to crush the moment in his fist. The music opened up. It reached the treetops. It pushed into the leaves. The twang of them singing out of tune together swallowed the afternoon in one boyish yawn. Max wished he knew every word to every song they sang, and he pretended he did.

LATER THAT NIGHT, THE BOYS pushed a cooler off the back of a Ford pickup truck and carried it down a red dirt road. The night was tar black with stars punched into it. Something unsettled Max about the smells: like rotting wood, wet hair, and skin that'd burned and blistered. He tasted mud on the roof of his mouth. There was a strand of grass in his molars.

Davis said: Feels like we're walking on a dog's tongue.

All teeth and heat and sweat.

The sound was running roaches smashed beneath steel-toe boots and wind slapping at the bushes and the kind of deadened silence that only comes past midnight in rural parts of America. Country ballads lifted from the speakers somewhere in the darkness ahead. A fire snapped. It guided the way like a door cracked open at the end of a hall. The field, which belonged to Cole's father, careened into black-black for acres on either side. It had taken nearly an hour of winding down skinny roads with many right turns to get here. Nothing had been marked. The boys just knew the way.

The fields had once contained cotton, but Max didn't see any white heads reaching up from their stems. He saw shadows. He saw his hand only when it was in front of his face. The land was undressed by all the darkness. Like it'd been stripped down. Like it had been left to go wild.

The boy Max rode with said, Where the ladies at?

Max thought girls would be at the patch of bald earth that'd been trodden down to something worn and grassless for socializing. For late-night whatevers. A pit for fire had about a dozen boys from the team circled around it. No girls. A few logs. A shed with a broken window. A four-wheeler and some old barrels that looked like they were there for sitting. The same song from the barbecue was still playing. Or was it a different song? The chords were so full of long-ing, Max felt like he was right beside the girl singing about her sexy man and his tractors and his fishing lines and his big red dogs.

A boy named Price put his elbow on Max's shoulder and leaned in so he could whisper. The bill of his dirty ball cap edged into Max's forehead.

Price said through his stutter, Looks like someone brought the god-damn witch.

Max's eyes found an image on the other side of the fire. The shock of Pan in fishnets. Pan's legs were crossed at the knees. He sat on the back of the four-wheeler next to Lorne, whose hair was orange as the flames. Lorne's wide chest was covered in a camouflage shirt with deer running across it. *Lorne.* The Judge's son. Lorne was a sluggish and muscled boy who seemed to have as much personality as a blade of sun-dead grass. Nothing like his sinewy father, whom Max had seen on the sideline of football practice, clapping and whistling. When Lorne had joined his father near the watercooler, Max had watched them huddle in what Max had come to recognize as prayer, hands clasped to shoulders, heads bowed.

Lorne prodded Pan with his hooded eyes. His lips opened and closed in something Max recognized as hunger. Lorne was quiet and cagey anytime Max had been around him, but that night he seemed to have a lot to say to Pan. Pan stroked his own tuft of coal-colored hair as he listened to Lorne, nodding occasionally. Pan's back was ramrod straight; he moved from his core with an elegance that seemed acquired from other worlds. Movies maybe. Or books on dancing. Max wondered if he was a dancer. He pictured him spinning in the middle of an empty room with four beautiful white walls. He might leap into the air and land spinning or land in a split or land on the tips of his toes. Max thought Pan would look beautiful in a room with four white walls because his features were so drawn and heavy and dark. There was something in them that sprung out like they were shouting the word *look*. His mouth was as red as a cherry pit but that night it was painted even redder. Max could see, or did he just remember, a black mole shaped like America beneath his left eye. He tapped at the four-wheeler's bumper with the heel of his fat army boot. He and Lorne appeared to be flirting. The flirting seemed clear to Max. He glanced at the other boys. *Did they see the flirting, too?* The longer he watched, the clearer it became. Pan scooted from his seat and led Lorne into the tall grass.

Price watched Max watch the two silhouettes disappear.

Jesus H. Christ, said Price. He thinks he's a frigging princess. Look at that outfit.

What? Max said, because the snap hiss of the fire ate the words from the boy's mouth and plus, he was distracted. Can you please say it again?

I said princess over there wants to be a freak and sometimes we let him.

Price shrugged as if it were an inconvenience no one could do anything about. He spat a kernel from his mouth into the fire. The small black stone smoldered, and Max wondered what kind of a freak Price let Pan be.

A freak for sure, said Wes. Once he lit his feet on fire and just laughed as they burned. We could smell it. We poured beer on it or who knows what would have happened to his toes.

Yeah but the freak didn't have any burn marks, said a boy named Boone. Like what the actual F?

I think he liked it, said Price. You know? He likes the pain.

Max understood. He bit down on his tongue to remind himself how much he liked pain. Price's eyes, which were the striking green of a Mountain Dew bottle, danced with mischief. Had Price said *you'll know*—as in, one day, Max will know, too? Max wasn't sure he heard it right. A cold sweat broke out on the back of his neck and under his armpits and around his cock.

He's only been like that, all freaky, for a year tops. Maybe two. He used to look preppy as a frigging boy scout. It's some kind of weird-ass phase or something.

What is preppy? asked Max.

Preppy, said Price. I dunno, man. It's like fancy. It's like buttoned-up and kind of rich or something, but you don't have to be rich to look preppy.

Preppy is like boat-riding clothes, said Knox.

Max couldn't believe it. He tried to imagine Pan preppy, peering from under the same swoosh of bang that hung over the eyes of the boys beside him. The thought made him smile.

What is happening next? asked Max. He wanted the boys to tell him everything they knew about Pan.

Beats me, said Price. He's going to grow out of it. My dad says it's a call for help.

That's about right, said Knox. A big-ass call for help. I don't know why Lorne bothers with him at all right now.

Wes shrugged. They used to be tight, he said. I bet he's trying to save him. He doesn't want him in the fire pit of hell. Roasting and setting his feet aflame like we know he does. Lorne can be sweet like that.

It's about time he takes some rat magic, said Knox. See if God's gone from him or if he's still in there somewhere sleeping.

Price jabbed Knox in the side.

Ow, said Knox. What the fuck, man?

Keep your trap shut. We don't want to freak out Germany.

The boys were lit in orange by the fire in front of them.

Davis handed Max another beer. The necks of the bottles were sweating. Max touched the cold glass to his forehead and wondered about the rat magic.

Hey, Davis said to Max. Say y'all again.

Please, Max said, flashing a smile. I would not like to.

He sound like a goddamn Nazi, don't he?

Max decided to laugh with them this time. They could call him a Nazi, he guessed—though it made him wince. The fire in front of Max smelled sweet. Like tree spine and tree blood and tree brain. Like a log of cedar splayed perfectly along the groove. Max thought of Pan's feet on fire and how the burning must have stank of shells and keratin and human skin. He saw Pan roasting on a spit in a pit of hell as flames licked his charred calves. He saw himself on the same spit. He popped his neck. The coals in the fire turned white with heat. A boy picked up a can of gasoline and held it in front of his crotch and spurted it on the flames.

Cicadas buzzed in the background from their secret spots. The air was heavy as tea steam. Wind didn't move it. Max steeped in it. His feelings brewed until they were strong as a tannin. He sipped his beer, which was going warm, and searched the grass, through the stems, through the black-black, for a sign of Pan and Lorne.

Excuse me if I need to go to the bathroom, said Max. Where is it?

Urinal's right there, said Price, pointing to their field.

Max walked to the edge of the field. He tipped a stream of beer into the dry split-up dirt as he urinated. He was afraid to get drunk, to unclench his mind in that way. The field bunched together and seemed to release an outbreath of air that cooled him, as if the stalks themselves could offer their own shelter from the sweat and swamp of sky. He noticed a dead worm half buried in the dirt. He directed his urine right onto the worm. Then he bent down and touched it. The pink slime wriggled back to life.

Max flexed his biceps and balanced on his heels. He admired the smooth skin of his ankles. His shinbones dusted in white blond hair. He didn't believe that Lorne wanted to save Pan. He'd seen the way he looked at him. He knew that look.

Back at the fire, Knox came up to Max with a plastic bottle. The liquid inside glowed a strange green.

Made this myself, Cheeto, said Knox.

The mouth of the bottle smelled astringent. Even a whiff was potent enough to snap shut his eyes.

Please thank you, said Max. But not tonight.

Aw really? Cause you're scared? said Knox. It'll put the moon in you.

Knox pointed to the moon above them. It looked like the bottom half of a smile.

Please, Max said. I don't want the moon. Not tonight.

Knox studied at him. It was an expression Max had never seen, something between suspicion and intrigue. If he could pluck a thought from the hulking boy's head and read it, Max would. Knox took a swig of the moon juice while staring Max right in the eyes. Then he sat on the ground and began to hum. The song sounded familiar. Knox hummed as he began to crawl a circle in the dirt. Max felt someone grab his arm. He turned, and there was Davis with his set mouth. Davis ground his jaw at something in between his teeth.

Don't mind him, Germany, Davis said. He needs to be in private.

⁓

WHEN LORNE emerged from the stalks, Max was sitting on a log by the fire and Cole was sprawled out on his back in front of him. A beer bottle stood on his chest. Cole looked graceful in repose as his muscles relaxed against the twigs and pebbles. The same music played, and Max sailed through it just the same as he had all night, reliving the same feeling over and over again, the soulful shudder.

Lorne walked toward two boys huddled near the shed playing War on a turned-over cardboard box. Max did a sweep for Pan. But he wasn't there. He hadn't returned. It was just Lorne, who still looked hungry. Maybe he would always be hungry. Even when Max hunched down in the bed of the pickup truck and it bounced over the dirt road back toward town, Pan was still gone.

Dawn was revealing herself over the treetops like a lady pulling up the hem of her skirt. Dawn was a headache that was as pink and light blue as the veins that ran over Max's eyelids. He watched the fields for Pan, watched to see skinny hips shake through the tall stems, but he saw nothing. Knox was curled up in the bed of the same truck singing, moaning for Jesus, calling out for Jesus like Jesus was a woman he could love. Max lay on his back when they hit the main road and let the air from interstate lift the night off his clothes and he shut his eyes, so he couldn't see the clouds or the telephone wires or the billboards with their fine font and pornographic pictures showing off everything he could ever want to eat.

MONDAY MORNING. Lifted trucks and beat-up sedans and jeeps with roll bars filled the school parking lot. Girls from the cheer squad applied makeup in the back of a pickup. Max's mother dropped him off by the front steps. It smelled like hash browns. The sun shone bright as orange juice. Pan stood on a curb that gave way to a hill that sloped down to a freshly mowed practice field. He pouted beneath a black tiara perched in his black hair. It seemed people at school mostly ignored Pan's weirdness.

Pan drew in a deep lungful of his Virginia Slim and shot out a clean blue line of smoke. Max had to stop himself from grinning. He had worried all weekend. He had made up scenarios in his head of Pan being left for dead or Pan hitchhiking home on the lone highway and being picked up by an ax murderer or a truck-driving rapist, all of which could happen here in America. He had imagined Pan getting lost on the back roads and deciding, why not, to just take up home in a shack somewhere forever as a runaway. He had thought: *Might not see him again.*

Pan wore mesh gloves and his bangs hit his eyebrows like they meant it. He combed the gridiron where two boys were running suicides. He turned his head in Max's direction as if Max had called out his name. He pulled at his cigarette and dialed his eyes right into Max. It sent fish swimming through him. Max averted his eyes, pretended he was thinking of something that made him look at a variety of objects without realizing it. He pretended Pan was one of those objects. He turned and walked toward the school and its sullen brick face. He climbed the red stairs into the red building. The heat drew a smell from his armpits. Or at least Max pretended it was the heat.

In Physics, Pan sketched concentric circles on a paper between them. What are you doing tomorrow night? Pan asked.

Me? asked Max.

No, the girl behind you, said Pan.

Max looked behind him to an empty chair and realized a joke had been made.

Lol, said Pan. You're funny. Yes. You. You got plans or what? After practice, what are you doing?

Dinner with my parents like is usual.

We need to find a time to work on this project. I was thinking it's a nice idea to do it outside of school. My house is a wrecking ball right now. So, can I dinner at your abode?

You want to come over?

Can I come over to work on our project? asked Pan. To your house?

Pan sat straight and did not move his focus from Max. The boy's attention unsettled him. Pan dug at his cheek to get at a mosquito bite as he waited for Max to respond. The bite bled and Pan's finger took a smear of makeup away with it.

You can please, said Max. Yes.

THE YEAR BEFORE, MAX HAD attended a Gordon Parks photo essay exhibition on a school trip to Amsterdam. The exhibition documented the segregation of the Deep South. Later, when Max's parents told him they were moving to Alabama, it was this exhibition that came to his mind. He would not live in the America of New York or California. His would be a different America. The idea delighted his father, who had grown up living in many of Europe's biggest cities and found the American South to be a mysterious location for a family adventure. Max had never lived outside of Germany, though his father had taught him to speak English like an international, preparing him for such an occasion. His parents had given him what his father called an international name. *Anyone in the world can pronounce Max.*

Max remembered one photo from the Parks exhibition where under a sign that read ICE MILK SOLD HERE, a black girl drank from a water fountain marked COLORED ONLY. A line of people formed behind the girl but to her right stood an empty fountain. The sign painted on its front said WHITE ONLY. He had felt the white ice of the milk travel down his throat as if he had drunk it himself. Kept it only for himself. Sweat brimmed on the brows of the men and women who waited. Max knew people became the place where they lived and made up all kinds of reasons to justify their becoming. He knew normal kids whose grandfathers had been Nazis. Max wondered what kind of a man he would become if given the choice. No one could tell him that yet.

Another photo at the exhibition showed two black boys and one white boy playing with plastic guns, grinning straight into the lens. The hand of one boy had extended with a pistol that pointed at the viewer, one eye closed in a squint like *bang*. It had surprised Max to see the black boys and the white boy playing as friends, as if they liked one another. All three boys looked poor, and Max wondered if it was the poverty that had united them. There were many things about Alabama he already didn't understand. Max brought the photo to the front of his mind and placed it beside the image he had of Wes and Davis, their helmets in their hands, staring at him like he was the camera, walking toward him. This didn't seem like the same Alabama from the photos.

Wes said, We're going to stay late today and I'm going to teach you how to catch.

First game's coming, said Davis. You might not start, but we don't want to lose those legs of yours. They can be, like, a secret weapon.

Wes stood before him in his blue practice jersey. Not the hunter green school colors they'd wear on the first game.

Wes ran him into the ground. He arced ball after ball into the air and Max missed them all. Max looked over his left shoulder just in time to hear the ball crash into the grass over his right.

Wes said, Let's go again.

Patience came easy to Wes, who explained the rules two times. Three times. Seventeen.

Wes showed Max the three-point stance. How to burst off the line of scrimmage. Wes crouched beside him.

Now try it a dozen times, said Wes. Then a dozen more.

The sun tipped behind the trees and the blue above them slanted into orange and then purple. Wes kept throwing. Fireflies turned on and blinked like stars in the space over the field.

You're getting it, said Wes.

Never cradle a ball to catch it.

Hold your arms away from your body to receive.

Keep your thumbs together, spread your hands as wide as possible.

Beautiful. Yes, that's how you catch. That's how you do it, son. Three in a row. Beautiful!

MAX HAD NEVER KNOWN PRIVACY like the kind he had in Alabama. His bedroom was giant and had its own bathroom attached. He could regard the green lawn outside his window. Down the street were houses just like his. Rows of them. He could see, if he looked, the same blue television in the window of each living room. The trees that lined the wide, well-paved lanes grew to the same height because they had been planted at the same time. These were nothing like the unkempt forests that lined the country roads.

At six o'clock every evening, an old woman with a stick for fending off stray dogs would stride down the road in front of his house. Walking was so out of place in Delilah that the sight of her caused Max to pause whatever he was doing and observe her from his bedroom window. There was something rebellious about the sight of her. That night Max did not see the woman because he needed to get ready for Pan to come over.

His thighs and hands ached, and Max welcomed it. Wes had called him *son*, had said he was *beautiful*. Max combed his hair slick to his head. He spat at his reflection in the mirror and watched the bubble cry down the glass. Max did not see beauty. He tussled his curls. Nothing sat right. Max's face usually pleased him but now it made him want to rip his own shirt from his shoulders. An ogre stared back. Pan was scheduled to come any minute. They had planned to build a magnetic field that was stronger than the earth's.

Pan arrived late. When the doorbell rang, Max sprang from the recliner he had been sulking in as if nothing was wrong. Pan didn't apologize for his tardiness. At dinner, he would only eat potatoes. *Vegan.*

Aren't you supposed to live on red meat and friend chicken around here? asked Max's father.

I don't identify as around here, replied Pan.

Max's father stared at Pan for one long beat, perhaps unwinding the meaning of what he said, perhaps wondering if he should probe further into the subject of around here. Max and his mother stuck forks into the meat on their plate. The blood had been baked brown. The texture was the right amount of chew.

Take whatever you like, Max's mother told Pan.

So, what do you eat then? asked his father. If not meat?

I'm a fan of Spaghetti Hoops, said Pan. They're my favorite. My number one. The perfect portable food item.

Max had been relieved at the sight of Pan in Carhartt overalls, not leather chaps or a lace bodice or even a delicate dark chemise. He did not want to sit at the dinner table with Pan in girl clothing and his father stroking his khaki beard. Max could almost see the boy scout Price had told him about. He noticed the hint of another person, a previous self, in the way Pan wore the overalls almost like a man. His stubble was coming through on his chin.

I was going to order a bucket of thighs from the Chicken Shop but now I'm glad I didn't, said Max's mother as she passed Pan more potatoes. I get so nervous when I think about cooking Southern food. You know I read in a regional cookbook to sprinkle potato chips on top of casseroles? For the topping.

Common as apple pie, said Pan.

I was maybe a vegan once, Max's mother said. But I couldn't manage to get the protein.

You never were a vegan, Max said.

I was, she said. But I ate eggs and fish. Does eggs and fish count?

I'll let it slide, Pan said.

What will you let it do? Max asked, wondering if this was part of the American politeness he'd heard about. But she was not vegan. Egg is not vegan.

I'll count it, said Pan.

And where are you from then? Max's father asked, as if he couldn't help himself any longer. Originally?

Max looked at Pan, at his high cheekbones and deep tan. The way his genes came together on his face meant foreign, but foreign from where was hard to tell. Max would have believed it if Pan told him he had appeared from somewhere spectacular like thin air.

Mexico? His father asked, settling back in his chair with his glass of milk.

Max stared into his lap. He'd never felt embarrassed by his father before, but now the sensation was as real as the meat on his plate.

I'm not from Mexico, said Pan. I'm from right up the road. Born and raised. Unfortunately.

Where are your parents from then? Max's father asked because the answer didn't satisfy him. Mexico?

Pan said his mother was from Puerto Rico.

Puerto Rico, said his father. Bingo! He said this with pride, like he'd won a prize, like Mexico and Puerto Rico were the same thing.

He smiled and tugged at his beard but let it go at that.

When Max shut the door to his room upstairs, he apologized for his father.

He doesn't care actually where you're coming from, said Max, feeling his face heat up again. He wants only to know because he's curious.

Honey, said Pan. It's as depressing as a jail cell in here. You seriously need to decorate.

Max stared at his blank walls as if seeing them for the first time, and at his bare dresser with the lone blue comb atop it, his clean beige carpet, and the T-shirt folded on his bed.

Pan asked Max if he had ever met a witch in real life. When Max said he guessed not, Pan asked if he believed in witches.

In ghosts I believe, said Max. In dead things I believe.

Thought so, said Pan. That's close enough by me.

Is it? Max said.

The way Pan stood in the center of the room, so calm and confident, made Max fidget. He tried to stand in the most normal way possible, hands tucked into his pockets, chest pitched proudly out. In his head he repeated: *Not nervous, not nervous, not nervous.* It was a mantra. A manifestation. And it worked zero percent.

Want to learn how to cast a circle? asked Pan.

It was Max's turn to speak but he had no idea what a circle was or if he wanted to cast one. It was quiet in his room. Max heard the foundation settle and the walls creak as they breathed out.

Say something, said Pan. His hands hung at the end of his pin-thin wrists. They fell stunningly by his side. You look nervous as a cat in a room of rocking chairs. You scared?

Max felt like he was on a date, but he knew he wasn't. Maybe it was that he wished he was on a date. But he didn't know what a date even was or how to do that here or anywhere.

Pan unzipped the jacket he'd been wearing over his Carhartt's. Beneath his overalls was just skin, no undershirt at all. Pan wore a Band-Aid over each nipple.

No, said Max.

Mascara clumped in the corner of Pan's eyes, and Max fought the urge to reach out and clean him.

Course you aren't, said Pan. Now sit down and be still.

What is circle? Is that like a prayer? Like rat magic?

What did you say? said Pan. Did you say rat magic?

No, said Max. Fear replaced his curiosity.

Pan smacked his thigh.

You almost sound like someone who's been here a minute. Have they started on you yet? Are you saved yet?

Saved? Asked Max. What does it mean, saved?

He thought of the Judge falling from a cliff and not dying. *Was that saved?*

Okay, said Pan. So not yet. That's good. Now just sit down. Why be saved when you can just be safe?

He made Max cross his legs on the floor and focus on his breath as it traveled in and out of his lungs. Pan ordered Max to concentrate on the feeling of air entering the chest, expanding, and scraping through his throat and nose on its exit. Max opened one eye long enough to watch Pan point to the four corners of Max's room and recite a mantra at each cardinal direction. He pointed up and down and then Pan flicked his own chest.

Circle is opened, said Pan.

Pan spoke nonsense words, a guttural sound, a spew. Max became light-headed but maybe it was because he held his breath for a long time. They sat for what seemed like ages in complete silence. Max became bored. He wondered if he could fall asleep sitting up. He wondered if Pan had any real power or if this is what he meant when he'd said he was a witch. He peeked again at Pan and his eyes were wide open.

This is the question-and-answer part of our séance, said Pan. Time to go deep into the tangles of our minds. Ready?

We go into the tangles, said Max.

What do you really want from life? Pan asked.

I don't know, said Max. His throat tightened. I have not so much thought about it.

That's okay, said Pan. That's normal. It's the answer I expected. No one really considers what they want from life. Unless you're brainwashed. Then you think you know. But you don't know. We all just walk around like robots doing what we think we're supposed to do and then we die, said Pan. It can make one very depressed.

Max thought he understood what Pan meant.

Max said, I think what I want is the exact same thing as what everyone is wanting.

Pan scrunched his forehead.

No, you don't, he said. I know you don't. I can already tell. So, don't say that and start lying like a liar.

Sorry, said Max. What is it you can tell?

I said you're not like the others. I can see that plain as the day is long.

Pan wrapped his jacket around his skinny shoulders like a lady tightening her shawl in the cold.

Max tingled from all the attention. *What could Pan see?*

What kind of witch are you? asked Max.

Have you ever seen the television show *Psychic South*?

Max hadn't. Pan explained how during the show the producers made psychics compete by taking them to places where horrible things had happened: churches, steel mills, piers on the edge of an ocean. Then the psychics had to reconstruct the event that happened in detail—the rapes, the murders, the burnings alive. Whoever recounted the event the closest to the truth won.

I saw a woman tell of a stabbing like it happened right before her, like she was there. She's that in touch with the spiritual realm, said Pan.

Pan was training that same power by going to crime scenes in Alabama and standing in the energy and concentrating on his visions. He was learning how to detect trauma in the molecules of the air.

I went out to a gas station last week where a group of men murdered a woman they knew, he said. I stood near the dumpsters and felt my whole body beginning to bruise. My legs left the ground and I started to drift up to the power lines like something was going to tie me to them. But when I opened my eyes, I was alone. No one was with me except for the wind and the rats and the trash.

You are being serious? Max said, unsure if Pan was telling the truth.

I was inhabiting the past moment. I was reaching back toward the killing and for a moment I was close. I had visions. But I never got there completely. I hit a spiritual wall.

Is this what witch is? asked Max. Is psychic and witch the same thing?

Basically, yeah, said Pan. Basically.

Pan riffled through his purse and handed Max a pair of scissors to hang at the entrance of his door. The scissors had red plastic handles.

For protection, said Pan.

Protection from what? Max asked.

Pan ignored the question and said, If you decide what you really want from life, there are visualization techniques you can practice to manifest your destiny into reality.

Pan said, You can learn to make a force field. To be a magnet.

And Max walked right up to Pan when he said it, so how could he not believe him?

That night, Max thought about the odd Pan and his odd words. *Toodalooooo* was how he'd said goodbye. He'd kissed his cheek like he was French. *Strange.* Max stretched out in bed and felt the humidity raise acne on his neck. He jerked the sheet off his stomach and considered the question *What did he want?* Had he ever thought about it? Max had forgotten to ask Pan what he wanted. He wished he could travel back in time and ask him. He would stare right into his odd face and say *What do you want anyway for this life?* It seemed like Pan had thought about it, like he would have an answer. It would be different if Pan had wings, if he had fangs, if his nails were pointed, if his tail were wide, but he was only a boy.

During class, Pan wrote something in his notebook just for Max to see. He scribbled: *Ignoramuses don't even believe in the big bang theory or the evolutions. They think God put dinosaur bones in the earth's crust to trick us. How about the earth is 5000 years old? So much for science. Bet it's not like that where you come from. Is it?*

Max didn't know what to say.

Pan swallowed a laugh. He wanted Max to step inside the joke with him. The joke was that an ignoramus was teaching them, and that science was real. Max picked up the pencil after Pan put it down. The utensil was warm from his touch. Max wrote: *Wow. Would make my mom freak. She loves science.*

Freak, a saying Max had recently picked up. Along with *flip your shit* and *go mad.*

Pan wrote: *Tell me about Germany.*

Max wrote: *Very different in Germany. Also not so different.*

Then the bell rang, and time was up.

At lunch, Max ate with the football team. They placed chips that smelled of vinegar inside their ham sandwiches and smashed the white bread, so he could hear the sound of something break against a layer of mayonnaise. The fruit punch they drank turned the tops of their tongues neon. Max watched their tongues go flat in their mouths as they haw-haw-hawed about how they shoved a melted chocolate bar in a boy's boxers during gym so that it looked like he had shit himself. The boy had to go home for a new change of clothes. He had been chosen as the target because years ago he had farted during history class and when he stood up shit had slid down his leg. The boys would never forget.

He cried like a baby, said Knox. A baby who shat himself.

The boy hadn't come back to school yet with his new clothes but when he did they would be ready. They would redo the candy bar incident but worse. The boys would jump him in the locker room and shove the candy bar up his butt and pull a pair of shit-on boxer briefs over his head. The new candy bar was naked of its wrapper and sealed inside a plastic bag. It sat in the middle of the table like a centerpiece. Graham bragged about how he snuck into the girl's locker room the week before and jacked off into a shampoo bottle in their showers.

Max had vaguely heard of the concept of American hazing. His gut clenched. He jabbed at the layer of marbled ham hanging from his sandwich, hoping no one was going to ask him to do something like that. But he enjoyed the sound of the boys' laughter. It soothed him the way the sound of autobahn traffic did, whirring when his dad went particularly fast. Max could close his eyes and get lost in the drone of wheels purring over pavement and engines vibrating at fast speed. But there was always something threatening running underneath the highway rumble. It was harmless until it was not. All it took was one turn and the traffic became dangerous and the laughter became cruel.

Max plowed his fork through a lump of just-add-water potatoes that the ladies in hairnets had applied to his plate. Sandwich and mashed potatoes and chips. Max found the combination intriguing. White on white on white. A woman with purple nail polish had given him an extra cookie. Taking it made him feel bad for her. He hated watching elderly ladies stand on the other side of the buffet in lab coats and serve him. It was worse when they grinned, and lipstick was smeared on their teeth. Sadness could crush an appetite.

Lorne joined the table. He slammed down his tray and started to make his way through a footlong. *He's still hungry*, thought Max. And Max felt hungry, too. Lorne held the sub in both hands in front of his face and opened his freckled lips. He didn't seem to be listening to the conversation at the table, but then he smiled. It startled Max.

He *was* listening. Lorne dotted his mouth with a napkin, guzzled an energy drink, and continued through his sandwich with a kind of ravenous precision Max was sure did not leave any room for pleasure. It was about efficiency. It was about consumption. He noticed Max watching him and raised one finger like *hello*.

MAX STOOD IN FRONT OF the weight room mirror and lifted a barbell to his shoulder. Let it drop to his hip. His bicep swelled. In the mirror, he watched Wes bench-press. Knox stood above Wes, spotting the quarterback in case he buckled under the load. Max switched arms. Davis did legs in the corner. Boone worked out his shoulders on a stationary machine. A vein bulged in his neck.

Coach came in and leaned against the door frame. He said, Max, you got a minute?

A half-eaten ham sandwich sat on Coach's desk. Mustard leaked from the crust. In a painting on the wall, Jesus lifted his hands above the bent heads of a crowd that had gathered. Purple rays shot down from Jesus. Jesus was a white man with rosy cheeks and long brown hair and a sharp angled chin. Max scanned the rest of the office. If God's Way had won trophies, Max figured they would have been displayed on the bookshelf. The only achievements Max noticed in the windowless room were a framed diploma with the Coach's name saying he had earned a BA in exercise science, a heart-shaped photograph of his wife and Hayes, and a taxidermy raccoon Max assumed Coach had killed himself.

Son, we sure are glad to have you this season, said Coach. Even if you aren't starting, you are an asset to our offense. Wes needs a good backup receiver. Someone he can rely on. You keep practicing, and I think you'll surprise yourself with what you're capable of. I see determination in your eyes. Speed in those legs. Now that's not something we teach. That's something God gives you.

Max nodded.

Coach opened the playbook and turned it toward Max.

This is Wes, said Coach, pointing to a square with the letters QB in it. Wes, he's the focal point of the offense—the one who starts every play. Knox, center, snaps him the ball. Wes drops back. This here. This would be you.

His pen landed on a circle with the letters WR in it.

You're nimble. You're fast. You got to move quick. Zoom. Zip. In and out.

Max nodded again. He let the sport sink into him. The plays he'd need to know. He tried to grasp the fundamentals. Coach leaned in closer, and Max leaned in, too.

A text message found Max standing in his kitchen about to slice the midsection of a lemon. The sight of Pan's name on his screen caused his stomach to rise into his sternum. Pan sent a selfie of himself drinking diet Mountain Dew with just his lips showing: bright green on skin where drink met mouth. The next text showed a pink tongue extended. A blue Skittle sat in the center. His cat, Mr. Sprinkles, was curled up on his shoulder.

Protection, Max thought.

Before going to sleep, Max listened as the protection scissors above his door swung from a string hammered into the crown molding. They seemed to sway mysteriously. No breeze touched them. The tip scraped the wall and started to chip away at the paint. It was like Pan was in the room with him picking at the color, tapping on the door. *Pick, pick. Tap, tap.* Max didn't need protection. He rolled over in bed and dreamed of suicides on the wet field in the wet wind with the strong boys.

In Physics, they wrote notes back and forth in the margins of Pan's comic books. Pan took a Sharpie and drew a dress on Superman. He gave Mary Jane Watson a huge dick. He outlined thought bubbles that climbed from their lips.

What should she say? Pan asked Max. He wanted to put words in their mouths. What should Mary Jane say to Spidey?

Pan spoke of himself like he was a loner, but Max saw he was engaged in many social scenes at school. Girls especially seemed to like Pan. One girl was always by his side. The girl appeared to be enduring a lecture whenever Max spotted them together; a smile perched on her mouth as if everything Pan said was slightly funny. The pair passed Max at his locker one afternoon and Max strained to hear what Pan said, but he couldn't hear anything but the slam-bang of lockers hitting their hinges. Max thought he might walk up to them and say hello, but what would he say after that? He didn't know. Max leaned against the locker. Lockers. In Hamburg, you took all your books home with you from school. But this was just like the American TV shows. Just like *Saved by the Bell*.

At practice, Max watched Pan wait in the parking lot in his tiara. Max threw the football with Wes for warm-up. A man arrived on a motorcycle to pick Pan up. Pan climbed onto the back and held the other man's body. They flew away. The motorcycle engine lingered like a scream in Max's ear.

Distracted? asked a whisperer.

Lorne stood behind him.

He pushed on Max's shoulder pad. The weight of him was much.

No distraction, said Max. Just ball throwing for warm-up.

Good, said Lorne. Big game coming up. First game's a big game. Always.

He winked at Max like he knew him. Max felt the sweat on his face turn cold.

DAVIS INVITED MAX TO ATTEND a campaign luncheon for the Judge. It was a small affair in a backyard. The heat had begun to lift into a temperature that felt almost pleasant against his bare arms. Pan texted. Max knew enough not to tell where he was, but he didn't know where this intuition originated. If he could trace the source of his intuition, Max would say it was a spot lodged under the curve of his right rib.

His instinct told him: *Don't reply to Pan*. And then: *Look up*. Lorne stood in the shade of a ginkgo tree alone. He took his phone from his pocket, stared at the screen, grimaced. Or was it a grin? Max's instinct told him: *Pan's texting him, too*. A crowd descended on Lorne, surrounded him with smiles and sagging paper plates. He put his phone away and shook the hands held out to him. A swing creaked in the wind—a plank of sanded-down wood that'd been hung from two old ropes tied to a high branch. There was something unsettling about the way it moved back and forth, wildly, with no one on it. A cloud traveled across the blue. It was skinny and long and hopelessly white.

There was a good turnout of faces. The faces smiled over red-checkered tablecloths where food gleamed in plastic bowls. Davis orbited among them. The faces smiled as they smeared spoonful after spoonful of pimento cheese onto butter crackers and spread mayo over thick-cut tomatoes. Max had learned to dress exactly right for occasions like this. He chose a bright yellow button-up. Yellow as in happy. Happy as in what he hoped to be. He rolled up the sleeves so that his forearms showed. He wore shorts that cut off midthigh. He blended into the pastel.

Max overheard two men talking beside him on the porch. One was lanky with a face that made Max think of cobwebs. The other was hulking with jowls that dropped.

Listen now. It's clear as twenty-twenty the Judge has that Midas touch, the lanky man said.

That's the touch of God, the other man said. There's nothing Midas about it.

Yes. The touch of God.

The longer Max watched the lanky man, the more he began to look like his own father. The protruding brow. The pointed nose. The long front teeth. What else?—there was a kind of spiritual symmetry.

The men talked about how the Judge had traveled up and down the state, made speeches, attended fund-raisers exactly like the one that afternoon. The Judge read to ladies at the retirement center, took boys on fishing trips and visited the cemeteries of steel mills, and prayed with the workers who had black lung. He'd been traveling to churches and Bible studies and NRA meetings because he cared about community. He wanted to know the people he would represent, so he could help them. You can't help who you don't know. Simple as that.

The Judge, the thick man said, is the new face of Alabama.

We need God-fearing individuals in office if we want to save this state. It's not right, the secularization that's sweeping through the South, through America. It's downright terrifying.

The other man nodded, It's a sign of the times.

The man acknowledged the Judge had formidable trouble on the horizon. A young liberal had been riling up a crowd of professors and intellectuals and leftists on the college campus. The liberal wanted women to marry each other, advocated for access to abortion, and claimed there should be a state tax on carbon emissions. The liberal had started a petition to outlaw bump stocks, a small device that transformed semiautomatic weapons into automatic ones.

Owning a gun does not make one a psychopathic killer, said the thick man. If one is a psychopathic killer they will kill, gun or no gun. A psychopathic killer will eat a man's face off with a fork and knife. He doesn't need a gun. So, my point is—why take away my gun, a gun that protects me and you and all us here, just so people who don't know better can feel better, in theory, about being safe and protected? I'll tell you one thing. Everyone I'm around is safer because of the gun in my holster.

The man patted his side, and Max noticed, for the first time, a handgun attached to his belt. His arms prickled. He told himself: *Feel safe.*

Over my cold dead body will a spine-shucked immoral step into the governor's seat in Alabama, said the one who reminded Max of his father. Know what Sara Beth told me?

Sara Beth told him her history teacher at the university was a man who had assigned the class an article that advocated for the removal of Confederate monuments across the South.

And wouldn't you believe that she claimed to agree with him? said the lanky man.

Am I surprised? The thick man said, pantomiming shock, bringing his hands to his cheeks. Listen. Schools aren't even for teaching facts. They're fantasy-making machines. You go in to get your brain good and washed. You put perfectly open kids in one way. They come out tumbled and confused. It's moving so far away from the way God wanted things. People are so far away from God. I'm tired of people explaining to us how to live, and I've had enough. If God wants the planet to heat up and burn, there's nothing recycling a plastic bottle is going to do about it.

I like this idea about everyone registering with a church, said the other man. Even if you don't go to the church, you got to get yourself registered. Church brings people community. I don't know what Duris would do without her church group, and many people do not know the resources a church would give them. I'm talking even outside the love of Jesus Christ. I'm talking free meals when you're hungry. Someone to play cards with when you're lonely. No judgment either. Just come however you want to be.

You are speaking to the converted right now. Could not agree more. The way to heal is through relationship.

The Judge was inside, but his body was visible through the sliding glass door. He was making his way to the porch. Max watched him work the room. He gripped a woman's shoulder in a way that seemed to convey a spiritual message. Max could not hear the laughter, but it brought joy to his own mouth. The Judge was everything Max wanted to be: confident, speaker of the right words, comfortable in the body that was his.

Lorne walked across the grass, passed Max and the men on the porch, and met his father at the door. The Judge's presence struck the small area around him with a kinetic charge. He was so close now, Max could reach out to touch his arm.

Bless the day. It is good to lay my eyes on you, the Judge said to a woman near Max.

The Judge's voice sounded like a hero from an American movie. It was sweet yet somehow tough as a boot. Nearly everyone in Alabama sounded like that. Max sometimes felt like he'd walked onto the set of a Hollywood Western, but he had not. This was real life. People dropped their r's when they spoke and let the vowels linger on their tongues. Max practiced speaking in this way, but he couldn't manage. Not yet.

The Judge's laugh was a breeze that spread his warmth around him. He wore a ring, a ruby stone, on his pinkie. No rot stained his teeth like Max had seen on people in this town. No sign that he drank too much soda. His hands were gentle and giant and strong. His black felt cowboy hat sat like a crown on his head. A large golden belt buckle showed a scene of a cowboy kneeling before a cross; a horse stood by the cowboy's side as if he had to journey from far away on horseback just to get there.

The Judge took Max's hand and held it.

You are a mighty fine runner, son, the Judge said. I've seen you practicing out there with my Lorne.

Max flushed at the compliment. It was so direct. He didn't know how else to handle it except to stand straighter, as if by perfecting his posture he could rise to meet the Judge's praise.

I am so not good at the catching, said Max. Only my running is good. But it's so, how to say it, hot.

Sure, said the Judge. You are adjusting to a new place. That takes time. He kept Max's hand between his own muscular ones. He stroked the back of Max's fingers, almost like he could heal them. Max looked at his hand captured in the Judge's embrace. The touch sent a tingle down the back of his head and relaxed him.

After Nils died, Max had stomped on his hands with his boots. He had wrapped them in medical-grade bandages until his fingers could not get free. The doctor sent him home with slings for the sprains, once with a cast for a broken bone. They were not safe, the hands. Max longed to stop the power they had over him. If he ran and did not heal, he could cope. He could forget what they could do. But here in Alabama, he could not forget. His cravings were out of control. His old balms did not work as they once did. And now the Judge's touch. How to describe its magic? How to put words to the first thing to soothe him since he'd stepped off the plane?

You have to learn to love the heat, said the Judge. You have to like to get a little burned. It feels good to burn. I used to love the first few minutes getting into my car in August after a day spent swimming. My car would have been out baking, all day, and I'd just sit in it for a moment before cranking on the engine, rolling down the windows. I'd just sit in that heat, let it wrap itself around me. Like a hug, you know? I used to need a hug so bad. Never knew how to just ask for it. I left it to the heat to touch me.

Max nodded.

Anyway, son, it's going to cool down quick enough. Just wait. This ain't the Bahamas. It'll cool down soon.

The Judge let go of Max. More people came to stand near him, but he kept staring right at Max, as if he had something more to say. Max pictured the Judge's younger body twisted, panting, barely alive at the bottom of the cliff from which he had once fallen. Barely alive and then completely dead. He had broken his arm during the fall and still couldn't use the thumb of his left hand. Max glanced at the Judge's thumb now. It looked normal.

Germany, the Judge said. You're from Germany, is it? Fine country. Fine country indeed. You can stay, he said, making his hands into imaginary guns and cocking them at Max's chest.

Boom.

Christians, right? asked the Judge. That a Christian nation?

Christians? asked Max.

They worship the Lord? Try to do right by him?

Max didn't know how to answer this question. There were big, beautiful churches in the German cities and small villages, and all of Germany closed down each Sunday. But Max's parents were atheists, and he knew nothing of what Christians did or didn't do in Germany, if they did or didn't do right by the Lord. Whatever that meant.

They try, Max said. I think they try for the right way.

Good, good, said the Judge. That's what I thought. What I'd heard. *Good.*

The fund-raiser had a theme and the theme was freedom and life. It sounded American to Max. When it was time for his speech, the crowd gathered on the trampled yard before the Judge and the flag. The Judge remained on the porch above and the people circled around a few steps below, listening attentively as if he would tell them the secret that would bring the win. The Judge had a way of making Max feel special for a reason that was so hidden even Max didn't know what it was. But it seemed the Judge deposited this feeling into everyone gathered. His posture told the crowd that he saw something in each of them and if they stayed close enough to that gaze, they might see it one day, too.

Freedom, the Judge said, is absolutely under threat right now. Freedom is something you have to fight for every day so that other people can take it for granted. You hear? People want to take our freedom. They want to write the rules for us. But brothers and sisters, they don't know us. And they sure don't know our God.

The man who looked like Max's father said, Amen.

Life will win, the Judge said. In the end, life will win. Know why?

The people stared on. Max, too, stared on.

Why, Max heard himself say.

The Judge looked at him.

Because, son, we are doing the Lord's work. Jesus is the way the truth and the light. Jesus himself is life. Jesus will win. No one ever said following him would be easy. No one said it would make sense. That is what faith is—it's mystery. It's being content with half knowledge. With living in the dark. Faith is believing in mystery even when the rest of the world tells you that you are wrong. You are crazy. You are lost. Even when the rest of the world says you are evil. We, brothers and sisters, are not those things. The rest of the world says, We know the answers. They say, We've solved the question. Science told us this or that. Well, listen. Science has been wrong before, and science will be wrong again. Once upon a time, science told us the world was flat. That the sun revolved around the earth. But we know more now than we did before, and such will be the case again. But do you know who has never been wrong? Do you know who knows the answer to any question our hearts or minds could ever hope to ask?

The crowd nodded. They knew, and Max, in that moment, felt that he knew it, too.

Well, listen everyone. There is an answer to the question. To every question. There is an answer you can know.

The smiling faces went still.

I don't have to tell you. Because you know it in your hearts. God. God and our Jesus. That is the answer.

The Judge spoke about war. First, he said there was a war on Christianity. *A war on our kind of people.* He talked in fragmentary paragraphs and nestled interesting verbs into interesting sentences. He spoke in a cadence that drew emotion from a place Max couldn't see. It intrigued Max, how easily the Judge could increase his pulse, how in just a few minutes he could cause his mouth to dry up. His mind to spin. The Judge spread out his arms to silence the people's moans. He bent his head, so Max could see the dip at the top of his black cowboy hat.

The Judge told the story of his anointing. He'd been high on paint with his friends in the forest before the healing occurred. His awakening. He spoke of it as both. The Judge and his friends had set up a moonshine distillery out of a few dozen fermentation barrels they hid under pitched tarps near the Gulf.

I did shameful things, said the Judge. I am here to show my shadow to you, so that you might have the faith to expose yours, too. Integrate into yourself so you've got nothing to hide. There's nothing so low-down that the Lord cannot lean in and meet you there. When you expose your shadow to yourself and to your God, you are set free.

The Judge told how he and his friends had huffed paint, shot squirrels with BB guns and roasted them for dinner. One night, the Judge wandered off in search of berries, something raw and fresh to add to the rodent feast. But he found something else.

He woke up at the bottom of an overhang without a memory of how he got there. His head hissed. His eyes shown back into the blackness of his brain. Blind. Or, as he discovered later—dead. The hospital ran tests that confirmed the Judge had been dead for three whole days in the woods before he woke up and found his way back to the moonshine distillery, his truck with keys still in the cup holder, and the country road that led to safety.

Before he found his way out, the Judge had had a vision. He had come upon a shed covered in mirrors. The mirrors caught the sun and the glint called him. In the shed sat a can of poison. The voice of God said to him, Drink it. Gulp it down. Swallow the magic.

A crazy thing, the Judge said. Faith can be a crazy thing. Faith can ask impossible things. I had none of it until that moment. But suddenly, I had faith entire. I picked up the jug of poison. I held it to my lips, and I swear to the Lord on high, I have never felt more alive. The poison went through my veins. It touched my heart. And I did not die but live.

I walked through myself and found God in the thing that should kill me. I trusted God, and he revealed himself. I saw him in all things—in the weeds and the bushes and the dirt, in the big blue morning that opened up just enough to let me breathe. In the cracked red mud. In the wet black trees. In the silence of space. In the salt-brined soil of the land that was soggy from its closeness to the coast. The moon was full when I finally found my truck. That same moon that pulls the ocean toward it and breaks men only to heal them. It lit my path, the moon did. God's lantern. His clear way. His eye on me always. I have never felt freedom more than I did in that moment, drinking that poison and living. It's freedom that we all want in the end.

A boy picked at a pimple on his chin as he listened to the Judge say that God's way would bring freedom. And that freedom was as important as love. As the moon. Max watched green ooze out of the boy's face. He watched as the boy pinched the ooze from his chin and wiped it onto his neck.

Real freedom, the Judge said, isn't the kind of freedom you're thinking about. He seemed to be looking at Max when he said this, but Max hadn't been thinking about any particular freedom. He had been wondering what the poison tasted like, what it meant for faith to come suddenly and entire, how a green ooze existed under every man's skin.

Orations flowed fully formed from the Judge's mouth. More than his words worked to hold the crowd captive. Something else moved them, some subtle thing. Power, maybe. Because it was power that radiated off the Judge like a kind of profound, supersonic vibration. Max could feel its buzz, like the hum of a microwave when you put your nose against its screen.

It's the kind of freedom you find only after you find your Lord and savior in Christ. When you make the conscious choice to follow him.

Max's mother wouldn't believe the Judge had spoken to God in a shed covered in mirrors, anointed with a cask of poison. She would say the Judge's vision had been summoned by the paint fumes, the shoe polish in his pocket, or from the near delirium of death. She would say it was the same as people who are pronounced dead in the hospital and see a divine light at the end of a dark path. They think it's God. They hear spirits say their names before they are drawn back to life. But science has proven that theory incorrect. The light at the end of the tunnel is a reaction to chemicals in the brain: a splattering of synapses, nothing more or less beautiful.

Max wondered, as he often compulsively did, how science would explain his ability. He wasn't sure. Might never be. He questioned if a god was indeed *out there* and if God had bestowed this power, this curse, upon him. A chemical collision in his brain, a possible origin story. No more or less beautiful.

Max would ask someone if he didn't suspect he'd end up in an asylum, snatched up for a series of medical tests. *Whom would he ask even?* Not sure is whom. No one is whom. Max conjured an image of himself on daytime TV shows, Oprah making him resurrect a girl's dead hamster in front of a live television audience. The applause. The cruel applause. The pure happiness of the girl. The love of what Max could do. Not ever the love of Max.

Better to ignore it. Better to pretend it doesn't exist, Max thought, *and then maybe, quite possibly, one day it no longer will.*

The Judge stood beneath a white flag with a big red X through it. The flag of Alabama. In Germany, one could not love the flag like one could love the flag in America. People would worry you were becoming a nationalist. It would spark memories of the war, of what could happen when one loved their country blindly and too much. The flag was for government buildings and sporting events. But here in Alabama, Max saw many flags in front of many houses, on the front of many shirts, flying from the bed of many trucks. His class saluted the flag each morning, placed their hands over their hearts and spoke words of respect to it. It was an honor to raise the American flag up the pole in front of the school, to know how to fold and unfold it, and never once let the fabric touch the ground.

We're going to pray for those who have lost their way. We're going to pray that God uses us as his warriors in this love-lost world.

Lord, boomed the Judge's voice. Father God, use us as your army on earth. We're building up an army. We will not be swayed by the ways of evil. We will be your face in government. We will do your will on earth as it is in heaven.

This is Alabama, said the Judge. A state for you, Lord God. We are not great if we are not doing your will. Help us reach the hearts of sinners. Let us judge people on nothing but their love for you and how they reflect your will in the world. We will not stand by and watch the world take you from us.

When the Judge got on his knees on the well-laid oak porch, Max almost expected a beam to shoot down from the heavens. Light him up or smite him, Max wasn't sure which. He closed his eyes. Was that what prayer was? Just closing his eyes? He wasn't sure what was supposed to happen after that. No God spoke to him. But for the first time, he wondered if he could find a God there, in the black silence of his own brain. He made his mind say *God?* It was completely silent. He was alone with himself, just like always.

Max squinted at the Judge through his pretend prayer. It unsettled him to see this noble man on his knees mumbling to himself. It moved him. Max wanted to get on his knees, too. He wanted to humble himself before something great. The Judge began to shake, so Max closed his eyes. He didn't want to see it. The Judge had the ability to change people. The bodies in the crowd had been changed. They shook and trembled in the same way the Judge did. It was as if the Judge possessed the power to twist and bend the will and the bodies of the people before him, the people who watched. Max wondered if the Judge knew the limits of his own power. The Judge's power reached out and grabbed Max by the heart. He felt the Judge wrap around his beating pulse. Power entered him. Was that God?

I have seen death, my friends, the Judge said, quietly and slowly. I have seen death, and I have seen the devil. I've looked him straight in the red of his eyes. And I am here to tell you that the way of the Lord is not easy. But it is good. The world is a battlefield, and the right path is not always kind, but it will make sense in the end. God never promised us ease. He promised us love. He promised us himself in exchange for eternal life. Commit yourself to him and be free.

Praise Jesus, the Judge said. Amen!

The prayer ended and people were released back to conversation. Some strange and unsettling thing roiled through the bodies beside Max. One man began to act hyper. He laughed too loud and spit flecks of chewed burger onto the faces of the other men while he talked. Max wondered what it was the Judge just did to everyone. Max wondered because he felt it, too—a surge of cortisol cruising his veins, swelling them thick as they could go. Maybe that's what God was. Maybe God was power. Max wanted more of it, whatever it was, even though it scared him. It scared him the way drugs scared him. It scared him the same as when a girl at school smashed a plastic bag of Ritalin into dust and licked the bag until it was a slick sack of saliva, and the girl's teeth began to grind.

The moon remained even in the daylight. A moon so bright the sun couldn't wipe it away. Max concentrated on its craters, the blemished and intricate topography he could trace from the backyard. He might not understand science, but it still made him feel small.

On his way out, the Judge walked past Max. He stopped. He raised a finger above him then drew it through the air and touched Max's chest. With that gesture, Max felt like the Judge had taken some of the sky and put it inside his body. He expanded into blue.

People like you, he said, are the people we need here. People like your father are doing good things for our economy. Cars are Alabama's biggest export right now. You need to invite him to church. We would love to see y'all come with us to celebrate the good news.

The good news? said Max.

Jesus has risen, son, said the Judge.

THE UPCOMING FRIDAY was the first game. Two days away, and although Max knew he would not start, the attention was getting to him. God's Way did not have a strong football team. They would not go to the state championship, but people still treated the players like minor celebrities. Earlier in the day, a girl had walked right into Max's History class with his teacher in midlecture and placed a homemade brownie on Max's desk.

Max needed alone time before the pep rally. The word *pep*, a mood that felt far away and uninhabitable. Pompoms would fly. The cheerleaders had memorized a dance that ended with one of them tossed into the air spinning. They would perform it for the boys to bolster them with luck and confidence. God's Way did not have a marching band, but music with trumpets and cymbals would crash from the gymnasium speakers while Max stood arm to arm with the boys on his team, his inherited family, even though he'd known them for just a short time.

He needed a run. He needed to find a dead yellowhammer. Max pushed through the glass doors at the back of the hallway. Sun filled his lungs. Outside, relief. End-of-summer smells. Cut grass and clover. Dirt scattered by the wind. Heat hit his face. At the far part of the field, a playground. Wood chips scattered in clumps below a long stretch of monkey bars.

Taking a break? I get it.

Max startled to see Glory in her pants and polo sitting on the sidewalk. She fiddled with a pink quartz at the end of a golden chain that hung from her neck. A spread of playing cards fanned out in front of her.

Max had seen Glory around school, but they hadn't talked since that first time, when she had appeared before him, evaluated him, and then left him to the boys.

Why aren't you in the gym for pep rally? asked Max.

I think that question is better served to you, said Glory. People won't miss me but they sure as heck are going to notice your absence.

I go soon, said Max. Just fresh air for a moment.

Uh-huh, she said. Take your time. I'm not here to judge. I'm just saying.

Max waited for her to ask him if he was excited about the first game, but she didn't.

Want me to pull a card for you? she asked.

A card? asked Max.

A tarot card. You ask me a question, I'll ask the cards. They'll divine an answer.

No thank you, said Max. But the cards drew his gaze down. Their paper looked worn thin. The plaid pattern on the back flaked off in patches.

These were my grandmother's, said Glory. She taught me to read them.

And all I ask is one question, said Max. He couldn't help himself.

If you want. Or I can just pull a card of the day and you can use it as a guide.

Later perhaps, said Max.

Whatever you want, said Glory. She shuffled the cards. They purred.

I should go in, he said. Before it's later.

He turned to open the door and then paused.

Remember when you said I can ask you things and you have the answers, said Max.

I do indeed, said Glory. She stopped shuffling and spread ten cards facedown in front of her crossed legs. She bent over them. She arranged them in a curious pattern.

I can now ask something? he said.

That's right.

To you and not to the cards, said Max.

Sure. Whatever you want, said Glory.

What do you know about, um, rat magic?

Glory stopped arranging her cards. Her hand hovered over one. She remained still and didn't speak.

I don't know much about it except that it's crazy, she said. And a rumor.

A what?

It's like a rumor people made up about drinking poison. If you drink rat poison and it doesn't kill you, then you got the soul of Jesus in you or something. The nickname for the poison is rat magic. Like a pet term. People in the country used to drink it and then they all died. People still talk about it to sound radical, but no one is dumb enough to do it.

The Judge he has done it, said Max.

Nah, she said. Nah. He hasn't. That man's just real good at storytelling.

Okay, thank you for so much information, said Max.

He pulled the door open to a blast of cool air. Goose bumps jumped onto his arms. Before he went inside, he looked down at Glory's cards. She turned one over. A woman tied and blindfolded. Ropes encircled her torso and bound her arms to her sides. Surrounding her were eight swords. They sung up from the ground and closed her in, trapping her, it seemed. Behind her, far away, a castle looked on.

After the pep rally the players headed to the field for practice.

Davis said, Get a load of Graham. The boy's a freaking nutball.

Max was only half paying attention as they walked through the parking lot. He was thinking about the last text Pan had sent him: a black heart. *A heart*. It wasn't until they reached Graham, the beefy defensive lineman with a nose so smashed you could practically look into his brain, that he realized what Graham was doing. Graham held a dead squirrel and was skewering it, mouth first, through the radio antenna on his truck.

Max wanted to reach out and wrench the squirrel from Graham's hands, but he cast his eyes to his cleats. His thighs were not thick, and they trembled, tender and sore, under his padded football tights. Davis began to chuckle, low and mean, then it pitched higher and turned inviting—a big, whooping laugh. How Graham got the squirrel, Max didn't know. Found it dead or made it dead, did it matter?

Pan tore across the blacktop with a black cape bellowing behind him, cinched at the neck above his God's Way polo. He let out a howl that mimicked how the inside of Max felt. The girls who had gathered around Graham's truck, smacking gum in cheerleading skirts, also howled, but theirs was the howl of girls mesmerized by the meanness of their boys.

Jesus, said Davis. Here comes the High Priestess of Weird to rain on our parade.

Graham cocked his hip to the side, so comfortable in his body. The squirrel was fully impaled now. The antenna protruded from its butthole.

Little Miss Crybaby, said Graham. What do you want?

Pan was out of air and shaky.

Don't cry, crybaby, said Graham. I'll give you the squirrel when I'm done with it, and you can use it for one of your little voo-doo-doo's. You can go all *The Craft* with it or raise it from the fucking dead.

You're not worth the shit in your asshole, Pan said.

Graham smirked. He approved of the insult.

You're a bunch of soulless cowboys, said Pan. He swirled to take them in, as if he were tallying them, counting roll. Max closed his eyes, hoping Pan wouldn't see him and think he'd been involved.

A violent mob, Pan muttered.

The whole scene reminded Max of something he'd recently witnessed on another of the school's playing fields after a practice. A bunch of senior boys had lured a swallow into the batting cage and swung their clubs at it. They had stomped their feet and climbed up the sides of the cage. They had stuck their hands through the links and shaken the fencing, trying to scare the swallow closer to the ground so they could beat its body to death.

Max had stood with the players from the football team as they held their helmets in their hands and watched. They had jumped a little. One of the football boys had chucked his helmet toward the cage and made a *woop* noise, edging them on. Their bodies had tensed, and their knuckles struck the air like *Get it dead*. Max's lips had widened until his mouth was a perfect oh. Oh, as in *Oh shit* or *Oh no* or *Oh dear*. Max's Literature teacher, a man with a concerned acne-riddled face, had come running out of the school and yelled at the seniors torturing the bird.

He said, YOU ARE PSYCHOTIC. What the hell is wrong with you? Are you serial killers?

This made them double over with laugher. *Hahaha*. They had to hold their guts in their hands. The laughing did not relent. Their laughing made Max laugh, too. It got its claws in him.

Now, Graham's mob of boys disbanded, leaving the squirrel bayoneted, and Pan defeated at its feet. And Max, now one of them, left, too. On the field, the boys ran into one another at high speeds. They ran faster, energized, maybe, by the spectacle they made of the squirrel. Max couldn't concentrate. He kept thinking: *violent mob*. The squirrel flashed in his mind: *dead, dead, dead*.

In the next drill, a boy pummeled Max to the ground. Impact ripped the worry from his head and snatched his breath from his chest. Max and the boy collapsed in a pile together, their bodies glistening raw and torn for two golden seconds as they lay on their backs in the grass. Coach blew his whistle, like get up, and they obeyed.

Max hobbled the sideline.

Forgot something inside, he told Coach.

Max trudged up toward the locker rooms, then veered right in the parking lot, toward Graham's truck. His mouthguard dangled from the metal cage in front of his face like a piece of his own mouth. He took off his helmet and placed it on the truck hood. The paint burned him when he tried to steady his hand on it. On the other side of the windshield, Graham's stuff was mounded into heaping piles. His rumpled school polo, a folded pair of aviators, a party-size bag of chocolate peanuts, gray sneakers. A wooden cross was suspended from the rearview mirror. Max wrested the squirrel from the place it was impaled. He laid it on the asphalt. The parking lot held no one but him. Max massaged the squirrel and kneaded it slowly along the spine. He blew against its fur. The small thing raised its head. It ran away fast, a dash, a living thing again.

Holy Mother of God, called a voice behind him.

Max turned to see Pan. His face open and questioning. He looked at Max like he was a riddle.

He thinks he's a princess.

Lorne lets him be a princess.

Calves roasting in the flames.

How long are you there, said Max.

You just brought the squirrel back to life, said Pan. I saw it.

It's different than what it looks like, Max said.

How did you do that? asked Pan.

Max shrugged, the truth. It happens sometimes.

Pan nodded. His face scrunched as if he were seeing Max materialize before him for the first time.

I never have shown a person, said Max.

You're scared, said Pan.

Max didn't know if this was a question or an answer. He looked at his hands. He wanted to hide them in his pockets. He wanted Graham's truck to run them over.

Max was not alone with his secret. Fear blurred the eyes. Fear lived in the ears. Fear tunneled through the holes in his nose. He had let another human see him. Pan lifted a corner of his mouth. *A smile means he's not angry.* A dimple dug into his cheek.

Don't tell, Max said. Please don't tell.

Strangeness was what Max saw when he looked at Pan. Strangeness sat in Pan's throat and waited. Strangeness recognized itself and called more strangeness to it.

You look sad, said Pan. Why are you sad? Why would you be sad?

Pan's voice was edged in tender tones. His lipstick, which had dried into the cracks of his mouth, chipped off in red flecks. Pan came to Max, knelt beside him. He placed a hand on Max's back.

What I am is not sad, said Max, though he was. What I am is scared.

Don't be scared, my little witch, said Pan. He rubbed Max's back in circles. Don't be a Sad Sarah. This is like a miracle. You might be a miracle. I think you are.

DON'T LOOK NOW, said Max's mother, as she drove toward their house. We have company.

Max was zoning out in the passenger seat beside her. His glazed eyes affixed to nothing. His mind replayed the scene from the parking lot. The squirrel ran away. Then died. Then ran away. Pan had called him a Sad Sarah. He felt like a Sad Sarah. He would like to be a Sarah. Unremarkable. Just like everyone. Sarah, the name of girls who dated football boys. Sarahs were like Katies. Sarahs and Katies roamed the halls of God's Way in droves. Sarahs and Katies came in such quantity no one could ever think they were wrong.

Hello to Max, she said.

Sorry, he said. What?

What's gotten into you these days? You feeling okay? Are you getting those headaches again? You napped all day on Sunday.

No, he said. I'm fine.

If you weren't fine you wouldn't tell me. That's why I have to pry.

Mom, said Max, I'd tell you.

The back of his thighs stuck to the leather seat. He crossed his legs like a Sarah would do. He placed his hands on his knees and sat straight and proper.

I'm really fine, he said.

His mother pulled their car onto the driveway. Next door Miss Jean tended to the hibiscus bush near her yard trellis. His mother cut the ignition.

Another text in his pocket. A buzz against his hip. Pan's name on the screen.

I am n service to ur power.

Don't tell any people, Max typed out again. Please.

Duh, Pan texted. DUH. Don't be Sad . . . Sarah.

Promise?

Duh!

Duh didn't reassure Max at all.

Pan texted him a picture of Mr. Sprinkles the cat.

Mr. Sprinkles, the text said, haz a crush on u!

Mr. Sprinkles keeps good secrets? Max texted back.

Well, hey there! said Miss Jean when Max and his mother stepped from the car.

Y'all defrosted yet? she asked.

Excuse me? said his mother. She opened the trunk and picked up one of the grocery bags and handed it to Max. He had convinced her to buy him Hot Pockets, a small, ham-filled victory. He stared at them nested on the top of the bag. The Hot Pocket freezer ice melted into the paper. *Defrosting.*

Max beamed at the neighbor and shifted the bag higher onto his hip. A headache stretched from Max's neck to his temples, but Miss Jean loosened it. Her lightness distracted him. An ointment to his mind.

Miss Jean left her garden and strolled into their driveway as they unloaded. Max sensed his mother's dread with each inch that closed between them. She slammed the trunk door.

I said defrosting because y'all got yourselves a tan. And y'all about to be defrosted right in time for winter, too.

Oh, said his mother. I suppose we do have a tan. She raised a browned arm and stared at it.

I mean you're vibrant, said Miss Jean. The both of you. Practically vibrant. How's that for vitamin D?

I am enjoying, said Max. The heat is nice.

I know, it feels good doesn't it? said Miss Jean. That's cause it's a vitamin. All you got to do to get it is sit yourself outside while it's sunny. I don't know how people live in that place Seattle. My god-daughter lives out there and she tells me it rains three hundred days out of the year.

Well, said Max's mother, not every place is Alabama.

That sure is right, said Miss Jean. That is the truth if I've ever heard it.

Miss Jean waved her garden shears in her right hand while she spoke. With her left hand, she clenched a dead hibiscus head. Max's mother slammed the driver's door shut. Miss Jean took a step back, as if just noticing Max in all his glory.

Oh my! Look at our future football star, she said. He's transforming into a star athlete before our very eyes. I do believe his jaw has become even more prominent overnight.

He was already an athlete, said Max's mother. A runner on the track team—

Oh, sweetie, I don't mean to offend you none, but I was talking about a real sport. You must be beside yourself with pride. First game's Friday, isn't that right?

Yes, said Max. I will not probably play.

Well now, honey, that's not a thing to be ashamed about. These boys are seasoned. You're just learning.

His mother rolled her eyes with her body. She carried her bag up the front steps and disappeared into the house. The screen door clattered behind her.

Sorry, said Max. My mother is, how do you say, shy.

Oh, honey, said Miss Jean. Everyone goes at their own pace, has their own way. Don't you worry about it. I am not one bit offended. You just be yourself and let your mother be however she needs to be.

And you are doing just well? he asked.

I've been fine, honey, just fine. Mighty kind for you to ask. Now I have this spot here on my face the doctors want to look at. But they can burn it off in a minute if it's cancerous.

Okay, said Max. Well, that's good.

Sure, it is, honey, said Miss Jean, who was already headed back to her yard to tend to her luminous hibiscus. Make sure you get you some SPF, she called over her shoulder.

MAX OVERHEARD A FIGHT between his parents. His mother wanted to move back to Germany. His father thought she should give it time. Anger built its way through her. She climbed it like a staircase. She had gone to pick litter in town with a volunteer group and discovered dead puppies in a garbage bag tossed to the curb.

The bag stank, she said. The puppy heads looked like wet tennis balls. It took a minute to realize what I was looking at. Then it clicked, and I will never not see it. The maggots stuffed into their eyes. The fat tongues.

Her fellow volunteer had shrugged, said, Oh, sweetie, it's not the last of that you'll see. We find them each week at the river walk.

Football is going to destroy his brain, his mother added. Do you see the force with which they tackle each other? It disturbs me. I saw a program on the television about how the sport caused chronic traumatic encephalopathy in nearly all players.

Okay, let's move back to Hamburg because you watched a television show, his father said.

She was being dramatic, and he had told her as much. She needed time to adjust.

Max likes it, his father said. Can't you see?

Max's mother accused his father of liking the place, too.

You're getting fat, she hissed. And don't fake to me that you like this stupid American sport. You don't want to go back until you get your promotion.

Max's father suggested something called Taco Tuesdays at the plant that his colleagues' wives put together. She could go to that.

You want me to eat tacos because you think it'll make me feel better, she said.

It will make you feel better, he said. And tacos are delicious.

Stop trying to fix this, she said. This isn't about me. It's about Max.

I think if you would find a community, it would take some of your focus off him. You might relax.

Their voices dimmed, and Max lost the conversation.

FIRST GAME. FRIDAY NIGHT. The football soared into the sky. All eyes watched the ball bounce twice off the bright grass. A player from the opposing team scooped it up and ran. Somewhere in the stands sat Max's parents. Thinking what, Max wondered—a cultural experience. During halftime, girls tumbled across the field in taut green skirts. They glittered above the anointed grass. Their legs kicked high, panties exposed, pep proliferated. A student hoisted the American flag onto his shoulders and ran it back and forth across the gridiron. Cheers rose from both teams. The flag was a thing that bonded them. Max remained on the sideline for the entire game. Part of things yet separate. The offensive and defensive lines took turns rising up and sitting down. They traded places, sweating, hulking. Their chests heaved with exertion. The field did not need Max. The team demanded someone who could catch what Wes threw. Wes looked divine that night, like a star. The offense from God's Way united to protect him. They hit other players so Wes might stay safe, might let his arm sing. The football hummed from Wes's hand like an arrow finding its target. It sailed with accuracy. It had assured velocity. The thrill of the game, Max did not know it until that night. His heart ran even when his legs did not. Coach marched along the sideline. He yelled until his voice changed, rattled in his throat, and retreated into rasps. Max looked on, amazed at the spectacle. He pinched the head of a dead daffodil, hidden in the frayed dirt near the watercooler. He put the bloom between his teeth and kept it there, smiling.

Among the collected: roadkill, dead neighborhood dogs, a lifeless cat. Pan lined them up along the edge of the gravel. He had amassed a dozen dead animals. Max wondered for a sick moment if Pan had snapped the neck of the cocker spaniel or drowned the tabby cat in the creek himself. How else could he come upon so much death? But the way Pan used his dry, sandy arms to arrange their bodies upright, even as their heads dangled off the end of their limp necks, moved him. Max remembered how Pan had gawked in horror at the dead squirrel. Pan could not have killed these animals. His movements were so full of good. He arranged the dead like a mother bird tended her nest.

They had convened in an old lot outside town where no one would see them. Pan wanted to test Max's abilities. Max stood there squinting. His neck throbbed like a fresh bruise. He massaged it and stared at the flies gathered and floating above the bodies.

The sky had a faint red bleed, especially at the bottom, at the spot where the tips of the pines sank into the sky like a row of jagged bottom teeth. That's what it looked like to Max, like fangs dug in and blood dripping down the chin of the sky, pooling at the horizon. The heat hung steady and dank without any wind, and the heaviness and the stench from the animals made Max's vision skew red. Everything had that tint.

Max had tried to keep from using his power like his father tried to keep from eating salt. It tasted too good to be good. An X-ray of his midsection might present a radioactive glow. It had to go somewhere, all that rot and death. Maybe it started in his toes, and it filled him from there like someone was holding a bucket of death-water above his head. With each animal he healed, another soul deposited in the bucket of death-water. He had a word for it now, since the

Judge's BBQ, all the darkness swirling around inside of him. Maybe it was *sin*.

Do it, Pan said and stood back.

Max wished Pan would come closer. Place an elbow on his shoulder to steady him. What Max needed was a body against his, even if he couldn't ask for it. *Move closer. Step in.* He needed to be grounded into the bigness of the moment. He needed Pan to tell him this was okay. That he was okay. He never realized how much that mattered to him until now. It mattered that someone could watch him use his power and not think: *wrong, contaminated, criminal.*

Pan's pink shirt collected the sweat from his back and stuck to him. Max studied Pan's neck and the scales of dry skin behind his ears, the pimples on his shoulders that peaked through around the tank top. He'd never tried to heal so many animals at once. He stalled. Max reached out to stroke the neck of three different felines: alley cat, tomcat, black kitten. The shock was ultrasonic. He knew it in his jaw. After seven healings, his mind went one hundred miles per hour toward something he could not see. The smack of cinnamon burned the roof of his mouth. It was sweet and hot, and Max's face dripped, and Pan wiped it with the bottom of his tank top. He was on his back in the unmowed grass.

Pan stood over Max. He stood in the middle of his blinking and drilled a feeling of wordless wonder down on him.

He said, I knew it. I just knew you were magic.

Max heard a dog whimper. Out of the corner of his eye he observed a black kitten walk across the lot.

Did I do it? he asked, but he already knew the answer.

His temples hummed like a quiet country song, like a bonfire snapping and flaming. Puppies barked in his inner ear. A robin sung against the back of his eyes.

Pan leaned down and kissed Max on the cheek.

PRACTICE WAS CANCELED ONE AFTERNOON, and Max hung at Davis's house with him and Boone. Max enjoyed the *hanging,* as they called it. Hang: to be suspended in time together. His head still hurt from the mass animal healing. His cheek still hummed from the kiss. Max had to stop what he was doing and touch the skin, try to calm the pain. He didn't know what to worry about more, the fact that Pan knew he could heal things or that Pan had kissed him.

Kissed. Him. Kissedhim. On the cheek, but still. Like a friend. Like the French. Or more?

Pan had been elated after Max healed the animals, as if it was something to celebrate. Maybe it was. Max had started to think maybe it was. For the first time, Max had felt proud of what he could do. They had gone for celebration sorbet. Pan called it vegan ice cream.

We can start a coven, Pan had said. He had looked at Max like he was some kind of angel, some kind of real special.

They had sat on the front of Pan's mother's car. Its cloth upholstery had come unstapled and sagged down almost to the crown of their heads when they drove in it. They reclined on its hood like it was a metal blanket rolled out for them at the edge of the Atlantic, but no waves had licked the sand at their feet. There had been only asphalt and car exhaust. The hood was boiling to the touch. Max tapped every smashed bug on the windshield until they were buzzing in the air around them and Pan was howling with crazed joy. Max had made Pan happy. His power had made him happy. Max and Pan put the ice cream in their mouths, not even using a spoon, just licking the melting balls that were almost too cold to eat. Above them a billboard said JESUS SAVES and beyond that was the Judge's face, his blue eyes watching them.

Max sat in Davis's living room and observed Boone mash the Xbox buttons. Boone held a Capri Sun between his knees. He huffed like it was him and not his avatar who was running through a bullet-laced landscape with his gun barrel pointed in front of him, dodging the orange blasts of bombs, searching for a war enemy to kill. Boone grunted. His avatar's boots crunched over the destroyed, rubble-strewn ground. Nazi flags dropped down from the façade of a building in the distance. *Oh*, thought Max. *Oh*. His heart sped up to catch his excitement. He sucked his own Capri Sun dry as Boone navigated the war-torn terrain on screen. The helicopter blades slashed audibly and the screams of troops killing or getting killed rippled through the heroic background ballad that set the tone of the game. The animation looked so real. Max stared at the body of two German enemies as they ran toward Boone's scope and were thrown back, caught in Boone's fire.

Double kill, said the game.

Boone clenched his teeth. Fuck yes, he said.

Boone had given Max a ride to Davis's in his old Chevy. They'd stopped by Boone's house on the way, so he could feed his pit bull, Dog. Dog was old with bad hips, and he struggled to walk. Boone explained this as they drove. He had to check on him and feed him. The house had looked older than it probably was: a dirty ranch home missing its shutters. Max was careful not to walk on the piss-colored grass of the lawn as he followed him toward the front steps. Inside, a man with the same curly black hair as Boone sat catatonic in a wheelchair, watching a daytime law program. The TV judge stared at screaming defendants and asked questions that seemed to expose them as lazy or as liars.

Max had stood in the doorway, not daring to come all the way in, and watched the man sit straight as a beam in the spine, mind folding inward, and not registering a thing, not him, not Boone. Boone carried a plate of food to the man's chair and set it down beside him. This was the real reason they came.

The man, eyes still on the TV said: Not a goddamn vegetable on the plate, Bo. You trying to deplete me?

Then without looking at Max, he spoke to him.

He said, Who the fuck are you?

Max and Boone left without saying a word.

That's my oldest brother, Boone had explained when they were back in the truck. He's been in that chair for a few months now. Doctors say he might not walk again. He was doing a construction job and fell from a third-story window. Should have died but didn't. It's a miracle. A miracle from God.

And his legs will not work now, said Max. Or ever again?

Well, that's the saddest part. Yes, probably not ever again. And he wanted to be a dancer. A ballet dancer. He turned our mom's old bedroom into a studio, hammered a barre right into the wall. He'd dance for hours every night.

Boone grinned and Max glimpsed the little boy he had been. The image of the dancing brother pleased Boone. Pale veins wound through his forearms. Boone fastened his eyes on the truck's dashboard, as if he could see an image superimposed over the mileage meter. What was he looking for? A shadow spilled over his face.

He said, Not no more though. Now he just sits in that chair and watches TV. Used to hate the TV. Called it the brain drain.

Max didn't ask where Boone's mother was because it had been explained to him that Boone's sister had killed her when Boone was still little. His sister had been fighting with the mother over whether or not she could spend senior week at Gulf Shores. His sister had pulled out a shotgun that had been wrapped in a towel and hidden under the mother's bed. In the story, she never meant to pull the trigger, just scare the mother, show her she meant what she was saying, but she shot her in the chest. She'd called the police after the accident, screaming that three hooded men had broken into the house with a weapon. The police found the sister in the driveway on her knees crying, face nuzzled into the grass. The following day, right on the spot where Boone's sister had cried into the lawn, a long-stemmed rose had bloomed. Max had looked for the rose as they left the house, but not a single flower lived in the yard.

While Boone played his video game, Davis leaned against the dark wooden bookshelf, where biblical fictions about the end of the world stood spine to spine beside romance novels named after different Southern locations—*Nantahala Nights, The Prince of New Orleans, Natchez Blues*. Davis's doorbell rang. The ring interrupted the explosions of video game bombs and presented to the living room three girls. Davis grinned. The girls looked bored as they surveyed the room and pined their eyes on the three boys waiting for them. Davis clapped his cracked palms together, and one of the girls jumped.

There was one girl for each of them. Max did the math and understood the consequences immediately. One of the girls would be his. Max recognized a girl Davis regularly talked about in the locker room. Renata. The girl who let him ejaculate on her naked breasts. Davis called Renata his experimenter. What they did sexually was experimenting, not serious, but practice for the people they would one day marry.

It's not sex unless you name it sex, Davis had explained to Max. Sex is an intentional act. What we are doing is playing. Experimenting. Getting good.

The boys were supposedly babysitting Davis's half brother, Duke, a toddler with a demonic laugh, but mostly the baby went untended. Left to his mischief. As if to greet the girls, Duke marched around the room. His nose leaked green fluid. Davis grabbed Duke, picked him up, and shook him until his hands unclenched dirt from a potted plant.

That's nasty, Davis said. Don't be nasty and eat plant matter, he growled, nose pushed to his brother's cheek. Your mom will ground my ass if she knows you're eating her plants under my watch again.

Davis must be excited about the girls, about the nearness of his experimenter, Max thought, because he's showing off and acting cruel. Normally, he'd ignore Duke.

Stop it, said Davis. Stop crying.

He put his brother back on the carpet and pretended to kick him but stopped his cowboy boot just before it would have made contact with the face.

Y'all sickos, said one of the girls. Quit your yelling. You're not going to fix anything by screaming at a baby. What you're going to do is make it worse.

She walked over to Duke and scooped him up, bounced him on her hip. Max couldn't imagine how she knew how to do it, because after a few moments the baby cooed and grabbed at her ears and dribbled chewed dirt from his mouth.

You got something it can color with or whatever? she asked.

She patted Duke's sweaty hair. On her thumb was a giant Ring Pop like the kind Pan sometimes wore. The baby tried to shove it in his mouth.

This was how it went: Davis and Boone disappeared with their respective girls. Davis went to the basement. He appreciated it because it was insulated. No one could hear what happened down there. The Christmas lights that hung year-round from the rafters made for romance. The big-screen TV could be set to a station that played love songs. Private was how Davis liked it. Boone claimed the girl called Amy Grace. Renata and Amy Grace both had hazel eyes and high ponytails and lipstick the color of pink fruit with a smell between cookie batter and ripe flowers. Renata left a binder behind on the coffee table. Inside the see-through sleeve was an illustration she'd drawn of a Widespread Panic song. The lyrics exploded in an acid trip of color. A school bus flew over a rainbow. The sun gazed stoned and cross-eyed from behind a purple cloud. A dog sprinted across a mountain.

They gave Max the plainest yet prettiest girl, Billie, and he felt like it was an act of kindness on their part, as if Davis extended an olive branch for pummeling him into the dirt during practice that week. Billie was square-faced and tiny-eared with eyes set far apart. Remnants of baby-bang, scant wisps of hair, clung to her forehead. There was something boyish about her that Max liked. It didn't even have to do with her name. She drank water out of a metal canteen, and her house keys dangled from a purple carabiner that hung from a loop on her shorts. Her wrists were wrapped in macramé bracelets she made herself. She yawned to reveal a gap between her front teeth. It was the kind of gap a girl on TV might have. She pushed her tongue into the gap. It seemed like a sexual provocation.

Billie was the girl who had come to the aid of Duke. She still bounced Duke on her bony, cocked-out hip. The on-pause noise from the video game played on repeat in the background. The steady fire of a machine gun set to a threatening tune of chords signaled an enemy could be around any corner.

Want a Capri Sun? Max asked. He knew there were a bunch of the fruit crush flavors in Davis's fridge, and he wanted to get out of the living room.

Sure, said Billie.

Max's mother hated the word *sure*. She said it lacked commitment.

In the kitchen, they sat beneath crocheted curtains and talked about nothing. She was not a boring girl. Max decided it was him that was boring. He couldn't think of a single interesting thing in his head that he could unfile and hand to her. He realized then how little talking out loud he did with the boys and even with Pan. He might be limited, he thought, in his capacity to distill an original thought into a sentence.

Billie set Duke down on a towel and Duke smashed his toys together and laughed maniacally to himself. The smell of shit came from his diaper. They ignored it. Max had no idea how to change a diaper or clean a baby butt. Billie spoke about Renata, whom she called her Ultimate Best Friend. She seemed vaguely worried about her Ultimate Best Friend, who was now in a soundproof basement not drawing stoned suns or flying dogs but enacting her role as the experimenter. Billie told of how Renata had created a recipe for purple hair dye. That weekend, the painting of hair would happen.

Max listened to Billie talk and wondered what kind of things Davis and Renata did in their experiments, and if Billie also wondered or if she already knew it and knew it better than Max. Max understood he should be admiring the distance between Billie's eyes and the slow rise and fall of her chest bones beneath her white shirt that so clearly showcased the outline of her jersey blue bra. He should want to put his fingers between the young, muscular legs that extended from her jean shorts like two brown relics of summer. He should want to take her as his experimenter. If he were a girl, Max would not mind looking like Billie. If he were a girl, maybe he would even want to kiss her.

What's it like in Germany? said Billie.

I don't know, Max said. How to describe a place you're from. You see it too close to see it. I cannot think of anything to interest you.

I'm sure there are a dozen things that would interest me.

She told Max she wanted to move to Paris to be a writer when she grew up. She said it like he should know all about Paris, even though Paris was in another country. Max had only been to France a handful of times, and he had been a kid then and he couldn't speak more than a few sentences in French. Either way, Max told her she would love Paris, though he knew nothing about this girl or what she loved. But he wanted Billie to love Paris, because he felt grateful to her for sitting a respectable distance away from him and not looking at his lips when she talked to him. She looked right into his eyes or right into her own hands, which were opening and closing in her lap. Or she stared at the curtains. She read a lot of poems, and she showed Max the side of her sneaker where she had inscribed quotes from her favorite dead poet, Sylvia Plath. She asked Max to repeat a line to her in German. She nodded at Max's sentence and tried to say it back but what she said did not sound like German.

Very good, Max told her. Almost there.

Billie did not smile when Max praised her, but she wanted to. Max could tell.

Max decided he liked her and hoped that Renata was okay. He was glad that even after Duke had fallen asleep on the kitchen tiles and dusk's shadows had slipped over them, that he was there with her.

THE BOYS LOST THEIR SECOND football game. The dark mood dissipated once they left the locker room and emerged into the steamy night outside. It had to do with the absence of Coach, whose disappointed admonishments receded into the back of their brains as soon as they were out of his earshot.

Let's eat, fellas, said Davis.

Max rode in the bed of Boone's pickup because Davis called shotgun. Davis spit sunflower seed shells out of the window. The wet shards hit Max in the face, but he didn't mind. He'd played for the first time in a Friday night game. The team had been too far behind for it to matter if he fumbled a ball. But he had not fumbled. He had caught what Wes had thrown, and, for a moment, the crowd had sung for him. Roared. They chanted *God's Way, God's Way*. Max had turned. He had dug his toes into the field to push off. But he had delayed, taken a long moment to orient himself before running. He had let the mind slip in and overwhelm his instinct. The tackle that had come for him sent his head back. A white, hot star slammed against his eyes. Grass stained his nose. His helmet seemed without cushion. The world did not have cushion. What it felt like to be tackled. He had stood up grinning and initiated.

Wipe that smirk off your face, Germany, Coach had yelled. This isn't funny.

Max leaned back against the side of Boone's truck bed, elbows hooked over the edge, as they sped into town. Max's lip was busted straight open. The restaurant signs blinked their neon and the streetlights overhead made him feel like he'd entered a real city in America where important things happened and stores never closed. But here, all anyone did at night was drive around or eat, which was fun enough for Max. When Lorne and Knox pulled up next to them at the stoplight, Knox stood up in the truck bed, held up his football jersey, and howled. Lorne hit the gas when the light flipped green. Knox doubled over in the back, still howling and waving his wet jersey like he wanted to surrender something. Lorne turned his truck down a one-way road going the wrong direction. Max gripped the metal edges of the truck bed, terrified. Boone was trying to find a shortcut to the Chicken Shop, so he could beat Lorne there, get there first and win. Max felt Boone accelerate, the engine let out a grinding metal sound, and Max knew they were going to race. He slammed his eyes shut.

The two trucks slowed when they drove through the treeless streets behind the mall. Davis turned up the Pink Floyd song that charged the air around their truck. They rolled through a stop sign just because they could and idled in the road for longer than Max expected. Davis switched the music to the local rap station and slid the windows down. He yelled *wooooo* into the night.

At the Chicken Shop, they piled their trays high with fried food. Chicken strips with extra pepper sauce and waffle fries and tots. They each ordered their own refillable extralarge soda cup. The sizes still amazed Max. They each held at least a liter of liquid, and everyone would get seconds.

Dude, said Knox, pouring two extra packets of salt onto his fries. Did you know that someone found a rat's head at the Chicken Shop off Fifteenth Street?

Shut up, said Lorne. That's a bag of baloney.

A bag of baloney, thought Max, and he filed the saying away in the must-use section of his brain.

Oh, it's true, said Knox. I saw pictures. They got pictures. It's nasty. It's like you can see the fried little rat head and its little rat teeth. The woman who found it, she was just about to chomp down when she looked and saw something staring at her.

Nasty, said Lorne.

She could have gotten rabies, Knox said. I'm fixing to check every last fry and tot before I bite.

Knox dumped the contents of his fry sack onto his tray and started his search through them.

She couldn't have gotten rabies from eating a fried rat head, said Davis. It doesn't work like that.

Hold up, said Knox. You do you, and I'll do me. Good luck not eating a rat head.

Whatever, said Davis. He dipped a fry into a swirl of mustard-ketchup-barbecue he had blobbed together.

Well, well, ladies. Fancy seeing you here, said the voice of Pan, who stood before their table with his tray of fries and diet cola, Max knew it had to be diet cola, steady in his hands.

Sitwithus, Max said in his head.

Davis started to hum the theme song to the TV program *Psychic South*.

To what do we owe the honor, Lord Darkness? Did you need some chicken for your cauldron? said Davis.

You should really try stand-up comedy, Davis, said Pan. You're freaking hilarious. Scoot your fat ass over. I'm joining you.

Oh wait, I'm sorry, said Knox. That's right, you don't eat chicken. Cause you're a vegetable-tarian now.

Davis made room for Pan beside him.

Yep, said Pan. A vegetable-tarian. That's right.

See these, Knox pointed to a sharp tooth, crooked and stained with a fluoride patch. We got these because we are predators that are made by God to kill and eat animals.

Well, said Pan. Thanks for the biology lesson. Looks like I'm evolving at a higher speed then.

Max didn't know what to do with Pan among them. He looked to Lorne, who seemed more engrossed in his sandwich than in Pan's presence. Lorne uncrossed his legs and opened his knees.

Hey, said Pan, staring right at Max. Good game tonight.

Thanks, said Max. We lost.

As if you even watched it, said Lorne.

Not a chance in all of hell, said Pan. But I'm being polite and I'm assuming it was good.

We lost, said Boone.

He's just being a gentlewoman, said Davis, mouth full.

Max watched Davis's molars come together across strings of chicken thigh. Flecks of it hit his lips. Pan folded into their conversation with an ease that girded Max. Pan knew how to talk to them, even though they said nothing. It seemed to be a conversation strung together with pantomimes and insults and jokes about how sweaty testicles could get. Boone farted his armpit into Pan's face. Pan spit a chewed fry into Davis's lap.

Cars pulled in and out of the lot outside and Max's nuggets stayed uneaten, though he had unskinned them from their crispy batter, which now lay in crumbs around his wrapper. He sucked the sparkle of his soda. He wanted, already, another one.

I got a serious question of some kind, Knox asked.

Lorne leaned back in the booth. Max thought he saw Pan look at Lorne.

How long do you think you have to put your dick in a girl for her to get pregnant? said Knox.

How is that even a question? said Davis.

Like where did you put it? asked Boone. The ass or the other place?

I don't know, said Knox. The other place.

Davis rolled his eyes. You got to be careful, brother.

Like longer than a minute, right? If it's under a minute, it's probably safe, right?

Pan put his head on the table and shook with laughter. When he lifted his head, his eyes were streaming tears stained black from his liquid liner.

Knox's going to be a daddy, Pan said.

Why don't you shut that piehole, Pan? said Lorne. He needs advice not a freaking psychic fortune-teller.

Psychic fortune-teller?

Max wanted to leave.

Maybe Pan could stir up some abortion juice in his cauldron for your girlfriend, said Boone.

That's not funny, said Knox. You know I wouldn't do that. I'm against all that stuff

Yeah, Lorne said. Don't even joke about that.

Boone put up his hands like *Don't shoot*.

I'm only being practical, fellas, Boone said.

No one's pregnant! said Knox. Jeez. I'm just asking hypocritically.

Hypothetically? offered Lorne.

Yeah, said Knox. Hypothetically, how long do you think the thing has to be in there to, you know, do any impregnating stuff?

Depends on the man, said Pan.

As if you would know, said Davis.

The edge of Max's soda cup was red from his broken lip. He ran a tongue across it. It looked like lipstick.

Did she want it? asked Lorne. If she didn't want it, I don't think she can get pregnant. The body doesn't take it. So, if she didn't want it. You don't have to worry.

Knox shrugged.

I think she wanted it, he said. I couldn't really tell. It was late and stuff. We'd been sipping on the moon.

A family-shaped group padded to their SUV outside the window. The night caught the light from all the fluorescence in town and glowed with it. Max wondered if there might be a world not long from now that never gets dark at all.

My ride's here, dudettes, said Pan. Thanks for the titillating conversation, but I'm about to blow this proverbial popsicle stand. Knox, success with fatherhood.

F you, dude, said Knox. No one's a father! It was under sixty seconds. She might not have wanted it. No one's a daddy.

In the parking lot, a girl with a bowl cut stood next to a silver Honda. Pan waved at her. *His ride*. She held a skateboard to her side. Her pants were baggy, and her chin nodded when she saw Pan push through the glass doors.

So, even if it's under a minute, it like counts and stuff? said Knox.

I would feel bad for you, said Davis, if you weren't such a tater tot.

FOOTBALL PRACTICE ENDED EARLY. Pan stood in the middle of the parking lot waiting. He adjusted his plastic Dracula fangs and waved at Max. Max walked over to him. He shoved a hand into his pocket and fiddled with a pen cap. He usually showered after practice, but he hadn't that day. He could smell himself. Maybe Pan could smell him, too. He wondered about the flavor of his pheromones. He held the handle of his gym bag, something tidy and all black from Germany. Not cool like the brands of America.

Honey, Pan said, I'm taking you to the mall.

You are? Max said, trying to sound normal. But my mother is usually my pickup.

Yeah, well, call her and tell her change of plans. My mom has the car today, but I got a ride coming in a few. You can be my escort to the comic book store.

Do you like Tintin? Max said.

Never heard of her, said Pan.

A motorcycle descended on campus streaming blackness behind it. Pan's ride. The man on the motorcycle flipped up his reflective sunglasses to reveal eyes of different colors.

Pan, half powered, said, This is Uncle Quaid.

Max arranged himself on the motorcycle behind Uncle Quaid. A truck filled with beefy defensive linemen slowed as it passed them. Max tried to pretend he was busy getting adjusted into his seat and did not notice Knox in the truck scowling and curious. Max felt the stares, the watching, even with his back turned. But he thought: *This is fine. They're friends with him, too.*

Pan folded into the sidecar of the motorcycle. His knees stuck up so that he could wrap his arms around his thighs and make himself into a small package. He looked like a present of a person. Max held tight to Quaid's body which stank like a barn of hay. He was sour and animal. The man's leather jacket felt freshly dead, and Max worried that if he held too tightly to the hide, he might startle life into it.

Quaid's long flowing hair was drawn into a tight tail. When he took off his jacket in the mall parking lot, Max noticed the puckered scars and welts on his forearms and hands. It looked like he'd survived some kind of attack.

Nice to finally put a name to the face, said Quaid.

Max had heard his accent around town. It was gentle and flamboyant but distinctly Southern. Something in it sounded rich.

A name to the face.

Quaid held out his hand. Two fingers were missing from it, and Max shook it. Quaid talked a bit more, but all Max heard was: *Pan's been saying my name.* Max spread his lips. He had been told by many people that his smile was a knockout. He liked to share it when he could. An armor to the world.

Quaid leered at Max, flipped one leg over the motorcycle, and left them there.

Inside the mall, Pan went into the bathroom to change out of his God's Way uniform. He emerged, ready to show off his new mesh top and lace gloves.

What happened to his fingers? Max asked.

Snakes got them, said Pan.

Snakes? said Max. A snake bit the fingers away?

Yep, said Pan, grabbing the bottom seam of Max's shirt and pulling him deeper into the department store they had to travel through to get to the mall corridor.

You'd be surprised how unsurprising it is when you live here long enough, he said.

At the entrance to the comic book store, magazines showcased muscled men in electric spandex with fierce coiffed hair. SHAZAM! said a superhero in a blue-clad onesie as he high-kicked a villain whose face was painted ghost white and whose mouth was a grimace of shining monster lips. Pan hovered over the rows where obscure titles had been filed side by side and touched each one. He lifted them gently. Occasionally he would shriek with joy at some rare edition.

Max paused to look in a mirror that hung over the fifty-cent discount bin. The light from the overhead fixtures drew attention to all the perfections of his face. He ran his hand over his flushed cheeks. He loved his big mouth and square jaw. His eyes he did not love. Tiny and darting and set back in his head. Another thing wrong with his head was the hair on top of it. His hair should fall in a blond wave, like his father's hair did. But Max's hair curled. It cowlicked and greased and made him look silly. He usually sheared his curls down to the scalp so all that was visible was a thin film of fuzz. But he hadn't shaved it since Alabama. He just let it grow.

A song played overhead, something well-known and sung by a fabulous pop star whose voice sounded like it was screaming the words *fun* and *sex* and *danger* at the same time. Max bobbed his head to the fun and sex and danger and imagined what it must feel like to be her: to dance before a crowd under blaring electric lights and have people yell your name as you stripped down to nothing but the spandex clinging to the beautiful body you were born into. To prowl like a glimmering, shimmering goddess under video images of yourself prowling like a glimmering, shimmering goddess. To lift your goddess limbs above your goddess head and swim your goddess hips back and forth across a stage that was built for people like you. For boys and girls to rip at their hair and sing with you and sing at you while trying to make their lips match your lips, their voices match your voice. That was what it meant to be American, Max thought. To be able to stand on a stage and sing so loud that it rushed through every radio in the country and made the world want to dance and cry at the same time. To make music that lingered above swimming pools in the summer. Music that people swam through as they cut strokes across the clean, chlorine squares in their backyards. Music that people fell in love to and out of love to and became bored to while walking through the mall.

Sure, Max knew his face was okay, but he was not beautiful. He was not the kind of beautiful that people wanted to cut out of a magazine and fasten to their wall with metal pins. He was not the kind of beautiful that became a poster looking out over a bed as two boys touched each other quietly beneath a quilt knit together from one of their mother's dresses.

Max turned away from his reflection and considered the rows of comics. The mall space and its sweet-cookie smells seemed to trivialize and commercialize the feelings looping up and out of him.

Hey, Max heard himself say. You're not going to tell anyone, please remember, about what you saw me do?

No way, Jose, Pan said back. A hundred percent no.

Okay, Max said. He leaned closer, realizing, for the first time that Pan was shorter than he was. He loomed so grand in Max's mind that he hadn't noticed. He came up only to Max's eyebrows.

Because, Max said. I've never told a person. It's a secret hugely.

Aw, said Pan. You don't have to worry. I'm not crazy. I'm telling absolutely zero people, Maximillian.

Why is everyone calling me that? Max said. My name's just Max.

Max picked up the newest *Superboy*.

Can I ask something else? said Max.

Sure, Just Max, said Pan.

What is up with Lorne? Max heard himself ask.

With Lorne?

Max turned the page of *Superboy* as if he were reading it or interested.

Why are you asking?

I don't know. I notice you two talking in the field at that party and wonder because it looked like friends. Like close friends.

What if I told you Lorne was crazy? said Pan. A disturbed human.

Max tightened the comic he held. Pan would never give a normal answer.

It's true. Lorne's a family friend. I've known him since I was practically in the womb. So, I would know if he was disturbed, and he is. He's messed up in the brain sauce.

He seems only a little angry, said Max. I don't know about disturbed.

Pan shifted under Max's gaze. Pan's eyes were the lightest brown, almost gold.

Everyone in that family is disturbed, said Pan. Just look at his father. You know they kill animals, right? That's like the number one symptom that something is mentally disturbed with you.

Max picked up another comic. He needed to hold more things.

Don't you wonder why they're so interested in you, huh? asked Pan. Why they are so enamored by their new German princess?

They are not so interested, said Max.

Oh god, come on. Don't play dumb.

I'm the fastest runner on the team, said Max.

Sure, sure, Pan said. He started laughing. Don't you think if you were so good at football, you'd be playing more? Don't be stupid, Sad Sarah.

Pan laughed maniacally. His eyes snapped into slits.

What is so funny right now? asked Max.

They want to save you, hon. They want disciples. It's easy to see it. I can see it from way over here.

The laughing rolled Pan's shoulders. Pan laughed as if Max was silly, silly to think he could be special. Pan's laughing peeled back the scab of something still sore. At him. Not with him. Max had been laughed at so many times in Germany. Walking into school with his hands wrapped in gauze, needing to miss days because of migraines, going into the girls' bathroom instead of the boys' because his brain was somewhere else, always somewhere else.

Laughter ran down his spine. Max cracked his neck. His head hummed with the memory of the smacking on the fields. It did feel good, the pain. It did. And what had Price said? That Pan liked pain, too. Feet on fire. Feet in the flames. Laughing like a knife to the peel.

He wondered what would happen if he leaned in and kissed Pan on the mouth. Right then. Right there. In front of the mall people. If that's what Pan wanted. If that's what this was. They would be physically removed from the premise. Max touched the shelf in front of him. He breathed deep to induce calmness. Pan was so strange. It didn't make sense.

But to me, you're special, said Pan. More than a disciple. More than a warm body to put in a pew.

Pan bent over and shuffled through a pile of comics on the floor. His butt tapped Max's hand. *On purpose?* Max wondered.

I think you're special, Pan said, not looking at him, still riffling. For the record.

You do? Max said.

There was something different about you the very first time I saw you. Yeah, Sarah. You have that special sauce.

I do?

Found it, Pan said. He held up the vintage *X-Men* comic for which he'd searched. As Pan flipped through it, Max almost expected some kind of animal to fly out.

MAX STOOD NEXT TO LORNE during stretches. When they lifted their arms, their shadows held hands. Lorne ran toward Max during the scrimmage. Tackled him. Max stumbled up. Lorne pushed him back to the ground and sprinted off. Cold sweat streamed down his hot flanks. Lorne slapped Davis's butt as he ran past him, and Davis yelled *Woo* into the pink dusk of the horizon.

Max limped to the bench for a break. *Fiver* was what Coach called it.

He took off his helmet and shook out his bangs. Wes walked past him, gave a tight nod, and pinched his lips into a smile.

Hey, buddy, he said. What up, Germany.

Max knew by now this was a greeting. Wes did not require a thoughtful response from Max. He nodded back.

Sup, he said.

Max filled his paper cone with Gatorade. He sipped and watched the yellow jerseys scrimmage the red jerseys. Yellow was offense. Red was defense. Red versus yellow. Yellow versus red.

You guys in red! yelled Coach. Keep your feet moving!

The American flag snapped and rolled on a skinny metal pole, always above the field, always looking down. Max thought he'd never experienced an afternoon of such searing blue or boys as real as these boys as they ran with busted noses and sore knees toward one another, their arms outstretched, their fingers reaching just a little farther.

He heard a voice. The Judge stood beside him. His straight-backed body, his regal black Stetson hat, and his Ray-Bans. Max couldn't believe how excited he was to see the Judge.

Good moves out there, son, said the Judge. He seemed to purr as he spoke.

Or did he say *God moves out there, son?*

Max couldn't tell, but he thanked him anyway. Thanked him even though Max had not played well in any scrimmage. But he had won the suicides again. The suicides he would always win. Max felt the Gatorade stiffen into a mustache above his lip.

Son, I'm not going to beat around the bush, said the Judge. I have a favor to ask of you.

Me?

Yes, sir, said the Judge. I'm looking for some more volunteers for my campaign. I came here specifically to discuss this with you. And you know, I am a busy man. I don't take my time lightly.

I will do it. Anything I can, Max said and realized he meant it.

That's kind of you. That's real kind. I need someone to join my canvassing team on the weekends, maybe make some phone calls. You're new to town, so I was thinking it could be a good way to get you involved. My son says you are a team player. You'd be going out with him and the boys. Riding the state going door to door. Maybe sitting in the HQ and placing some calls to voters.

His son. Team player. Max's sides ached from where Lorne had hit him. Max shook on it, what else could he do? The Judge came all the way across town to see him, to see Max.

I'd like to get to know you, son, said the Judge. Would you like that?

Yes, sir, said Max. I like that.

He tightened the grip on the helmet in his left hand.

All right. Now terrific, said the Judge. Terrific.

The Judge paused, like he wanted to say something else and wanted to say it right.

This is part of something bigger than just you or me or one office. You understand that, right? This is about the heart and soul of people in the community. This is about goodness and the great love of God.

Max said yes that he understood because he wanted to understand, and he hoped that if he feigned understanding long enough that the understanding would find him. What Max knew was that he wanted to be around the Judge a little longer. Just a little longer.

The Judge smiled that smile.

He said, Good, son. That's good.

Max heard himself agree to go hunting with the Judge and Lorne the following weekend. He heard himself admit to the Judge that he'd never been hunting. Never even held a gun. The Judge seemed to have expected this and the thought also excited him.

Shooting a bird is just like shooting a skeet. Just aim a little out ahead of it and bang.

Bang.

Bang.

Sounds fun, said Max, but a great fear filled him.

I know it! said the Judge. I know it does!

The Judge marched back to his truck through the hiss of lovebugs that clouded near the bleacher puddles. The man's attention felt too good but not good enough to stave off the foreboding feeling that had entered him and would not leave.

PAN HAD BEEN TO MAX'S HOUSE for dinner three times in two weeks, and each time he brought Max a present for *his sterile, strait-jacket room.*

Get the juju buju moving, if you know what I mean, Pan said.

He gave Max a quarter he left on the train tracks. The train smashed it into a golden flower, a sun ring, a perfect metal petal. He presented a satchel of dried lavender that he told Max to leave in his underwear drawer. Then came a smooth tiger stone whose middle stripe glowed the same golden brown as Pan's irises. Pan didn't want anything in return as he curled Max's fingers around the tiger stone and said: Just hold this when you need it. Just kiss it when you're scared.

Pan brought a poster of Kurt Cobain pouting into the camera with his hands clasped against his knees.

The most beautiful girl in the world, Pan said, as he affixed the poster over Max's bed.

What I wouldn't do to that tortured sulky sulk, said Pan, stepping back to admire it. What I wouldn't do.

This was the first time Pan said something so explicitly sexual about anyone, much less a boy, much less a boy Max thought looked like Max would look if he let his hair grow out, let his true feelings float to the surface of his face. *How brave. How brave Kurt's eyeliner looks.* It made Max shudder, run his hand along his jaw, and cast his eyes away from his witch.

MAX IMAGINED HOW PAN'S HOUSE might look as his mother drove toward it. They passed through the center of town, which wasn't a center at all, but a collection of shopping malls, a sprawl of chain stores, Italian restaurants that had nothing to do with Italy, and Mexican dives. The car headlights blinked on.

His mother remained mostly silent. Paint stained her jeans, a sign that she had spent the morning in front of a canvas. Her new project captured her thoughts. Max could tell by the way she pulled at her top lip. Her thinking face. She was doing a study of the packaged foods of America. In her series so far, a Pop-Tart on a plate, an Eggo sliced down the center, one of Max's prized Hot Pockets oozing orange cheese.

You should paint sour straws, said Max.

A what?

It's a thread of candy coated in sour powder. It makes the face pucker. It's fun. You can slurp it right in.

Max mimicked the slurp.

Fun food, said his mother. Now that is America. I like how that sounds. Title, perhaps?

A little on the nose, don't you think? said Max.

A smile found his mother's mouth. Amused. Miss Jean was right. The sun had changed her. Her hue had deepened. The new tan looked healthy. She cleared her throat as if to clear the moment, as if to scatter Max's gaze, which took in his mother's flared nose and swoop of onyx hair with its strip of white running through it in one contained band. She called it her badger streak. Sontagian, his father would suggest. Nah, his mother would say—badger. She reached over and patted Max on the leg.

If they turned right at the Chicken Shop and kept driving for fifty miles, they'd hit the university campus, another world entirely. The university had a coffee shop that roasted its own beans. It had a bookstore. It had rows of colonial mansions that housed fraternities and sororities. The road that led to the stadium was lined with life-size copper statues of the former football coaches.

Pan kept saying that he'd take Max to the university to drink a chai latte at the coffee shop, as if that was the most exotic thing he could imagine. The way Pan said *chai*—like chia, instead of chai—made Max wonder if Pan had ever even tasted one. He called it a coffee. *A chia coffee latte.*

Pan lived just outside of Delilah toward the scrawled edge of the county line, where the football boys went mud riding through dried creek beds and drank warm beers in cotton fields and where many of their fathers and grandfathers had once stood, huddled around a fire, spitting secrets into the dirt. The two-lane forest road became a red dirt one, and the trees and their twisted limbs ignored them, couldn't care less if the car sped beneath them or not. His mother turned left at the wooden board nailed to a rusted fence post that read JAM FRESH N SWEET. They went right on Lower Snake Road. Max's thighs ached and pulsed under his shorts. Sore from practice. From running each morning before school. He had a craving for a cold glass of water. He was used to craving. He would put honey in his water. Drink it down.

Max liked it better when Pan came over to his house. He could anticipate the order of events—how his mother would say *Dinner's ready* and what serving spoons she would use. He and Pan would sit on his back porch. The sun would slant in through the screen. He could picture it. They had started a routine. Routines eased him. But his routines needed to be handled with care. Once Max did something three times in a row, he could do it forever. The smooth tracks of familiarity soothed him. They added guardrails to his life. But here was so much new. Here he was coming to Pan's house for dinner. Here he was turning toward a clump of trailers perched at the end of a road he'd never seen.

Pan reclined across his front steps like they were a chaise longue. His legs were crossed, and one hand was flung over his eyes as if to protect them from the cruel angle of the setting sun. A comic book lay unfolded across his lap. He was pretending to be busy. Pan looked up only after the car hummed into place on the loose pebbles.

Max watched his mother wave to Pan. Her eyes swept over the house and took it in. A wooden porch extended from the mobile home, anchoring it into the plot of land under it. Its care was marked by the hydrangea bushes planted in the front square of the yard. Less care could be said of the adjacent mobile home, where starved kittens roamed from underneath cement blocks that lifted up the trailer.

Max noticed the white tips of his mother's knuckles on the steering wheel. Her audible exhale.

Well, she said.

You don't need to come in and say hello, said Max. Please.

Call if you need anything, she said. Okay?

When Max exited the car, he tried not to look at the woman who sat in a rocking chair on the neighboring porch, toothless and sunburned, and reprimanding a young child who seemed to be her relation. The words NEVER FORGET were penciled onto the back of a Bud Light box and taped to the inside of their neighbor's window. The space behind the mobile homes was a jumble of kiddie pools and lawn chairs and discarded wheelbarrows and buckets that once carried something but now held only rainwater.

Max anticipated Pan's impending hug as he exited the car. Before Max reached him, Pan bounded to his feet, jumped up the stairs, disappeared through the front door. Max had nothing to do but follow. Inside, the smooth laminate floors smelled stringent and clean. The walls were thin as dresses. The pictures that hung from them showed faces of smiling, Pan-shaped people. Pan's mother stirred a pot of hot marshmallows and Rice Krispies on the stove while something savory hissed in a skillet.

Pan's mother spoke Spanish into the phone clenched between her shoulder and cheek. It was a relief to hear someone not speak English. She looked younger than Max's mother. The youthfulness presented in the flush of her face, the bounce of her arms. She mouthed hello to Max. Big smile. White teeth made whiter by the red of her lips. She seemed more masculine than Pan. He was the lady of the house. He flitted and spun around his mother in his pink shift as if to prove it.

You ever eat plantains? Pan asked.

Max shook his head no.

I hope you like them, said Pan's mother, who was now off the phone. If you like fries, you'll like them.

She had scrubbed out most of her Puerto Rican accent. Max wondered how she'd done it, if he would ever be able to do the same. He hated the sluggish way he spoke, so tense and halting. Something felt sanitary about the shortness of his sentences. He wanted to hold those American sounds in his mouth, for them to exist in the air as they did in his mind.

During dinner, they ate from paper plates and wiped the grease from the fried plantains and black bean burgers onto red paper napkins bunched up beside them on the table. They drank grape juice from clear plastic cups and pinched off pieces of Rice Krispies treats. Max noticed flatware in the cabinet, sitting untouched, a whole tower of ceramic plates and bowls.

Plastic and paper is easier to clean, explained Pan. You just trash it when you're done.

Max found this to be a strange reason, but he let it go. He liked the informality of dinner. It didn't matter how slow he made his way through the pile of food before him or if he even used his napkin at all. He noticed Pan reach down and smear the sticky from his fingers onto the edge of his sock. Pan's mother saw it, too, but she continued to talk about a colleague at work who was going to get gastro bypass surgery. There was an intimacy to the dinner that Max envied. Maybe this is what happened when two people lived alone for a lifetime. What would that do to a person, to be the sole object of someone's affection? To be the beloved of a single mother? Max tried to imagine a world where he lived with just his mother, but he couldn't. Max wondered if anyone could ever know Pan as well as this woman cutting her bananas, coughing into the canvas elbow of her buttondown, smiling with those thick blocks of white teeth. He felt almost jealous of her.

Ma, Pan said. His voice turned serious. We don't care about your fat colleague. Tell Max about Grandmama.

Oh, said Pan's mother. You tell him. You're better with stories.

Pan let his head roll toward Max.

My mom's grandmother, said Pan, died last year at the ripe young age of 117 in a convent on the outskirts of San Juan. But her whole life she was the healer of her village. She cured sickness with her magic. She could lift the suffering off of someone. She was better than a doctor. We were going to go visit her. But she died. So, I never met her. But she was, you know, she had powers like you wouldn't believe.

A joke, his mother's face seemed to say, an exaggeration. But then her head nodded like, yes, it's true.

She was not a witch, his mother said. She was an herbalist.

She was a witch, said Pan. I come from a witch family. A whole lineage of witches.

No, no, no. Not a witch, baby, said Pan's mother. She was closer to a doctor. A natural healer. She just had a knack for the body.

That's what I said! said Pan. She would heal people. A witch doctor.

She could tell by intuition, said his mother. The exact reason why someone was sick. No one knew how exactly she could tell this, but she could. She never went to school. Of course, she didn't. But if she just took a look at someone's tongue or smelled their urine, she saw what was wrong with them.

A witch, said Pan.

~~~~~~

When Pan's mother left for her graveyard shift on the university campus, Pan took Max into her room, so he could try on her clothes. Her bedroom was smaller than Max's. Pan handed him a bottle of Smirnoff Ice and two Dixie cups. He brushed his hair with an antique bone comb and stared at himself in front of the full-length mirror hung from the back of her door. Max poured two tall cups. They ate chips for dessert. Pan's mother's slips, cardigans, and navy, flat-front slacks were soon strewn across her lavender dresser, the camel-colored carpet, the lumpy armchair pushed into the corner near the window. The furniture in her room was tacky and it didn't match, but it still made more sense to Max than the couches and chairs in his family's rental home. Here, the furniture felt lived in, where the pieces in Max's home seemed empty and without taste—the too big cushions and lumbar pillows with uplifting words and slogans stitched into them. *Joy! Peace! Blessed!*

In her closet hung a tough leather jacket and dirty black jeans. Pan fondled the clothes and made a face that said EW and GROSS as he moved through the white blouses and many shades of salmon. He held up a red workman shirt that Pan said his mother liked to wear to game days and college tailgating. He drew it over his arms and bunched up the bottom, so his belly showed.

Nice, huh? he said. It's like butch meets femme.

Max pretended to flip through a magazine on the bedside table but kept one eye always on Pan.

Super nice, Max repeated.

He watched Pan in his mother's clothes and thought of the Judge's words on TV: Imagine a boy in girl clothes in the locker room with your daughters. The Judge would not like him in this bedroom, even though nothing had happened. Max was a clean slate, a pure intention. But if the Judge and his God were real, then that God would be watching him watch Pan. God would observe the pleasure Max took in this boy dressed as a girl, how Max pined over the small hill of his hip and his smooth, hairless belly.

Have you ever known someone who died? Pan asked.

He held up a negligee to his torso and pivoted his hips.

The question shocked Max. He felt his lips move, an attempt to snatch a word that hovered just outside of his mouth.

Yes.

Pan nodded into the mirror. He gave himself a twirl, dropped the negligee, and examined the way the workshirt looked tied to the side with a scrunchie. Pan caught Max's gaze in the mirror. He cocked his head.

Girl dressed as a boy. Boy dead in a box.

Have you? said Max.

Nope, he said. But I saw a dead body. Tied up in a burlap sack ready to be hauled off somewhere in the night.

I am not following you, said Max.

Something in Max swirled, as if he'd been stirred with a spoon. *A burlap sack. Hauled off in the night.* Before Max, a winding road, a field encroaching, trees sweating above boot-torn leaves. His own death-filled torso overflowed with waste. Pan could set a scene with so little. Max wanted to know more but couldn't think of a way to ask for it.

Oh yeah, hon, said Pan. Scary shit, but I told you this place is a trash can. He mimicked a cheerleader and threw his hands into the air like he had pompoms. Can I get a T? Can I get an R? Can I get an A-S-H? Can I get a CAN? TRASH CAN!

Gothic AF, Pan added.

AF? said Max.

As fuck! Pan shrieked. Honey, you need a language course.

Pan walked over to where Max sat on the bed and looped a leg over his lap and straddled him.

So, who died? said Pan. Tell me.

Their noses were close. They would touch if they moved a centimeter. Max didn't know what to do with his hands. He let them rest beside him, useless and limp. This is what people meant when they said spark.

Who died that you knew? Pan repeated. Tell me.

Max blinked at him.

I'm a witch remember? I could tell someone died.

Pan held a cup of Smirnoff to Max's mouth and watched him drink from it. His eyeliner looked feline. A cat purred at him. Max pictured Pan drawing himself in with a black pencil, circling his eyes as if to confirm their presence.

Your aura's got a bruise on it. Pan flicked Max lightly in the middle of his forehead. Right. There. Bruised. So, tell me.

Max heard himself say Nils's name. The N was hard. It crunched in his mouth. Max heard himself start to tell Pan about the neighbor boy and the beet cake and the toothbrushes they'd shared. The blood in his mouth. The tongue he swallowed.

He needed me.

Max looked toward the window, no screen on it. It sat open. The bugs flew right in.

And I let him down.

The story came fully formed from Max's mouth as if he had been waiting to tell it.

After Nils had moved next door, it had taken exactly two weeks for Max to become obsessed with his new friend, the tow-haired Nils with a Nordic sheen to his skin and eyes as light as clouds. Eleven-year-old Nils had been so pale, he practically glowed in the dark.

Cause I'm made of star stuff, Nils had told Max.

But it was because he was recovering from leukemia.

Max and Nils became inseparable. Bonded like brothers. They roamed in and out of each other's houses as if they were the same. They built a castle inside a tree and made their wars there. They became princes and dragons and celebrated knights. They became soldiers who died only to be brought back to life. While the other boys bought skateboards, they ran through the streets of their imaginations.

Then they grew older, touched their teenage years, and stopped spending days in the tree. They traded their wooden swords for Tintin comics. They read about Tintin's adventures to Tibet, America, and even to the moon. Nils's mother served them apple juice in ceramic mugs and plates of homemade beet cake. They splayed their bodies on the floor of Nils's room, tangled together at the legs. Nils never slept through the night. The monsters in his mind stopped his slumber. He wanted to crawl into Max's dreams instead. That's what he told Max. Nils told him: The monsters are back.

In one dream, Nils peeled the skin from his face, layer after layer, but he never got to the bone. Even though the blood poured out, and his eyes rolled from their sockets and his gums released his teeth, he still couldn't make it to the skull beneath his skin.

In another dream, Nils ran through an old house looking for Max, but when he found him, Max was trapped inside a cage of thorns being eaten by a dog, and Nils couldn't get into the cage to save him. He had to watch Max be eaten.

Max listened to these dreams and repeated the phrase *It's okay* until the phrase meant nothing.

Time passed. The trees turned yellow and lost their leaves. The clouds bunched together and wept a black rain. The clouds cleared, and the earth was blasted with bright rays.

During winter, they built forts out of blankets. Nils rolled candies between his fingers before dropping them into Max's mouth. Malted milk balls. He sucked off the thick sugar coating and spit them out to examine the naked, mud-colored pearl. The heat from their bodies wrapped around Max. The fort became a castle of heat. Nils jerked his shirt over his head. His skin was meatless. A light rash covered his bare chest and bangs clung to his flushed face. He pushed a hot forehead against the pillow they shared. Max always let Nils make the rules for the games they played but, somehow, he knew this game would be different.

His touch made Max's veins move. Excitement and danger swirled in his stomach until Max felt like throwing up. Max held down the sickness that threatened to jump from his body and ruin the moment. They put their faces against each other. Nils tugged at Max, and Max shut his lids tight.

Stop, they both said at the same time. Or maybe just Nils said it.

They could go a hundred hours without touching, and then Max would be brushing his teeth in the bathroom and look up to find Nils behind him, his face watching. Max cleaned well, for both of them, as if by scrubbing his cheeks, he was scrubbing Nils's, too. Sometimes Nils would say *Lick my lips,* and Max would. Other times he would simply reach down in Max's underwear, past the elastic of his shorts, and cup him. Max waited for these moments, afraid of them beginning, but more afraid of them never happening at all. Nils would walk into Max's kitchen, and Max's breath would rush to fill his chest. His breath stayed there, trapped, until the touching began.

If Max thought, if he shut his eyes tight, he could reach the memory of the last time. Max had been kissing Nils's thighs. He put him in his mouth, and when he looked up, blood was pouring from Nils's nose. Max had never seen so much blood. Nils opened his mouth, and there was blood between the cracks of his teeth. There was blood on the front of his shirt, blood on the cliff of his chin.

What is happening? Max had asked, thinking he had done something awful.

Nils breathed his sour breath. He grabbed Max's wrist and handed it back to him. Nils stepped away, looked at Max, and said, I'm sorry.

Max clamped his teeth down on the tip of his tongue and watched Nils leave the bedroom. Nils's sharp, bony shoulders punched at his thin blue shirt like they were wings trying to extend. *I made him sick again*. Nils's spine looked geographic, its topography a ridge that divided his living back in half. Nils called out to his mom in the hallway. His hand slammed into the wall for balance. He tried to speak, but his throat was too weak for the weight and girth of that word he wanted to say. *Mother*. It sounded more like *other*. Max kept moving his teeth back and forth across his tongue tip, back and forth. The uneven ridge of his bucks chafed the muscle until he felt the tip sever—a tiny piece no bigger than the clip of a fingernail. There it was, a sliver of his tongue floating unrooted in his mouth. He swallowed it, then he climbed out of Nils's window.

It was odd how it had happened, how that day everything changed, as if they'd signed a pact never to speak again. Snow had begun to fall the day he left Nils's house forever. The flakes collapsed from the clouds like feathers slashed from a comforter. Nils's mother had taken him away to the hospital, where he stayed for weeks. When Nils came home, he wasn't allowed visitors, because of the germs they might bring. Or at least that's what Nils's mother told him. Max showed up on the doorstep one day, rebellious with beet cake, but Nils's mother had only said: I'm so sorry, sweetie. He'll be happy to know you stopped by.

A direct line of vision existed between the attic window of his house and Nils's room. During the days that Nils was home and not at the hospital, Max would stand at the window and spy on him in bed. Light from the TV screen would strike at the golden rind that stretched over his skull. In those moments, brief and fragile as they seemed, Nils looked like no one he knew. The sight of his sunken cheeks scared Max. It was too intimate. Nils had lost so much weight. It seemed impossible this was the same person who could once climb a tree.

Max shot messages straight to Nils's brain waves, sweet things. Things like *Do not feel sad. I am here even when I am away. You are a king and the bed is your castle. You are the real knight and knights die noble deaths.* Words from their younger games, words a fourteen-year-old Max could only say in his mind. Max would then duck out of sight to hide below the window through which he spied. He had been frightened that Nils would glance up at his house and catch Max's staring face, plump and boyish and beaming with the right kind of blood. After spying on Nils, he would peel a rotten orange just to see it come back to life. He would bite into the fruit, taste its living sugar and its juice, and it wouldn't make him feel better.

When Nils died, Max's mother sat him on the leather chair in the living room and expected him to cry. She knelt before him and placed her palms on his thighs. But Max didn't cry.

I know how close you two used to be, she had said. But now he won't suffer anymore.

His mother had drawn a picture of Nils and Max from the time they met. It had been a quick study to help her improve with watercolors. Nils and Max had posed with such poise, she'd praised them. Max loved how they looked side by side in twin blue button-ups. He kept it propped on his vanity. But after his mother had told him of Nils's death, he went to his room and tore the picture in half. He balled up the half where Nils had been drawn in careful colors and ate it.

Max tried to reach out toward the knowledge of Nils's death, that elusive, matterless thing, like it could be a banister guiding him down a set of steep stairs, but he felt nothing in his hands. He could not hold death's weight in his palm. He could not stuff death into his ears to block out the sound. He saw the mouse come back to life under his touch. He felt the mouse's death in his throat. What would Nils's death taste like? He might kiss his dead lips and make him sit up in bed. But fear held him captive. He couldn't act.

At Nils's funeral, snow fell again. It seemed like it had never stopped snowing since the day he left through Nils's window. Snow fell on Nils's casket and on the shoulders of Max's black jacket. It fell in the white hair of Nils's parents. Max placed his palms on the well-oiled wood of the box and tried not to remember how alive Nils had looked with his face on the pillow, his cheeks flushed, his eyes blooming with intensity. He tasted a fresh apple. Then suddenly, crushingly, the fear came.

Dirt thudded onto the casket's top.

One shovel.

Another shovel.

What had he just done? Max wondered. *Touched the casket? Touched the casket with his hands, his cursed, steal-the-dead-away hands?*

A sugar cube dissolved under Max's tongue. His nose burned with honey. In his mind, he saw Nils's eyes opening only to discover darkness. Nils screaming into the red carpet that lined the walls. Nils hearing the *thuck-thuck-thuck* of dirt hitting the lid above him.

Max sat there in a cold sweat, in a cold panic, in a metal chair. A headache thrummed low and mean. His mother dabbed her eyes and squeezed Max's hand against her stomach. Fear dilated in his heart until it rang out in waves through every cell in his body.

I'm sorry, Max had whispered. I'm sorry.

Shh, his mother said. She stroked his hair. Shh. It's okay. It's not your fault.

At the wake, Max punched through a glass door threaded with steel while people ate hors d'oeuvres, and his mother rushed him away. He hated himself for not saving Nils, and then for maybe saving him after all, but on accident and too late.

Max described Nils's sunken cheeks to Pan. He told Pan twice about laying his palms on the smooth wooden coffin, about punching through another window that night at home. Terror gripped him any time he remembered. The terror came dark and shadowy and flung itself over him without warning. He could be walking down the street and the terror would be hiding in a doorway. The terror would lay right on the ground, and he'd trip on it. The terror waited under bushes. The terror was dressed like a dead boy.

Sometimes he felt Nils's death spreading like a contusion beneath his skin, bruising him from the inside, corroding him to a cancer. Max wondered if Pan might decide to hate him, after hearing what he'd done, but Pan smoothed Max's hair back, brushed it down, and lifted the cup to his mouth again so Max could drink. Pan could open him like an oyster, suck out the pearl. That's what he was doing. *I've never said this out loud*, Max thought.

I've never said that out loud, said Max out loud.

Pan kissed his face now, wet lips on Max's wet cheeks. It almost tickled. The gesture made him think of his mother. Max shut his eyes and let himself be held. He saw his mother kissing his cheeks when he was a child, smoothing back his hair. Gestures that said *safe*.

I felt him in my mouth. I tasted his life go through me and I didn't do anything, said Max.

Pan kissed his chest now. He lifted up Max's shirt and kissed his belly, the white fur around his navel. Little wet sucks. Max looked at his ears, the small brown spines of them. Their skin colors together were a contrast. Pan kissed his way back up Max's chest, up his neck, until he met Max's mouth. His tongue felt quick and alive. They moved clumsily back on the bed until they were no longer sitting but lying. Pan banged his head on the wall. *Ow*. His hand examined the skull for a cut. Pan grabbed Max by the waist and pulled him in tight. *He's nervous, too*, thought Max. Pan's face was against his bicep, and he nuzzled it as if he wanted to get closer to Max but wasn't sure how. They kissed again and humped each other through their pants until that was no longer enough and their clothes started to fall to the sheets, to the side table, to the carpet.

Max moved forward from one desire to the next. A muscle twitched in his calf. He knew his pits smelled oily and sodden. And here was Pan so near to them with his nose shoving into his shoulder and then collarbone. Their lips touched again, and even a clumsy kiss felt exciting. Everything sped up until Max didn't know where his body began and Pan's ended. His pulse quickened, and his heart beat so fast he would have to run a million sets of stairs to find himself again. Max might be bad at this. The heat strung itself from dusk to dawn, and they tumbled through it. They moved through the hallway, found themselves in Pan's room. The tied-up dog howled outside.

You are you, Pan said, biting Max's lips. You are so you.

Max bit his lips back. There was a butterfly-shaped blotch on Pan's neck. *Hives from me*, Max thought. *I gave him a sex butterfly.*

They dozed together in a twist of sheets in the bedroom thrumming with damp air. Then they woke as one, gripped each other in the dark, and did it all again. Max had never let himself go like this—not with Nils, not ever—but there he was soaring through the vodka, sweating Smirnoff from his pores. Max opened his mouth to give something to Pan, a sonnet or perhaps the exact way it felt to be trampled by a body more delicate than his own, but his teeth caught whatever good he could have said. He went so deep into Pan he thought he might touch the bottom of his rib cage, feel the root of his beating heart.

Max had thought love would begin with a courting ritual: arranged dates, unbuttoned shirts, a first kiss, anticipated yet restrained, on the sidewalk before a house. Love was not a boy in Germany with blood pouring from his mouth. Love was not a witch in Alabama who slept until noon and ate cloves of garlic. But there in that room, Max wanted to buy Pan a house full of flowers.

Nothing bad will happen, Pan said, as if convincing himself, as if answering a question Max never asked.

He said this to Max, or he said it to the ceiling, which was where his gaze was affixed, which was lined with bone white plaster, which was the only thing separating them both from the stars.

Finally, Max said.

But this was always going to happen, said Pan.

MAX WOKE UP THE NEXT morning hungover and unhappy. He wasn't sure where the melancholy came from, but it sat in his jaw. He felt like a bowl licked empty. It wasn't a good empty. It just felt empty. His shoulders ached. The drunk cleaved his head. Pan slept beside him curled like a question mark. A spindle of drool hung from his lips. Mascara smeared across the paisley pillowcase. Pan's cheeks caved toward each other. Max saw that his own nails had been painted red, a detail he did not recall from the previous night. What else did he not remember? The sun was already washing Pan's bedroom white with heat. It exposed the dust gathered on the windowsill, the streaks of wet mold on the ceiling. A poster of a Valium pill was tacked above the bed. A shrine to Billy Corgan had been erected in the far corner next to a pile of Pan's thrift store dresses. Max heard the dog bark outside and the woman scream at the child. He listened as the woman threatened to tie the child to the bedpost or stuff her in a trash bag and take her to the curb. Vodka churned his stomach. He rolled onto his side and buried his eyes.

Max had hoped sex would make him feel better, closer to Pan in some way. But he didn't feel the tenderness he wanted. He just felt naked. He could not wash the image of Nils from his retinas. It was more present now. Max remembered the way his eyes had stayed on Nils as he undressed in the bathroom, the way Max's body had tightened with longing under the gaze of the first boy he had ever wanted.

ON A WOODEN CUTTING BOARD, Max's mother sliced black radish into lace. She recounted her latest Alabama annoyance. The woman from the corner house, whose husband owned all the Ford dealerships in town, told her *Y'all come on over now, you hear?* But when Max's mother had appeared at her doorstep, the woman seemed shocked, even embarrassed.

Oh, his mother had realized. She wasn't supposed to come over.

Being here is like a code you have to crack. She chopped the radish with a new fury. It's fake. They don't mean what they say, and I'm just supposed to understand the subtext.

Why do you hate it so much? Max asked. I don't think it's bad even at all.

The mothers feed their children Starbursts and call it fruit. A woman in the grocery store told me Starburst is one of her five a day.

You are being judgmental, said Max.

He had already told her his plans to go hunting with the Judge that weekend. *You have to be there at what time in the a.m.?* she had said, aghast, but according to her own parenting morals, she had not forbidden him from going.

I want to ask you about Pan, his mother said. She widened her eyes as if hoping to implant some psychic undercurrent directly into his brain. She set down her knife.

When Max said nothing, she continued.

I want to hear more about him. Like what does he do for fun? Does he have hobbies? A pet? What was his mother like when you met her?

Wow. Twenty questions, said Max.

Not twenty, she said. Just four.

I don't know. He wants to be, uh, a magician or something, said

Max. And he's got a cat named Mr. Sprinkles. Well, it's like a stray, but also kind of his.

What I mean is I can tell you like him, she said. I want you to know I like him, too.

Okay, said Max. You like him, too.

I wonder if you like him the way you liked Nils.

Nils made Max stand up straighter.

What is that supposed to mean, said Max. The way I liked Nils?

She brought the vegetables together on the cutting board with the edge of her knife. She watched the knife and not her son.

She said, That would be difficult here.

As if Max didn't already know. He yawned into his hand and acted bored. He caught his reflection in the kitchen's glass door, the one that slid open to the backyard patio. He looked normal enough, he thought, but maybe he didn't see himself right. Maybe his desire was obvious. Maybe he walked around with it written across his body and everyone could see. He felt exposed standing before his mother in the kitchen. Exposed in a way his new Alabama uniform of polo shirts and camo jackets couldn't cover up.

I think he's great, she said. Pan. For the record.

Max did not know what she thought she got, what she thought she understood about him or Pan or Nils. Max looked at his phone. It lit up like it was speaking.

LONG-DISTANCE CALL BETWEEN HIS mother and aunt as over-heard on speakerphone.

MOTHER: If only you could see our next-door neighbor.
AUNT: Tell me.
MOTHER: She's a certified nut job. And Max loves her.
AUNT: Loves her? Really.
MOTHER: She's always walking around in football jerseys holding dead azaleas in her hands and talking about Jesus.
AUNT: Max is curious. It makes sense that he likes what's different.
MOTHER: Well, everything here is different. So, he's in paradise. But, you know, he is more swayed by power than I expected. It makes me think he doesn't have strong enough self-esteem. Did I fuck up somehow?
AUNT: Show me a teenage boy that has strong self-esteem.
MOTHER: Kids with good self-images do not get swept up by some-one else's personality. They can differentiate.
AUNT: It's called peer pressure. It's called being a teen boy. He needs to separate himself from you. Build his identity in oppo-sition to yours. Of course, he's not going to be into painting or whatever. That's what his mom does.
MOTHER: This is different. Trust me. The boys he's become friends with—there's something not right with them.
AUNT: How are his headaches?
MOTHER: Fine. Better.
AUNT: How's therapy?
MOTHER: He hasn't gone since we left. But he's not sleeping the day away, and he's stopped wearing slings on his hand.

AUNT: Well, I don't see what's worrying you. This sounds good.

MOTHER: He wants to go hunting. Which, I tell you, terrifies me. I never would have thought hunting would interest Max. He's sensitive. You've seen him with animals.

It amused Lorne that Max had never held a gun.

Not yet, man, Price said.

Max followed Lorne and Price into the mudroom of the Judge's house, where Lorne laced his boots underneath the gaze of many decapitated animal heads. The doe appeared especially elegant with her long neck and black eyes.

The Judge kept a gun cabinet crowded with rifles and shotguns used for hunting. The doors of the cabinet were made of glass, so the guns could be gazed at and ready to access for home defense. Lorne showed him the bottom drawer, where his father stored cleaning supplies and extra ammunition. Price explained to Max that to have a gun was a right. Those long hard bodies were powerful things to hold. They were to be respected, tucked into an armpit, cradled like an infant, pointed far away from the body. They were for the event of bad guys, intruders, militia formation.

Max popped his thumb joint. His stomach clenched and unclenched.

These were real? Max asked, looking at a duck's green feathers, its wings extended into a kind of rigid eternal flight. He brought his hand toward it as if to stroke the wing, then thought better of it and shoved his hand into his pocket. He imagined birds shot dead into the dirt. He couldn't pick one up without it flying off his palm.

Course they're real, said Lorne. Killed that one myself.

He explained how he sliced the neck of the deer to stop its suffering, then hauled it into the pickup with his dad. It was his first kill, so his father had rubbed the innards all over his face and neck. The hot blood came steaming off him. He said you could taste her intestines in the air.

A picture memorialized the occasion. There was a little Lorne in a too big camo coat, cradling the giant deer's head against his thighs. It was nighttime, and the flash had the power of a searchlight. The animal had been smeared across his cheeks into a kind of war paint. Max fixated on the deer's tongue, large and pink.

We'll take you deer hunting soon, said Price. Ever get your teeth in some venison jerky?

He tried to hand Max a plastic baggy of twisted, leather-look flesh.

No but thank you for the offering, Max said and deposited the picture of Lorne and his kill back on the cedar shelf where it had been.

Suit yourself, said Price. He shoved a wad in his mouth and chewed. Dude, you have to stop talking formal as fuck.

Sure, Max said. Okay. He scraped his mind for something not formal. I'll try, he said. I'll try, man, he added.

Lorne snorted.

Been doing this a long-ass time, Lorne said. A damn long time, brother.

Lorne's eyes sought out another picture on the shelf. He picked it up and handed Max a framed photo of boys lined up to pose during what Lorne explained was a Youth Dove Hunt.

See? said Lorne. A long-ass time.

During the youth hunt, men took boys into the field and taught them how to kill. The boys aimed at branches to learn how the gun kicked. They aimed higher and higher until the kick hurt and knocked them over. They trained their eye at the smooth arc birds made when carving a flight through the blue cap of day. The boys returned with bags full of dead birds. Their hands were washed but their pants still smelled. The boys in the picture were reed and wire, not yet the bulk of body Max encountered on the field. In one picture, a boy whom Max recognized as Knox held a limp bird by its wing. His face was serious. Dead grass grew tall behind him and farther back skinny trees were scattered in thinned-out patches. The sunset blasted the horizon with streaks of red.

In the photos, the boys were dressed in camouflage shirts and pants and wore orange caps. This was the same outfit Lorne and Price each had on as they stood before Max in the mudroom. A kind of cartoonish twig pattern covered them: army green and tree-trunk brown and dirt tan. Lorne looked Max up and down, took in his khaki pants, and the new golf shirt he bought. He shook his head and chuckled.

You look like a fag, he said.

He riffled through a closet to search for a similar uniform for Max.

Just wait another month or so when it cools down and the deer come out. That's when you get them good bucks. Here, try this.

Max took the camouflage bib overalls. Their fingertips touched, and Max looked away, embarrassed. The tag called the pattern Bottomland. The undershirt was described as Shadow Grass Blades.

Max undressed in front of the boys almost daily in the locker room, but here it felt different. Lorne didn't pretend to give him privacy. He crossed his arms and leaned against the gun cabinet and chewed on a piece of mint gum that Max could smell from where he stood. Price paid no attention. He texted with a girl.

I like her, Price said, but her sister and momma look like they fell out of the ugly tree and hit every branch on the way down. I got no clue how she turned out so hot sauce.

He talked about how he was trying to persuade her to be his experimenter, but she would only let him make out with her. Price explained that if she didn't give in soon, he was going to move on to Betsy, who had been giving him eyes and was D.T.E.

Down to experiment, he said, exasperated, when Max looked at him like he didn't understand.

Max felt his legs hit the cool a.c. He thought he would shrivel beneath his new checkered boxers. These were not the form-fitting white briefs he wore in Germany. They held nothing in place. It took him by surprise, but Max felt himself harden while Price talked about experimenting. Lorne's eyes smothered him, and the stiffening moved down. His hardness struck at the fabric surrounding it, one quick *thump*, as if it were reaching out toward Lorne. Lorne must have seen it, because his gaze did not waver, and his eyes flashed hunger again. It was a hunger Max recognized. Lorne stood in front of the row of rifles. The guns made Max uncomfortable at first, but the longer he looked at them, the less scary they seemed.

Morning had begun to inch at the horizon when the boys squeezed into the truck with the Judge. It was so humid and sticky everything moved slow, even Max's mind. Max loved being up early like this. He clutched the thermos of coffee between his thighs and sank into the fancy leather seats. He felt like he was playing dress-up. He flexed his calves beneath his thick canvas pants. He was getting so strong. The truck sped through the morning. Everyone stayed quiet. Above them, a smattering of stars, the moon clipped high into place, far away from the sun.

The Judge turned on the evangelical radio station and the voices were like angels among them. *You're a good good Father.* The Judge hummed. Max closed his eyes and worry whipped through him.

You cold, Germany, he heard Price say. You're shivering back here.

On the edge of a cut cornfield, they ate breakfast sandwiches and drank from the thermos. Price explained how if you didn't kill a dove when you shot it, you'd have to pop off its head with your thumb.

The heads come off easy, said Price.

They sat on a fallen tree trunk, faces set to the field. It was hopelessly boring, and no doves came, which relieved Max. He put his eye to the scope and watched for a twitch or flicker of life. Still nothing.

Strange, the Judge said.

Max said a prayer to God. He said thank you for not bringing the birds to the guns. As soon as he prayed, a bird burst from the trees nearby.

The Judge rose gracefully and with speed. In the same gentle manner that he did everything, he shot the bird. The boys watched it fall from its flight path to the ground. Max could taste gunpowder, burnt and lingering. Now there were birds, many of them. The Judge whispered in Max's ear and helped direct the barrel to where he needed to point it. Max kept his breath in his mouth. The gun nudged into his shoulder. Max could sense the lives of every animal that had fled the earth. His mouth watered. He hated the gun in his hands, heavy as a limb. He closed his eyes when he fired, but he knew by the gasps around him that he shot the dove. He felt it, too. The smell found his nose.

The Judge led him through the clammy air to collect their slain birds.

Simple as one, two, three to run out and get them, he said.

They found the Judge's dove easily. It landed right where it looked like it had. The Judge bagged it, tucking it into the back of his vest, but Max's couldn't be found. They looked and they looked. They walked through the weeds and across a blanket of loamy soil, past cut cornstalks, but there was nothing. They discovered a patch of hot blood in the dirt and a few feathers and the Judge said: Curious. How strange. Seems like it just flew back to heaven. Thought we'd have seen it fly away.

You some kind of witch, son? the Judge said.

Max shrugged. He felt nauseated and blamed it on the coffee when he excused himself and dumped his gut into the grass nearby. He burped and wiped his mouth with the back of his shooting hand.

Max didn't try to shoot another bird, but Price and Lorne killed a few dozen apiece. When they left, their hunting buckets full, they passed families walking toward the field. It was a small miracle no one asked Max to carry one of the buckets.

Stupid. He admonished himself. *Stupid to think coming here could be okay.*

In the truck, the Judge turned up a program that featured himself talking. Max sat in the back with Price, who texted with his girl-not-yet-experimenter.

The reason we have more school shootings isn't because of the Second Amendment. It's because people have lost sight of God. Prayer has fled our schools. They put sin on the television and endorse it. These secular, godless lifestyles. It's almost like we've asked for it. We've pushed God out of schools, so of course we've ushered in chaos, violence, and death. We need more love in the schools. More God. It's more God. Not fewer guns. You need to put in the good, and it will overwhelm the bad. These children, they are craving relationship. They are craving the love of their Father.

The Judge turned down the radio and looked at Max through the rearview mirror. His eyes were blue as crushed ice.

What do you think about all that now, Max? Make sense to you?

Max understood that he wasn't expected to respond, which was good, because Max didn't know what to say. How someone like the Judge could be wrong about anything seemed nearly impossible. Max agreed that more good was needed. He'd thought about what the Judge had said about mystery. Mystery was the constant in Max's life. To live with mystery made sense to him. To accept mystery as a part of things.

We're building up a Christian army, son, and not everyone is up to the task. But what do you think? You want to be a warrior?

A warrior, said Max.

He had repeated what the Judge had said, and that must have sounded like a yes. Max didn't want to be a warrior, but he did want to belong.

The Judge squinted at him. Max tried to empty his brain of anything bad, feeling certain the Judge was in there, digging at the gray matter. The Judge nodded as if he had glimpsed all he needed to know about Max from that one swift survey and, yes, oh yes, he had approved.

THE JUDGE DROVE MAX, Lorne, and Price to his HQ to make phone calls. He was needed upstate for a campaign dinner. Before he let them out of the car, he prayed for the boys. They bowed their heads. Max felt the Judge's palm hover just above his scalp. He fought the urge to clasp the Judge's hand and thread their fingers together. He wanted to touch him.

Father God, said the Judge.

Another language bloomed in the Judge and pushed its way out. His words slurred. The sounds approximated words but were not words that Max knew. Price drove his knuckles into the back of the passenger seat and groaned. Thin white scars crisscrossed Price's wrists. Price had been sent away to a rehabilitation program a few years ago for what Davis called the sad spells. The women who ran the program used horses to heal depression and rage. She claimed horses absorbed the ailments of those whoever rode them. The sad spells had receded. Price's wrists had grown new skin.

The Judge's voice lifted and fell. The mouths of the boys vibrated. But not Max's voice. His teeth caged the sound in. His lips sank shut. Holy noises left the Judge and became Price's voice. Lorne caught the end of the strange sounds. Max felt the Judge touch his head. Shivers spread through him. The Judge moved his hand over the crown of each of their heads. Price gasped, and the spirit fled him. Their prayer had finished.

Rise up, Alabama! Davis yelled when he saw Max, Lorne, and Price stroll into the office. Y'all look damn worn out. What'd y'all kill? Tell me. I want to relive it right here.

Max shot himself a magic bird that flew right back to heaven, said Price.

Damn. Look at you, Germany, said Davis.

I'm ready to make my calls, Max said, hoping to steer the conversation. His body still shook from the car prayer. The warmth of it hugged him. It gleamed in his mind.

Price punched Max in the breast and smiled.

Get you a Coke from the vending machine, Price said. Sugar up.

The college game played on the television set, muted. The players looked giant as they marched across the gridiron. The camera panned the audience to show the painted faces. Arms shook pompoms. Hands jabbed #1 foam fingers and threw rolls of toilet paper into the air. Max watched as an elephant mascot ran through the green field flipping himself and riling up the crowd. Max could almost hear the collective roar of the stadium. He'd been practicing this new sport nearly every day now, and he felt like he understood it, the fervor it stirred up in people. It gave them a common purpose, a good team and a bad one. People in Alabama, he had come to realize, needed things to be one thing or another. Their team or not. With them or against. He understood where the nickname for the team came from, because they did look like a crimson tide, sweeping over the landscape, covering everything in red, drowning anything that wasn't them.

The camera zoomed in on the quarterback with his parted, worried mouth.

Wish I had a body like that, said Davis who stood, hands on his hips staring at the quarterback, too.

Max admired Davis's triangle. His eyes slide down the backside of his thigh, the carved slab of calf, the thin ankle.

You will, said Max. He pulled out a chair. Just keep with the weights.

Max stared at a piece of printer paper lined with campaign promises.

Rules for making a phone call, said Davis. One: Mention God's name within the first two sentences. Two: Offer to pray for them before you get off the phone. Three: Tell them you play football. Rest is right here on this paper.

Pray with them? Max said.

Yeah, man. Listen, it's not rocket science, just make stuff up that sounds nice. Just follow what we say. After you've prayed once, you've prayed a thousand times. Jesus will take the wheel.

Max tried a few numbers. Each time the person on the other line hung up right away. He kicked the table leg after the fifth dial zone droned into his ear.

I don't know what is going wrong, said Max.

Davis smacked the desk in front of him. I know what it is, man. It's that Nazi accent! They think you're pranking calling.

MAX FINISHED HIS MORNING RUN and walked into the kitchen. He stood before his parents shirtless, adorned only in his green athletic shorts. He picked up his sweatshirt from the bench in the breakfast nook and wrangled it over his shoulders. GOD'S WAY was spelled out in block letters across his chest. His mother had not gotten used to the name. She looked away. He pulled out a chair at the breakfast table and sat down before an empty bowl and began to heap it with yogurt. He stirred in honey and jam. More honey. More jam.

Your sugar intake has skyrocketed again, said his mother. Can you maybe use two spoons of jam and not three? It's awfully sweet.

I like awfully sweet, said Max.

Max had not healed in a week. A test he placed upon himself. In Germany, Max had begun to experiment with his healings. He wanted to understand the symptoms of acting and of abstaining. What he had noticed: each healing sent him into a moment of pure, sugar-filled bliss, followed by a migraine stupor where he'd stay for hours, sleeping off the effects. At first, the comedowns sapped him of serotonin. As time went on, he realized that if he healed small things once every few days, he could build up a kind of tolerance. His hangovers would not be as bad, his cravings would be moderate, and his headaches only a slight bruise. When he went too long between healings, eating sugar was a proxy that kept his headaches and energy levels manageable.

After Nils had died, Max had sworn off his power for good. He had quit healing at once, with no plan for how to manage the sudden transition. The symptoms of withdrawal had nearly killed him. In the months of sobriety that followed, headaches and fatigue pinned Max to his bed. Sugar alone could not fix him. He would sneak downstairs when his parents weren't home and crunch handfuls of turbinado cubes and drink cups of maple syrup. But these had been small reliefs that lasted only an hour or so. His mother had taken him to medical specialists and cognitive therapists. None of them had been able to locate a medical reason for his behavior. *Grief,* each finally concluded.

After months of suffering, Max had finally detoxed off death. His hunger for sugar subsided. His headaches fled him. Running, he had realized, was another way to curb his cravings. It gave him purpose, a thing to do with the energy pinwheeling through his body. If he was moved to heal, he would run instead—or eat candy. When death stopped him in his tracks, he had comforts to turn to for relief. But Alabama left him defenseless. His old tricks did not soothe him in the same way. He had relapsed, and the only thing he could do was wait it out and see how his body would react. The rules could be different here.

Careful or you'll find yourself with diabetes, said his mother.

Max shrugged. I don't think so, he said. I run too much for that.

Are you feeling sad again? Lonely and displaced? Is that the reason for all this sugar? asked his mother.

You're projecting, said his father. Lonely and displaced. My goodness.

No, Max said, and he wasn't lying.

I heard the university has some excellent therapists if you want to see someone. Your father, he could get a recommendation.

I said no! Max had not meant to yell, but he did.

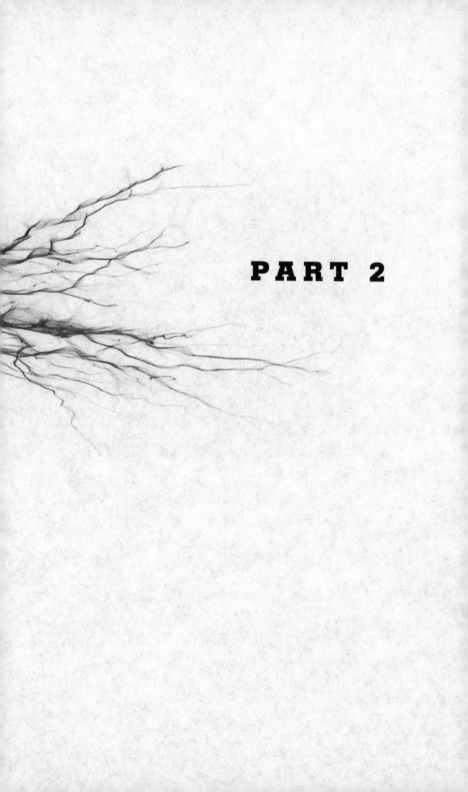

PART 2

THE BOYS WENT TO CANVAS for the Judge, and Max saw more of Alabama. They passed cemeteries where men buried raccoon-killing dogs in clean cotton sacks. The men had chiseled their names into bricks and placed them over the soil where their mutts lay. People came to scatter daisies across the graves. They passed an abandoned mill town where clapboard houses rotted in the woods. Bushes grew out of shed windows and kudzu crawled up the splintered sides. *Ghosts live here,* Max thought, *and nothing else.*

The boys dipped fries into chocolate frosties. They ate fried pork rinds and sugar and butter sandwiches as they drove up and down the state. They spit sunflower shells onto the truck's floor, tucked strawberry chew beneath their bottom lips, and let the open windows wipe all thoughts from their heads.

They passed a garden of white crosses where an evangelical had scrawled apocalyptic verses from the Bible on lawn furniture, busted cars, a washing machine, tree trunks, flags, and orphan parts of a jungle gym. White crosses and planks of particle board rose from the ground.

REPENT TO THE GOOD LORD HELL IS HOT
Jesus Coming Soon
JESUS Love You
JESUS is the GOD DOOR

Davis quizzed the boys on the capitals of foreign countries as they drove. He solved complicated long division puzzles all in his head.

A mind must be sharp as a knife, said Davis.

The boys passed a monument of white soldiers erected by Daughters of the Confederacy to memorialize the Civil War. Protests had sprung up around the South led by people who wanted to take the statues down. The protests morphed into mobs that ripped some statues right from the ground and destroyed them with sledgehammers. That's what the boys told Max. These protests convinced them of nothing but the rioters' own ignorance. The man running against the Judge led a charge against these monuments.

If he gets elected, Davis said, his face serious and still, he will systematically erase our history. He will take a black marker to the lives of our forefathers and blot them out. He's calling the Judge a monster. I mean. C'mon now, man. The Judge is a preserver. He doesn't think we should forget the past or pretend it was all one way or all the other. He knows that seeing the truth isn't easy. He's for all of us. It just might take some people more time than others to see it.

Lorne clenched the steering wheel with one hand, and Max saw his grip tighten at the word *preserver.*

Come at our statues and he'll see what happens, said Knox.

The truck they rode in had three bumper stickers on the back: Judge's name, a Jesus fish, and a slogan that said THE SOUTH WILL RISE.

Thing is, people in America are not educated correctly, said Davis, his voice dropping an octave. I don't know how it is in Germany, man, but the people here want handouts. It doesn't make sense. This country is built on personal responsibility. You heard of that, Germany? It means you get what you work for. You get what you put in. No one looks out for you but you. That's what makes America great.

And God, said Knox.

That's right, said Davis. God gives everyone opportunities in this country. If people don't want to use them, then that's on them. God knows where my heart is.

A flock of birds came together in the distance and formed an arrow. Each bird stayed in the line. The arrow forged forward. A bird broke off, drifted down, and circled toward the trees. Max watched the bird right itself and return to the arrow again. Max tried to understand what God had to do with this talk of personal responsibility. He studied Davis's profile to discern his mind, as if the answer to his thoughts expressed itself on the geometry of his face, in the deep pores on his cheeks or in the gentle curve of his lashes. The skin was raw on Davis's neck where he'd razored the hair away. He would be beautiful like this for only so long.

Thing is, said Knox. He turned from the passenger seat to face Max. His breath smelled of peanuts. People are going to get what they deserve.

Knox dug his knuckles into his thighs, slid them down to the top of his knee brace. You can't feel sorry when something awful comes down on a person. Fact is, they brought it on themselves. That's the fact of it.

Lorne had been mostly quiet as he drove, but he spoke then.

The wage of sin is death, he said.

Sorry? said Max.

You heard me, said Lorne. You heard me.

Lorne had a notebook of the addresses they were supposed to visit. The men whose doors they knocked on offered them sweet tea or skim milk and wanted to talk football. They visited a computer programmer who, Davis explained, had sunk into depression after his mother died. They had lived together, and he hadn't known what to do with her body when she passed, so he left it to decompose in her bedroom until the stench got so bad that he tried to move her to the shed behind his house, but her body began to fall apart, into pieces, as he transported her. The neighbors saw and called the police.

He didn't mean harm, Davis said. But he was charged with something because he had been cashing her disability checks even after she died. Judge's really been helping him out. Got him a good lawyer and everything.

And he also then brought it on himself? asked Max.

Nah, said Davis. This here is different. He was doing the best he knew to do.

They drove past plantation homes and under mangled oak trees. They drove past muddy rivers and clear creeks where water moccasins curled in wait. They drove past everything under that hot-as-hell sky.

A TEXT FROM PAN LIT up in Max's lap: Cum play with me PLZ.

Here is where I can get out, Max told Lorne as they approached the Chicken Shop intersection.

They had finished canvasing early. The evening was theirs. Davis wanted to take the boys fishing. Kill worms with hooks. Gut bass. Oil up and fry their scales for dinner. They'd pull blankets onto Davis's front porch and sleep outside as the outdoor fan cut the air above them.

Seriously? What are you going to do? Hitch a ride home from the fry girl? asked Davis. We're going fishing.

I'll pick u up. Text when they're gone.

You don't want fish? asked Knox.

Ttyl.

Fishing on Davis's dock was out of the question. He couldn't put himself through that again. He pictured Davis's face when he noticed that any fish Max caught stayed alive on the hook, stayed alive in his hands.

Walk on water, Germany. Go on.

Walk on the water.

Turn them fishes into wine!

Bread fishes. Sin scales.

He thinks he's a princess.

Damn, it's hot as balls, said Knox to no one, pulling at the crotch of his shorts.

The billboard near the intersection pointed a gun right at them. ARE YOU WILD & FREE?

Lorne dropped Max in front of the Chicken Shop. The truck idled at the red light. Knox spit out the passenger window. The engine revved. They screamed off into the fading day. Max bought a Dutch apple pie and an ice cream sundae. He inhaled them in almost one breath. He sat on a bench outside and waited for Pan. The parking lot before him was empty except for three SUVs and a red truck. Behind the parking lot a black road kept the cars backed up at a light. He watched traffic inch forward. Eating in cars was a thing that happened in America. He could have eaten his apple pie in the car with Pan.

Max had seen Pan only at school since their night together. But Pan had visited Max in his dreams, appearing in visions so strong and physical that when he woke in the morning, he'd been shocked to find himself alone.

Pan pulled up in front of Max, rolled the window down, and angled his head toward the half-mast of glass. Max blushed at the sight. A rose bloomed on the front of his throat.

Hey.

It was all he could manage.

Pan's car smelled of mold, which was the reason Pan had placed a Dove bar on the console. The soap soaked up the stink. Max grabbed the melted bar and brought it to his nose. It smelled like soap was supposed to smell. By neutralizing the odor, it hadn't destroyed its own essence.

Pan drove with his left leg tucked under his seat. Max liked being his passenger. He liked being driven by someone else to somewhere else. An image swung in front of Max's eyes. The two of them twinned on Pan's bed. As they got closer to Pan's, the land transformed just like he knew it would. No more manicured lawns and parking lot asphalt and signs blinking out desires. ICE CREAM. WARM BUTTER YEAST BREAD. FRESH/NOW. HOT/NOW. They passed tangled browns and sun-dead things. The car followed a perfect white fence around a bend and down a country road. A black crow sat on the telephone wire and turned its head at the car. Then another.

One crow sorrow.

Two crows joy.

Crows flew above them, trailing their car.

The smell of manure careened through the open windows. They passed a plot of land on their right, a place to dump junk. A woman emerged from a rusted pile of car parts and washing machines. A cascading blonde mullet. A sleeveless red sweatshirt.

That'd be a tough place to live in, Pan explained. Too cold in the winter. Too hot in the summer.

When they pulled up to Pan's trailer, Max was still thinking: *Too cold or too hot*. He hadn't registered that the land they passed, the junk dump, had been a home. In his mind, children climbed over weather-beaten couches, through discarded truck tires, and sat on rusted car parts. What world was this that he'd found himself in? He brought to mind the stories he'd heard of Alabama boyhoods: running barefoot over the hot ground, catching tadpoles in rain puddles, jarring the lit tails of fireflies, finding antlers in a pile of bleached bones. He imagined eating frogs for dinner like Knox had done.

What up, Ivetta, Pan called to the neighbor on her rocking chair, the one who was always on the porch. Today she did not yell. Her teeth were not in her mouth but in a glass of water beside her foot. Her dog whimpered and bit its own leg.

Ivetta shot Pan a look that was neither hateful nor good. It was just a look that said *I see you*.

MAX TOSSED AN EMPTY CHEETO PUFF bag into the can under the kitchen sink. He had consumed the entire family-size sack while standing in Pan's kitchen. He opened the refrigerator and stared into it like it held the answer to a question he'd just asked.

Hunger sat in Max's stomach, but Pan did not want to eat. Pan never wanted to eat. He consumed only Spaghetti Hoops and Chicken Shop fries and hardly even that. He starved off any trace of a figure. His dresses couldn't get tighter if someone painted them on. A cigarette smoked itself beside Pan. It rested atop the rinsed can he used for an ashtray. The countertop was bare, aside from a bottle of ibuprofen, a roll of paper towels, a neat stack of receipts held together with a paper clip, and a spray bottle of all-purpose cleaner. Three bananas turned brown in a mixing bowl on the table. The kitchen was as big as Max's kitchen in Germany, but the thick-legged table and heavy, meat-colored chairs gave the illusion of less space.

The morning after their sleepover, Max had woken up and eaten cereal at this exact kitchen table with Pan while his mother had brushed her teeth and dressed for bed. The cereal had turned their soy milk pink. They had held their bowls to their mouths with one hand and gulped, their free hands laced together between the chairs. Pan's thumb had rubbed and rubbed until it had bruised Max's skin. Now the bruise was almost gone. The sadness that had bristled through Max in bed upon waking had evaporated into a pleasant steam. Eating cereal at the table, Max had felt calm-shaped. Capable. He saw Pan in all his possibility. Mr. Sprinkles had slept in the chair beside them, tabby tail twitching and long.

Max eyed Pan sitting on the countertop, legs crossed and filing his nails. He thought of the places he still hadn't touched—the edge of skin between earlobe and neck, the hollow of collarbone, the pink pad of foot bottom, the long line of shinbone, the tendon at the back of the knee.

Pan snapped his fingers in front of Max's face.

Earth to Max.

Yes, said Max.

I said there's nothing to do in this godforsaken town but wander through the Walmart or drive out to the river to go inner-tubing and get drowned.

Is there? said Max.

You go to the river and you get drowned, said Pan. It happens ten times every summer. Some dumbo can't swim and thinks it's shallow enough, so it doesn't matter. Then he ends up dead. His body bloated and blue in the dam.

But Max had loved his trip to the river, the rope swing and the white-tipped water that pooled in eddies and spun off the top of rocks. The boys had taken him out to climb the sides of trees and cannonball off cliffs and nap on rocks slimy with water-hair. They had floated down the river with a cooler cinched to its own raft. They had spilled their beers like nothing mattered.

There is a plenty lot to do here, Max said. He unzipped a bag of generic taffy candy. Teenagers have cars.

He became embarrassed after resealing the bag and returning it to the counter next to the stack of receipts. Pan's mom didn't have money, and here he was eating her out of food.

It doesn't matter if you have a car or not, said Pan, if there's nowhere good to go. If I have to spend one more Friday night hanging out in the Walmart parking lot, I'll eat my own hair.

My mother she says only boring people will get bored.

Deep, said Pan. Sounds like this is her first year in Alabama.

Max shrugged.

You and your joking, Max said.

You know where I want to visit? Pan said. Mongolia.

Why would you want Mongolia?

I want Mongolia because I want to learn to be shaman, that's what. I saw a Discovery Channel documentary about a shaman in

Mongolia. He pulls liquid from people's necks with just his fingertips. They filmed him doing it. It's like a cleanse. He's extracting darkness from their aural body. He pulls out their suffering and their trauma with his fingers.

Pan held up his hand, spread apart his fingers, and stared at Max through the gaps.

Deep, said Max, hoping he sounded funny.

I could learn how to do that stuff, too, like, read energy fields, move cups of water with my mind. That's the kind of stuff shamans do. Battle darkness. Heal stuff, said Pan.

You want to heal? I trade you.

You might be a shaman, you know, said Pan. With your power. Maybe you need to go to Mongolia and see this guy. Maybe you need a guru.

I don't want a guru, said Max. He frowned at a cockroach that emerged from the light socket behind Pan.

Maybe you are a guru, said Pan.

No, said Max. I am not that.

You of all people should know that there's more to this world than we can see, said Pan. So, don't be looking at me like I'm the crazy one for talking gurus.

Sorry, said Max. I am not trying to look at you like that.

Don't you think you're trying to make a guru out of the Judge? Just a little bit. Don't lie to me now, Sad Sarah. This is a no-lies zone.

No, said Max. I do not think.

Max blushed, which meant lying. He walked through his mind and found the Judge in a cut cornfield with a gun to his eye. He shivered at the thought and shook it off. Why would he have gone there if he didn't want something from that man, if he didn't want his secret revealed, caught—absolved?

Okay, said Max. I'll give you maybe. Maybe I am just curious about what the Judge is saying. How he is saying it. Why it feels good when he talks with you.

Well, at least you can say it, said Pan. At least you can say it. Now that's good.

I don't know, said Max. He is against evil. He talks about love. So, I don't see what is all bad about him. I can maybe take what I want and leave the rest.

You don't know what to think, Pan said.

You're the one who said there's more in the world than we can see. Why can't the Judge see something you don't?

He sees plenty I don't see, said Pan. Fact.

Max opened the cupboard above Pan and found a sack of powdered sugar. Exactly what he needed. He uncinched the bag and poured a stream of sugar into his mouth. He swallowed it. Calmness came.

Pan kept talking.

You know their ancestors kept slaves as if it was normal, said Pan. He pointed at Max as if he needed a talking-to, as if Max were the one who owned the slaves. That kind of evil does something to a gene pool. You know what I think? I think we got a poisoned energy down here. It's afflicted us. I taste it in the air. We're just breathing in the violence. It doesn't go anywhere. The evil stays in the air, and we steep in it.

Pan waved the air toward him, as if he were smelling the evil.

Max knew a thing or two about an evil legacy, but he preferred not to think about it. In Germany, he'd hated visiting concentration camps on school field trips. It seemed like an unnecessary reminder. It had given him nightmares that made it tough for him to go on long runs alone. He would close his eyes and see his grandfather's face against the back of his lids. A person was capable of many things at once.

Bad stuff happens everywhere, said Max. He shrugged as though it didn't bother him, but it did. Doesn't mean it damages the energy of a place, he said.

Wrong, Pan said.

Pan set his nail file on his thigh. Nail dust on his dark jeans. White as sugar.

You feel it, don't you? The wrongness here? The badness. You feel that, right?

Pan titled his chin and placed it on an invisible ledge. He studied Max carefully as if daring him to disagree.

Max nodded, but truthfully, he didn't feel the badness. Not here. He saw something else when he looked around. Outside the kitchen window, forsythia bloomed into feverish yellow blossoms and behind that was the slick red mud of a creek bed. If he were to walk onto the back stoop and inhale, Max would smell the wisteria. Once you got far enough past the strip malls and the run-down BBQ shops and the gas stations and the trailer parks, beauty let her hair down. How could that be bad?

So, said Pan. Do you want to know a secret of mine? A history lesson? Insight into your not-evil Judge.

Max shrugged. He was tired of secrets. He wanted Pan to tell a joke.

It's got to do with Lorne, said Pan.

Max leaned back against the counter as if to say *Go on*.

Pan explained how Lorne used to ask Pan to dress up in his mother's clothes. And Lorne would dress up like his dad. Put on a tie and that belt buckle with the cowboy and the cross. One night, Lorne's big ranch house stood quiet and unguarded in the woods. The Judge and his wife were going to a cotillion party for a girl at church. Lorne and Pan had lobbied to stay home and play a biblical video game. Lorne had taken Pan into his parents' bathroom. He had wanted to pretend they were getting married, so they could be honored under God. So that their love could be honored under God. They had faced each other in front of the sink like they were at an altar. Lorne had been terrified to sin, so he pretended it was their wedding night and that God had blessed them, and that Pan was his bride. Lorne had worn his daddy's cowboy hat. Black Stetson. His hair had peeked through on the temples. It had looked like Satan was in him, coming out all hot and red in his hair. Then Lorne made Pan parade into the bedroom in this too big evening dress of his mother's, shimmering, a waterfall of sequins. Lorne had arranged Pan on the bed, sprayed him with Estée Lauder Pleasures, his mother's scent, and flipped Pan over. He had slid the dress over the moon of Pan's butt. Pan's bare back had touched the air. Lorne had glided the thick tips of his fingers up and down his sides. He had stuck one finger inside of Pan. Then Lorne had pushed all of himself in. Pan felt like he'd stepped foot on the sun. That's how he said it.

Max combed his mind for something to say. He didn't want the image of Lorne's freckled hands on Pan's body. Inside Pan's body. He held the scene to his chest. The ghost of Lorne stepped into the room with them, and he knew that ghost wasn't ever going to leave. Max wanted to say something that revealed nothing about how he felt, which was jealous and small. He searched for a response that might sound detached and interested at the same time but all he could come up with was a toothless smile that felt more like a leer.

And it happened only this one time? asked Max.

To this Pan laughed.

Oh, honey, he said. Oh, honey.

Lots of times, okay, said Max. I see.

Until the Judge found out, said Pan.

What, said Max.

The wages for sin is death.

You ready for the good news, son?

Well. Yeah. Well not found-out, found-out. But he suspected and that was enough. He never caught us. But one day, he stormed in yelling at Lorne that he was a sin creature. He tied Lorne to a tree outside, in their backyard. Tied him with ropes so tight his ankles and wrists bruised and bled. It looked like some kind of crazy stigmata something, that bleeding right there where Jesus bled. The Judge pierced his ribs with a hot metal cane, too, so his side would drip blood like Jesus. The Judge said it was about repentance and getting Lorne to work for his forgiveness. He needed to touch death in order to find life. He said he read on Lorne's soul his depraved desire. Said he saw what we had done in a dream. The vision came straight from God. The Judge wiped Lorne's tied-up body with a hot cloth. Got all his blood on this cloth and then burned the cloth in a pile with his clothes and spread the ashes of the bloody rag and soiled clothes across the lake. He said the past was burned up and the future would be clean and pure. You can burn the past down. So says the Judge.

What do you mean, the Judge just saw it on his soul?

Must be intuition, said Pan. But then, well, it was over. There's your history lesson. That's the kind of evil I mean. The Judge. He thinks life and death are connected by a fine thread. And I guess he isn't wrong. He thinks if you walk right to the edge of life, just like he did, like he did when he fell off that cliff and drank down a jug of poison, he thinks that can bring a person to God. He thinks it brings you right there into the light.

Max didn't know what to say. Pan and the Judge weren't so different. They both needed to believe in something. To have a purpose higher than themselves. Max wanted a purpose, too. He wanted to believe life wasn't for nothing. Maybe that's why he was drawn to them, to both of them. He wanted whatever it was they had found. Or whatever it was they wanted to find. Max felt the void open up around him again. The void was a huge black mouth with purple teeth. The void sounded like a shell to the ear.

Lorne couldn't take being two separate things. So, he chose one, said Pan. Wouldn't you? If your daddy tied you to a tree and left you out there all night in the dark, just howling at the moon like a crucified cub? If your daddy tried to bring you to the edge of life, put poison to your lips and hot metal to your side?

Max blinked.

He fed him the poison? he asked.

He was my first husband, said Pan. And I was his first wife.

Max let the void widen to the edges of the kitchen. He watched the void eat the fridge.

First husband, Max repeated. Okay.

You know, said Pan. Lorne was so embarrassed when he started to grow armpit hair.

Pan chuckled, like he was touched.

He wouldn't lift his arms above his head. He got bashful. I told him. I told him, they're just little whispers. Little spider hairs. They're cute!

Max ran his hand over the counter to clear off some Cheeto Puff crumbs. Pan was trying to get him jealous, he knew that, and it worked. He saw Pan's face in Lorne's armpit. Red spiders sprouted under the hinge of his arm.

You know, Pan said. I'm really wondering whose side you're on. Actually, I've been wondering that.

Whose side am I on?

Mine or theirs?

The question twisted in the air.

I can be both sides, Max said. I don't have to pick.

I don't think you can, said Pan.

Yes I think, said Max.

I want to tell you something else, but I shouldn't, cause it is secret, said Pan. But I really, really want to tell you. I need you to know.

Max tried to care about the secret, but he'd heard too much already. He rubbed his arms like he was cold, but he wasn't, not a normal cold. It was that tap-water feeling. He tried to focus on Pan's lips instead, chapped the right way, rough like how he'd grown to like. He felt so tired.

Never mind, said Pan. Later. I'll tell you later.

As if an afterthought, Pan said, Do you know how powerful we could be if we joined our forces together? Your healing and my psychospiritual capabilities? I think we could make shit levitate!

That made Max laugh. Pan's optimism had such charm. The laughter felt good. Who could explain how everything worked? The world had a mystery to it. The moon glowing into the night. The stars bunched into the black. Was that science? The ocean spilling onto the shores. Was that God?

Pan slid off the counter and swayed to his room. Max heard him turn up Nirvana and scream along to it.

Are you coming or what? he yelled to Max.

Max followed him in with a few fruit leathers and said, Want one?

Pan didn't, so Max had two. Max imagined binding Pan's wrists and ankles to the bedposts with fruit leathers and then eating through the candy to set him free. He pushed down the guilt that this was wrong, that the Judge could find him by reading his brain. *Skin him alive.* He thought of Lorne marrying Pan in the Judge's house. He thought of his first bride.

Pan curled up on the bed and pouted.

Aren't you going to come here? he said. I'm lonely with you all the way across the room.

Max flipped Pan onto his stomach and climbed onto his back. He wanted to love Pan until Pan got so used to his love, he could never live without it. *Fuck*, thought Max.

Are you afraid to get skinned alive? Max whispered into Pan's ear. To be a tree tied?

Me? said Pan. No. I'm going to get out of here too fast for that. No tree tying for moi.

Max didn't ask how he'd get out. He saw Pan lurching down the highway in a dress, lost as a scream in the wind, his thumb stuck out to the road.

Max slid off of Pan and onto the bed next to him.

Come here, baby, Pan said. What's wrong?

Max shook his head, Nothing.

Max spotted a dead spider, a clump of knotted leg in the sheets. Without even thinking, he reached out and grabbed it. He did that so easy now. Too easy. His mouth filled with a cloud of pink cotton. He felt the spider's legs move in his hand. It crawled up his arm with its pin-thin legs. Pan watched the bug walk. Then came the headache like a drum that started in the air just outside of Max's temple and traveled down the tunnel of his ear into the great open of his skull.

Beautiful, said Pan. Just beautiful. Now let's move him to the window so he don't bite you.

Do you ever think what we're doing is wrong? Max swallowed. Like do you ever think it might be sin?

The word had a bitter taste, like a penny rusted over and green. He wanted to take it back but taking back was impossible.

Sin, said Pan. He shoved Max almost playfully, almost-not.

IN THE LOCKER ROOM, the boys stood side by side beneath a row of shower heads and washed the stench from their pits and pissed into the open grates. Steam rose from their shoulders as they drew circles in the mirror's fog. They admired their faces of freckled skin and hamburger-shaped moles and smooth squares of abdomen. They spiked up their golden hair.

Coach let the team eat doughnuts to celebrate a recent win, even though he preferred they cut down on their sugar during the season. The boys raised the doughnuts to their mouths. Wes, whom Max had observed moving food around his plate at lunch and not touching it, consumed zero doughnut. He dressed himself slowly.

Max took one doughnut. Licked the sugar from his thumb. Wanted more.

Davis stood near the lockers, jeans splayed open at the hip. His zipper dangled. He talked with Graham about how Renata the Experimenter had taken to trailing him like a dog. Renata's last name was Sledgeworth, but everyone called her the Slutworth behind her back.

Renata.

Max held her real name in his mind as if that meant something.

Graham said he knew the feeling. The Slutworth's friend trailed him, too.

Davis and Graham assessed their relationships with their experimenters, whose big lips they liked.

She might be too skinny, said Davis. No cushion for the pushing. I need a lady with the curves.

Her jeans got those stupid rhinestones on them, said Graham.

Yeah, she put those on herself, like she wants us to know she's crafty.

The harsh lighting settled in the hollow places beneath the boys' eyes.

Watch out or she'll knit you a sweater.

Don't knit me a thing, said Davis. Or draw me another dumb picture.

The boys thought this was hilarious. They laughed so their gums showed. They said what the Slutworth and her friend liked and how they liked it, but Max got the feeling from the way Graham repeated the details Davis provided that he was lying.

I heard the Slutworth let the whole baseball team line up outside her daddy's pickup and do her one at a time, said Boone. Begged for more even after she'd had them all.

Watch this, said Graham.

He ruffled the palm of his hand through his hair until dandruff snowed down on his shoulders and shoes.

Nasty, said Davis.

Girls liked Davis, no matter how bad he talked about them when they weren't around. Davis winked at Max.

Don't worry, Germany. We'll get you a girl, too.

Oh, Max said, I do not worry.

Yeah, I bet you don't. You got a girl in Germany? What are those German tits like anyway?

The other boys chuckled. Davis's naked chest was flushed red from the shower. Max resisted the urge to reach out and place a hand on the heat of his rinsed skin.

They're beautiful, said Max, trying to conjure up an image of a girl in Germany. Any girl. But all girls receded from his mind. In that moment, the only thing he could see was Davis. Then Nils. And Nils, it was true, had been beautiful.

What's up with Billie anyway, Davis said. She cute. She's all right. And I've heard she likes you.

She likes me? Max said.

Aw, said Davis. Check out Germany blushing over here.

Billie? said Max, again.

Top choice for an experimenter if you ask me, said Davis.

Max left the steam of the locker room. He held two doughnuts in his hand. The chocolate sheen looked hopeful. It tasted like relief. Outside, the first cold pressed its palm into the air. It was subtle, sure, but it was there. Max tried to imagine taking Billie's hand, lifting her chin toward his.

LONG-DISTANCE CALL BETWEEN HIS mother and aunt, overheard on speakerphone.

AUNT: Maybe you're the one who's having trouble.
MOTHER: I wish. I mean yes. I hate it here. But it's more than that.
AUNT: More what?
MOTHER: Did I do something wrong? Was I a bad mother? I thought taking him here would be good after all he went through with Nils. I thought it would be, um, an adventure. Something that expanded him.
AUNT: He'll be fine! Let loose the apron strings.
MOTHER: This is different. The man manipulates people with religion. And Max has literally been making phone calls to get people to vote for him.
AUNT: You're sounding controlling, like Mom.
MOTHER: Max! Hello? Did you just get home?
AUNT: Max, is that you?!

On Fast Food Friday, the lunch ladies lined up bags of fried food in the cafeteria under signs that said CHICKEN FINGERS, FRIES, BURGER, CHEESEBURGER, CHICKEN SANDWICH.

So, you're a fingers guy, said a voice. Max looked and saw Glory behind him. I see you.

Max held his sack of fingers.

Glory reached toward the burger, then the cheeseburger. She selected cheese.

It is my favorite, he said. Chicken.

I see you've made it through the first few games unscathed. Even played, huh? Do you feel fully initiated now?

Yes, he said.

Glory focused on Max like all that mattered was him in front of her. She had a way of making him feel seen. She fiddled with the top button of her uniform. She had adhered a patch over the God's Way embroidery on her chest. The patch said PMS.org.

Max remembered the advice he'd been given: ask others how they are doing; they will know you care. He opened his mouth to ask but stopped short because the lunch prayer began.

A boy climbed onto the stage at the far end of the cafeteria. A portrait of Jesus hung above him. In the scene, Jesus raised a hand that seemed to pinion the crowd in place.

Oh Lord Jesus, our prince to be, the boy began. The cafeteria spoke the memorized prayer in unison. Bless this food you've placed into our hungry hands. Let us be filled with nourishment in body but also in spirit. Let our hunger for you never fill. Let our gratitude for you never cease.

Collectively, they said, Amen.

When the prayer ended, Glory was not beside Max.

He made his way to a table, and finished his fingers. He saw Pan appear, kicking his way through the swinging double doors. He barreled straight toward Max.

How is your animal flesh? Pan asked.

Max stared into the empty, shiny carton of once-chicken in his hand. Swallowed already. Gone.

Pan stood with his hands on his hips. His stubble was growing in on his chin and instead of shaving the shadow, he'd slathered foundation over it. Pan's fries scattered out across the tray he'd set in front of Max. He took a cold fry in the hand that said REAL and pointed it at Max.

You who brings the animals back. How can you masticate on the flesh body?

Not even whispering.

Shhh, said Max. He flung a glance over his shoulder. Don't talk about that here.

No one's even listening, said Pan. Don't be a paranoid.

It was true. The cafeteria contained few others. After prayer, most students had taken their lunch outside to the swings or front steps or dugouts or into the beds of their trucks. But they were not wholly alone. A cluster of girls still crowded the vending machine. *Diet Sprite Diet Dr Pepper Diet Cola?* Girls hear all things, thought Max. A boy hunched over a textbook at the far end of the table furiously dipping his bitten burger into BBQ sauce, out of earshot—or was he?

Pan should not test the line. Walk back away from the line.

It's hypocritical, said Pan. Meat is murderous.

It's not that he'd never thought of it. Sometimes biting into a chicken thigh felt exactly how it sounded, and he'd have a tough time swallowing. He visualized the animal turning into life between his teeth.

The flesh.

I need to get enough protein, he said. I am an athlete.

Protein, said Pan. Human beans baffle me. It's just crazy considering how much you care about dead things and tiny animals.

Can you please stop talking about this? Max asked. Please.

Pan stuck two fries under his upper lip and made them into fangs with which he hissed.

I bet Jesus wouldn't eat meat. He was a pacifist, you know, said Pan. Not a murderer. Stick that in your Christian pipe and smoke it.

Billie entered through the same double doors Pan just had, but her arrival exuded a calmness that Pan did not possess. She walked up to Pan and put an arm around his waist. She rested her purple hair on his shoulder and nuzzled him like she was an actual cat. Or maybe Pan was the cat. The makeup on her face made the makeup on his look strange. Her tasteful touch of mascara. Her barest hint of blush. The thinnest layer of gloss across her bottom lip. Next to her, Pan's features were a right angle, obvious and hard.

Ready? she said.

Totes, said Pan.

Hey, she said to Max, throwing him a peace sign.

Don't worry, Germany. We'll get you a girl, too.

Where you guys going? Max asked. His hands sat limp and awkward on the table. He couldn't think of a single thing to do with them. Open, close. Slide off the table onto the lap.

None of your biz-nasty, said Pan.

We're working on book reports, said Billie. In the library. Want to come?

Girl, said Pan. He busy.

Lunch plans. Max shrugged. Knox will be joining me any minute. But have fun.

Doesn't he sound like a Nazi? said Pan to Billie.

Pan, she said. She laughed. Quit it. You're mean.

Doesn't he!

HELLO, SIR, THIS IS MAX calling from the Judge's headquarters in Delilah. How are you doing this day? Is this a good time to call, sir?

Who is it?

My name is Max, sir.

Why do you sound like that? Funny like that. You from around here?

No, sir. I come out of Germany. But I do live here—

Why are you calling me from Germany?

I'm calling for the Judge, sir. His campaign. How are you today?

I been better. My doc's telling me the arteries in the left side of my neck are all clogged out. They're going to operate. And my daughter's late to change my shit bag. Everyone's late these days. Can't count on no one. World's going to all hell.

I'm sorry to hear that, sir.

Damn right you're sorry.

Are you planning to vote in the upcoming election, sir? We hope you will consider voting for—

Dial tone.

You cannot speak open and in public about my power at school, said Max.

No one heard, said Pan.

That's not the point. They could have heard. That is the point I make.

Okay, said Pan. I get it. You're like a broken record.

A what?

Scout's honor, said Pan. He held up two fingers. No more slippage on the subject.

Pan parked the car at the edge of the old downtown strip. The crumbling façade of an abandoned brick building loomed before them. Kudzu crawled up its side. Moss covered the skeleton of a once used train track. The slabs of a burned-down boarding school sat squat in the grass.

They walked beneath a bridge grown over with wildflowers. The flowers smelled like semen. Pan was leading Max toward the run-down shed he'd dubbed the Witch's House, where he planned to conduct his next psychic experiment. Max reached out for Pan's hand. He placed his thumb over the word LIFE.

Lorne's grandma had a house there, said Pan. He pointed their entwined hands to a road that curved toward a quaint, out-of-place strip with a pottery shop and a café called Shakespeare.

We used to explore around here when we were young, Pan said. One day we found this old shed. It looked like someone had been living in it. Every time we went to look at it, something was different. Like maybe there'd be a table set on the floor or a candle burning on the sill. Once the word *hello* had been written in hot pink paint on the side. The paint was still wet, like someone had done it just for us. Known we were coming. Lorne and I just took off running. We never went back after that.

Max rolled his shoulders at the mention of Lorne's name. Pan shrugged, lit a cigarette, and Max let his hand be drawn toward Pan's lips.

Ten minutes of walking took them to the shed. It was small and house-shaped. A person probably slept there at night.

There's still ghosts here, said Pan. I'm shivering. It's like there's a cold spot right here. You feel that?

Max shook his head. He didn't. It was hot as hell. October had arrived but still, it was hot as hell.

Pan opened the door to the shed and a mouse shot out. Pan shrieked and grabbed the green door to steady himself. Max peered over Pan's shoulder. A lace of a cobweb had strung itself from ceiling to side window. Dust collected on the floor. A few ancient, molded newspapers, a rake. A cracked open can of Coors Light.

Max stepped back while Pan prepared for his psychic reading in front of the door. Songbirds watched from the pines. Smoke left a chimney in the distance and disappeared. Clouds assembled. The wind moved the branches. The sun was at a mean, straight-at-you angle.

Pan raised his arms. The dry hinges of his elbows faced Max. Pan flung his head back and opened his chest like he wanted something to enter it.

A group of women were killed here, he said.

Really? Max asked. How do you know?

Shh, he said. There's a lot of them and they're speaking to me.

You're hearing something? Max asked him, not believing but finding it fun to pretend. Like they talk to you or something?

Shh, Pan said. His voice stretched out. I'm asking the energy to imprint on me, so I can read its vibrations psychically. I want it to enter through the tingling at the crown of my head.

Max walked toward the clearing and stood in the middle of it. He couldn't watch Pan fail at this. Pan had no power, and Max knew it.

Every town got a witch.

That up there is ours.

Wait, Pan said. Now I do hear something. He cupped his ear. *A voice. A singing.* There was a fight here. Yep. A bad brawl. I hear the screaming. The women were scared. Oh no. Oh, were they scared.

Max tried to feel it, too, the energy that people left behind. But he didn't feel it. He watched the auburn light soften into the red dirt around him. Now, here was beauty. A sweetness was in the air. The center of a flower. The trees thrummed up from the earth like they wanted to be climbed. It would feel good to let his legs loose and go somewhere.

Damnit, Pan screamed. Pan's boot hit the side of the shed. Again. Boot to shed. Boot to shed. *Bootshed.* Splintered into hole. Pan took the Coors Light can and punted it.

Max froze. He'd never seen Pan so upset—or anyone, for that matter. Pan ripped at his own shirt, tore the collar with his teeth. He took his hand and slapped his own face. Then hurled himself onto the ground and went limp. His back heaved.

Max approached him. Bent over.

You okay?

Fuck, Pan whispered into the crook of his elbow. He turned onto his back and flung an arm over his eyes. Can't you use your powers and try to bring those women back to life? Then we can ask them what happened here?

I don't think that is how it can work, said Max.

Fuck! said Pan. You're not willing to try anything.

Pan kicked his leg up and brought his heel down into the dirt. He cursed again, and Max stepped back.

After a few moments, Pan's breathing calmed.

I suck at this, said Pan. I got nothing. I didn't see anything really. I read it all on the internet. They said there was a shed in the woods that had been built over the site of a massacre. I have no idea if this is the place or not. I don't know anything.

Maybe you need juice or something? For the blood sugar?

I'm okay. I'm fine. It's over.

The tantrum had mellowed his eyes.

You don't look okay, said Max.

Max rubbed his back. The small bones rose and fell with his breathing. Max wanted to take care of him. Pan needed him, and Max liked how being needed felt.

Why don't you use your power for anything? asked Pan. If I had your power, I'd try to change the world. I'd use it for good. If I could do only five percent of what you can, I'd start a cult and move to the rain forest. I'd make my own police force and patrol the streets. I'd alter the course of science. There are a million things I would do with it. But you aren't doing anything! You're just sitting around eating stupid chicken wings and drowning yourself in sugar and playing stupid football.

I don't want it, said Max, trying to sound gentle.

Pan was quiet for a moment.

If I could give it to you, I would give it, said Max. I hate it. I never asked for it.

You're ungrateful, said Pan.

He thinks he's a princess.

It is too much. I wish I could go back to before I had it and never touch the mouse. I want only to feel normal. I am the wrong person for this maybe.

You could do so much good, said Pan. I would do so much good. Good is better than normal.

After I use it, it's like everything drains straight out of me. My happiness plummets and I feel like I want to die. Then I have to do it again to feel normal. The cycle does not ever end. It exhausts me. It makes me feel I have no control.

Pan shook his head.

You could make everything right, said Pan. You're a waste.

He brushed Max's hand from his back. Then he stood on his knees and let himself face-plant right into the ground.

Mouth to the dirt, he said: I surrender.

They made out in the shed before leaving. Max held Pan's shoulders against the plywood, and they covered their noses with their shirts because of the smell, and they blinked into the particles that floated toward them from the busted window. This was when Max felt most alive, when there was nothing between them, when they breathed in and out of each other.

Max tried to forget the look in Pan's eyes as they walked back to the car. A soft tantrum blue. The anger left as quick as it came.

You're a waste.

You'reawaste.

CHURCH: MAX WOULD FINALLY EXPERIENCE IT. He wanted to feel like he had that day in the Judge's car with the man's holy hand hovering over him. The electricity of the language they had spoken had made his forehead vibrate. Max longed to steep in the vibration again.

He woke early on the day of his first service. He rinsed his hair under the sink, slapped his cheeks with lotion that smelled like chemical pine trees. He unhung a clean polo shirt and positioned it on the bed above a pair of khakis. There was the shape of him, clothes with no body in them. Max turned to the full-length mirror behind his door. He was tanner than he'd ever been, and he admired what the sun had done. It burned him until he glowed. Football had changed him. Left eye puffy. His chest had thickened with new bulk, arms notched now. He loved the new weight. He liked what hung between his legs, too, and he cupped it in his own hand just how Pan had done. He humped at the air and made a face at himself, hands behind his head with his elbow wings out.

I'm a statue, he muttered. A statue and you like it.

His mother and father slid glances across the kitchen table when he emerged from the living room in his church uniform. His father picked up his coffee and blew at it. His mother cleared her throat and asked Max if he wanted toast.

I hardly recognize you, son, his father said.

Yes, sir, said Max. I feel good.

Don't call him, sir, said his mother. That's your father, not an army general.

Just think about this church thing like anthropology, his father said. Like exploring how other people live.

Of course, that's how he will think about it, said his mother.

Why are you worried about me trying to fit in? said Max. We're here because it's what you wanted.

I'm not worried, said his father. I'm not the one who's worried.

Maybe you should get a little more worried, his mother said.

In Germany, his family had visited churches during summer holidays. His father wanted to stand gob-smacked before the fact of history. It was what tourists did. The architecture was a work of art: something to admire, a thing to encounter, a monument to walk through. Max had seen catacombs in Italy, cathedrals on the coast of Spain, altarpieces in Bruges. He had stepped through marble interiors with his voice dialed low. He had observed light linger on dyed red windows and people on their knees in the silence, in a world carved from copper and stone. He had taken leaflets laid out by the entries and held them in his hands as he moved. He had touched a knob of incense to candles and meditated on a thought. He had run his eyes over the crosses carved into granite interiors but never had he tried to talk to God. His father would point out the details like how the feet of Jesus had been rubbed away; how his toes had been eroded to shiny nubs by something as simple as a repeated touch. His mother had said: Do you feel the energy? This is the power of thought. They want God to be here so badly they make it so.

The football boys worshipped in modern palaces, nothing like the European basilicas with their spires, clerestory windows, and engraved façades.

It's not like I'm going to some cult, Max said. I'm going to church.

When you say it like that, said his mother, it sounds like you're joining a cult.

His father turned his face to his toast and began to butter it.

He said: I'm not saying it's a cult. I'm saying be careful.

Ha, his mother said.

Max sipped his orange juice. Acid from the fruit sizzled in his stomach. Davis rang the bell.

~~~

CHURCH TOOK place in an old movie theater. The seats ascended and a thick velvet red curtain suspended in a scroll above the stage. A kind of kinetic spark kicked around the walls. Max felt it, a buzz gathering force and moving through the aisles like a flame collecting power as it goes. On the stage, a live band played rock music. The lead singer held his guitar in front of his cowboy shirt and baggy Wrangler jeans. He placed beautiful sounds into the microphone. Everyone knew the words to his songs by heart. They were catchy as pop songs, but they were about God's love. They made Max want to pump his hips forward and back. Side to side. They made him want to arch his back. The people in the row in front of him lifted their hands to the ceiling. The music moved through them. So good. So catchy. So nothing like anything he'd heard. It made him want to raise his arms, too. In the aisle the boys swayed. Beside him, Davis beat his chest.

Max stared at the back of the Judge's head a few pews up. Hatless for once and exposing his white hair, a puff of snow. Lorne sulked beside him. The Judge whispered in his wife's ear, then glanced over his shoulder. He looked right at Max as if he had known he was there all along. Max shifted in his seat and flinched his mouth into something he hoped didn't look scared. He waved. *Pan was wrong*, Max thought. *I can be two things at once. I can be everything I ever wanted.*

In the middle of the next song, a man burst from the pew and fell into the aisle. He began to shake while he sung. He lay his face in the carpet and began to drag himself toward the altar. The sounds that came from the man's mouth were familiar. Max recognized it as a prayer language like the one spoken in the Judge's car. Max watched the man stop crawling and go still. He turned over to his back. He convulsed on the floor right there. *Having a seizure*, Max thought. The Judge rose and walked into the aisle and bent down beside him.

It is all right, Davis told Max. He's all right. Everyone's fine. Just listen to the music. Just dance. Just let God do his work.

The spectacle of the man shaking on the floor disturbed Max, but he couldn't stop looking. The Judge swirled his hands in circles above the man's rib cage as if he could shine something from his body, polish him. Then the man stopped shaking. The Judge helped him up, and they rocked together in a half-standing, half-bent position. The Judge pulled a flask from his jacket pocket, water maybe, and the man lifted it to his lips. After drinking, the man's knees buckled. The Judge caught him. The man's mouth frothed.

Lorne stood beside his father with his head bent. The music played. People still sang. The man hugged the Judge and buried his face in the Judge's shoulder. When he stepped back, the man seemed better. The song ended.

During the sermon, the preacher stood at the pulpit and gripped its edges. The words he said didn't mean much to Max. He used a salt metaphor. Called the congregation the salt of the earth. He asked them what would happen if they lost their saltiness. How could they be made salty again?

The preacher asked if anyone wanted to come forward to get saved. All they had to do was accept the Lord Jesus. The boys of the congregation were already saved. Davis's gaze moved to Max. Warm eyes on his neck. Warm eyes on his chest. Max remained seated. Maybe if it was the Judge and not the preacher who had asked, his answer would have been different. Out of the corner of his eye, Max spotted Quaid walking the edge of the theater. He wore that same leather jacket. The same lustrous hair hung from his head. Quaid looked out of place and perfectly at home. Was Quaid walking up to get saved? No. He sat down in the pew.

After church, Max looked for Quaid again in the mass of people. Who he saw instead was Billie. She traipsed down the front steps trailed by two parent-shaped people. *Traipse* was a new word Max had learned, and it spoke perfectly to the condition of Billie's walk. She wore a flowy tunic dress with bell sleeves. He caught her eye and waved. She held up a peace sign in response.

The women moved around Max in the way that American women know how to do. They stood next to their thick-bellied men, men with chiseled features and studied masculine stances. The women wore beautiful pastel fabrics. *Silk*, Max thought, *or cashmere*. Max observed the beauty in the crowd and admitted to himself that he was impressed by it. He was superficial in that way. He wanted to touch something pretty as if, by proximity, the loveliness would wipe off on him. Max wondered what it would feel like to pull a silky blouse across his chest, to draw pumps onto his feet. He imagined standing next to the Judge, hand tucked into his elbow. He imagined whispering in his ear. The smell of Old Spice. Notes of cedar and spruce. Those rugged signifiers of virility that made him want to lick his teeth.

Last week Max had tried on his mother's lipstick in the bathroom. He had pulled at his ear and imagined a pearl in it. Ever since he'd met Pan, his imagination had expanded. His definition of boy had expanded. *A dress on his body. Pink gloss on his lips.* He touched his temples, felt growing pains, as if his mind were literally extending. *Boy on his back. Boy in his hair.* Max tried to sweep away the vision of Pan's glittering face, red neck, mouth an open O. O as in orgasm. O as in uh-oh. He didn't want the Judge to read his thoughts and see Pan in them. He didn't want the Judge peering into the smudged mirror of his mind and think: *Sin creature.*

Where's your father and mother, son? The Judge's hand tightened on Max's shoulder. Max leaned into the tightening. They didn't want to join us in celebrating?

Not this time, said Max.

The Judge nodded at him, a concerned eye.

Good that you came anyway, son. It takes something brave in you to do that. To see the truth. To see the light.

A FIGHT BETWEEN HIS PARENTS overheard at midnight.

It doesn't bother you that he's involved in a political campaign?

It's good to have him test his morals. Think about what is real to him and develop his own opinions. How can he know what he thinks, if he doesn't explore?

Do you hear yourself right now? The Judge man called his supporters a Christian army. An army? Says he's ready for spiritual war. He's trying to draft our son!

Have you noticed Max is not eating meat at dinner?

Good! Let him explore his morals. It's healthy for teenagers to experiment. Isn't that what you just said? I'm honestly baffled that you aren't more worried about the influence this man is having on our son.

Well, honey, I am trying to offer another perspective.

For the record, I think it's wonderful he's a vegetarian.

You know where he got it from, don't you?

Yes, and it's refreshing. I hope Pan does rub off on him.

What's refreshing is seeing him be part of a group. They're building his self-confidence. He's doing so well on the team. He looks healthy.

The team! When he gets a concussion, you're the one who's going to have to deal with the medical bills and the fact that you encouraged your son to destroy his intellect for a barbarian sport.

I just want him to become himself.

Do you want him to become a zealot?

A zealot! Listen to yourself.

A SCRAWLED NOTE ON THE WHITEBOARD: *Teacher Five Minutes Late Review Hmwrk.*

Students funneled in and claimed their seats around Max and Pan. They fidgeted like detained animals examining the edges of their cages. Nacho chips and peanut butter bites spilled from book bags onto the carpet.

If you want to romanticize those gun-wielding overlords, that's your choice, said Pan, after Max tried to convey the exact way it felt to run his cleats across the gridiron with the football players.

Church was a secret Max kept to himself, but he wanted to go there again. Stand in that music. Stand in the stranger's smiles until his body curved up like the lips of the approving crowd. The ballads still popped and sizzled in his throat. The Judge had explained to him how the music was the heart, the preacher's words the soul. And that big warm ooze that seemed to seep from the ceiling: that was the love of God.

The love of God seeps into you, seeds itself, and never, ever leaves. The love of God can dry out your sin. Replenish you.

I'm just saying. Sooner or later. You are going to have to choose, said Pan, his voice dialed to a whisper.

Why do you say it like that though? said Max. Why does everything have to so black and white with you.

I'm from the South, hon. If things aren't black and white, what the fuck are they?

Max tried to show-not-tell the feeling of sprinting in a formation beside a mayonnaise-white line. Nothing was bad about that. It felt good. It felt good to get hit so he couldn't think, to know that someone might knock his head so bad it broke his brain. There was a thrill that came from risk.

His teammates painted black patches under one another's eyes to protect their corneas from the sun. They unknit knots of muscle from each other's calves with their thumbs. They slammed their helmets together until their vision was strangled in hot white dots, stood ten to a row under the showers and let the pressure of the water sting them. That was friendship. He loved catching the end of Wes's perfect spiral and holding the warm ball with its raised, bumpy skin and running so fast no one could catch him. He loved jumping the heaps of fallen bodies, the pinch and snatch of hands trying for him. He loved finding a way to outrun it all.

To score.

Pan looked at him with an eyebrow arched. With one long nail, he dug food from a crevice of tooth. Max wished Pan would smile and say: I understand, baby. You do you.

Max willed Pan to squeeze his knee and let him know he could be both/and. Everything.

But instead he said, Cause you like to watch those tight-end asses?

Shh, said Max. Don't talk so loud.

Max did not explain the effect the Judge's grin had on his knees.

I just want friends, said Max.

What's wrong with no friends?

I have done that too long already, Max said.

You had Nils, said Pan.

This was the first time Pan had said his name and Max did not like the way it sounded, suffocated and drowned in Pan's thick Southern drawl.

That was different, said Max.

He wished he could untell Pan about Nils. He had given over his secrets too easily. And hungrily, Pan had let them be given. Max felt the loss of secrets. The lightness of having unburdened himself, but Max wanted something for himself again. He wanted Nils's name in his hand, to hold it to his ear. A sound no one else could hear.

That was actually different, said Max.

Why? said Pan. Because you loved him?

A WOODEN CROSS HAD HUNG above Nils's toilet. Max had stared at it while they kissed in the shower. He had been a normal boy then. *Normal hands no healing in them*. The cross, too, had seemed nothing special. Just two planks of wood that intersected at right angles. No one in Nils's house had talked about the cross. No one had used the words *risen* or *saved* or *sin*. *Jesus* was not a word they said in vain or ever. He had assumed Nils's mother bought the cross on a trip to Belgium, a trinket like the Day of the Dead skulls in the kitchen or the stone Buddha on their living room mantel.

But the cross in the Judge's office did not look like two planks of sanded wood. It appeared to Max like a noose or like gallows. A death instrument glorified. The wood had been shellacked until it shone. The color between brown and red and glowing. He watched it on the wall while he made his calls.

Lorne tied to a tree in the backyard.

Side pierced just like Jesus.

Lorne at the next table saying Vote for my dad.

I'm a student at the high school, ma'am, Max heard Lorne say. I am going to go to state college. I only want a fair and honest education. I do not want to worry that what I am assigned to read is going to put me on a path to sin.

The Judge came in with an old woman. The woman dragged a breathing device behind her. It attached to her nose with a long plastic tube. The Judge knelt in front of the cross. He stood on his knees and placed his forehead to the ground. The woman was beside him, her eyes tightened into wrinkles. The Judge pulled at the hem of the woman's dress, dried his face with its ruffle. He prayed. The woman wept. She hugged him, and they rocked together in worship.

The Lord has risen, Max heard himself read from the sheet of paper in front of him—a way to close the conversation.

Amen, said the women on the other end.

Her response startled Max back into his body.

Amen, he said back.

And will you like a ride on election day, ma'am? Max asked her. A quiver in his voice.

No, sir, I do not. But thank you kindly for the checking.

PAN TOOK MAX STRAIGHT DOWN the school hallway and into the parking lot and toward his car. The idea was to listen to music and drive around and *chill*. Max let the sun bake his skin through the windshield. The heat tightened his cheeks. It made him sleepy. He wanted to curl on his side in the passenger seat and pull Pan into his lap. But Pan was up to something.

So, you know it's impossible, Pan said. That you raised Nils from the dead. I've really been thinking about that, about raising up the dead. And I think you couldn't have done it with Nils. Reason numero uno is that there was a substance between you and his body. The wood.

When Pan said it, Max knew, somewhere deep in him, that he was right.

I mean, said Max, I've thought of that, too.

Reason numero dos, said Pan, if you really, truly, madly, deeply thought you'd brought him back to life, you would have stopped the service and said something. You would have cried out. You would have told your mom. You would have caved. You wouldn't have just let them bury him.

I guess, said Max.

This part he didn't yet believe. *Couldbetrue. Couldbefalse.* Coward was how he felt. Max placed himself back on the day of the funeral. There he was in the chair. His mother in black beside him. The crow circling the casket. The snow falling into his hair. The memory walked through him.

No, said Pan. Not *you guess*. You would have! And plus, Nils would have yelled for someone to save him, and people in the cemetery would have heard. Caskets aren't made of soundproof metal or something. They're boxes of wood.

Maybe, said Max.

Don't look so terrified all the time. You're going to give yourself wrinkles in your forehead, said Pan.

He reached into the backseat and lifted a shoe box from the floor.

Here, said Pan.

He popped open the lid to reveal a lifeless bird. Roadkill, it looked like, or beaten with a bat. An eye unblinked at Max. The bird's legs gleamed like wet roots. The feathers shimmered from dark blue into cloud. Pan shut the lid again.

Put your hands on the box, and the bird won't come back to life.

Max saw what he was up to. Heat welled under his cheeks and pinched its way toward his eyes. He placed his damp hands on the cardboard right over the word *Keds*. His mouth buzzed. It tasted like autumn, like cardboard, like a stain of grass on the tongue. It tasted like paper ruined by the green shit of a bird. Not sweet.

He lifted his hands.

Pan opened the box.

The bird stayed dead.

See, said Pan. Told you.

Then Max picked up the bird, and his teeth turned to peppermint. Stalks of lavender extended into his nose, and the wings flapped, and the bird squealed, and it would have flown right into the windshield if Pan hadn't grabbed it from Max and thrown it through the open driver's door. They watched the bird soar upward, a black smudge in the blue until it wasn't even that. It left no imprint behind. The sky forgot the bird. Then Pan crawled onto Max's lap. He didn't have a chance to catch his breath before their teeth clinked, and Max tasted nicotine.

See I told you, said Pan. You're not bad. You're not a bad boy.

So, the dye worked? Max asked Billie in the hallway.

The color was fading from her hair, but he could still see hints of purple intertwined in the mousy strands she tucked behind her ears.

I didn't say anything in the cafeteria because you were in a hurry, said Max. But it looks cool. Looks pretty.

The compliment just slid right out, and Billie ignored it.

Used to compliments, thought Max. *Shouldaknown.*

Davis walked past Max, pulled his arm back, sent a punch straight to the bicep.

Save you a seat at lunch, Romeo, he said in Max's ear as he passed.

What up, Bill, said Davis.

Billie kept her gaze on Max. Davis did not get a peace sign raised in response.

I've been trying not to wash it out, she told Max. I've been trying not to wash my hair because of the chemicals. I heard that when you stop washing your hair, if you wait long enough, you never have to use shampoo again. You can just use baking powder and vinegar. Au naturel.

Cool, said Max. If I had hair, I'd try it, too.

She ran her hand through his hair, held a piece and said—you have enough to go lilac.

Her touch sent warmth to the spine. *Hmm,* he thought. *Interesting.* The bell rang, and the hall drained through the cafeteria door. They stayed, small-talking, facing each other in front of a wall of windows that opened out to the baseball practice fields. It must be hamburgers for lunch. He could smell the beef.

Hey, she said, don't move. The shadows on your face are perfect.

She slung her backpack onto one shoulder and withdrew a manual 35mm Minolta.

It's beautiful, right, she said, holding the camera out toward Max.

The instrument took up her whole hand.

I'm in a photography class, she said.

She picked an aperture, adjusted the shutter speed, held the view-finder to her eye. Max lifted one side of his mouth.

Don't smile, she ordered. Turn your head a little to the right. Make it seem like you're thinking.

Click.

Cool, she said. Good shot. I think.

Really?

Yeah. It caught you in your element, looking stoic and strong.

She fiddled with the strap, a kind of hippy thing with a Mexican blanket pattern woven into it. She hung the camera around her neck. Max thought of his disposable camera in his drawer at home, discarded. The undeveloped pictures of the Alabama highway. An idea he had that he couldn't follow through on.

Saw you at church on Sunday, she said.

She held a finger to her temple and pulled the trigger of her thumb.

You hated it? said Max.

Didn't you? she said. Before he could answer she said, Come with me to smoke a cigarette. Let's get some fresh air.

Max didn't smoke, but he said sure anyway. He understood what Pan meant about auras then, because he sensed a force coming off her, a sadness. Max noted his intuition again, humming under the curve of his rib.

They walked across the baseball field toward the dugouts. He felt a panic about skipping lunch. It wasn't Fast Food Friday, which meant students were required to be in the cafeteria. He almost expected to see Glory under a tree turning over her tarot cards, but she was not there.

Someone could be watching us, Max said. Won't we get in trouble if they see us out here?

No one's watching, said Billie. Pinkie swear. No one cares.

You're not a bad boy.

She sat on the dirt floor of the dugout and pulled a metal canister from her bag. She sprung it open and revealed a row of self-rolled cigarettes, packed tight.

I feel like we're going to get caught, said Max, and a small part of him wished they would get caught. He wondered what would happen if they did. He wished that just once he wouldn't get away with something, that he'd have to suffer a consequence, make a penance, ask to be forgiven.

Nah, said Billie. Not going to happen. I do this every day. Plus, those teachers have bigger fish to fry than us out here smoking. It's small beans.

You are not hungry? asked Max.

She shrugged, held up her cigarette.

Lunch, she said.

Her eyes squinted at something in the distance. Max followed her gaze, but it didn't land anywhere. It struck some point on the horizon near the Burger Mountain sign, which reached taller than the pines. It was so clear that afternoon, a blue people write songs about. Billie reminded him of a bird. He'd heard everyone's face looked like a horse or a bird. Hers was bird. Pan's was bird, too. Nils had been a horse. Billie wiped her nose with her knuckle. Maybe she'd fly away.

I'm reading this book about the Holocaust, she said. In AP English. It's called *Night*. You read it? It's about Nazis. Kind of.

Max shrugged, a little annoyed.

It's good, she said. And depressing.

Yep, said Max. It's a subject that depresses.

I kind of like depressing stuff, she said. It makes me feel better. Like how sad songs make me happy. Like how tragic movies make me laugh.

That is funny, said Max. Sad songs only make me sad.

But this book has got me thinking, she said.

She handed Max the cigarette as if he wanted it, which he didn't. He puffed it quickly and handed it back.

What do you mean? Max said.

Billie inhaled like it was serious. She exhaled toward the ground. Max watched the smoke disappear into the dirt.

I just mean I read about all this suffering in *Night*. All the fucked-up things people do to each other. That shit people live through.

Well, Max asked.

He dug at his sole with a stick.

I think it's so easy to look at something bad like the Holocaust, you know, and say, that is evil, said Max. When Hitler was just one evil man who got famous for his evil, but evil is exactly everywhere.

That's what I mean! she said. Precisely. Evil isn't confined to the obvious.

He hadn't expected Billie to agree with him so easily. Max didn't know what to say.

Like bad isn't only Nazi stuff. It's not only burning people alive in ovens and genocide, she said.

You burned people alive here, too, said Max, repeating his mother verbatim, feeling almost defensive of the Nazis. You did all kinds of burnings, too, said Max. It is just you don't talk about it the same way. You put up statues of the people who did the bad stuff.

This was the first time he'd let himself take a stance against the Judge, and he realized he meant it.

Max's mother would be proud. Billie looked amused.

This isn't a competition, she said. It's not the oppression Olympics.

She passed the cigarette back. He took another drag. He held the smoke between his cheeks. He didn't want to inhale, so he left it in his mouth until he felt like it'd been long enough. He would never have said the thing about the burnings to the football boys, but he could tell Billie was impressed by his observation about the statues.

I bet you hate it here, don't you? Max said.

Pretty much, said Billie. But not everything. There's some good stuff, I guess. But I hate the fuckwads.

Max stayed quiet. He knew whom she meant.

You think somewhere else will be different? said Max. No fuckwads?

A hundred percent, she said. I met a guy on the internet from California. From Fresno. He told me about life out there. I know it's different there, because he's different. He's, like, so different.

Is the internet person your boyfriend? asked Max, confused by the jealousy he felt at the mention of this other boy. This *so different* boy. Max didn't want Billie. But he didn't want her to want anyone else either. He didn't want there to be someone else who was *so different*.

Billie shrugged.

Boyfriend shmoyfriend, she said. Who cares?

The bell rang. Billie stuck the lit end into her mouth and the ember died. She didn't flinch. She looked at Max with her pale eyes.

Time's up, she said.

It is not so romantic, said Max. Being somewhere else. In Germany, it is just fuckwads being fuckwads in another language, in another landscape.

Maybe, said Billie.

Certainly, said Max.

Certainly, she repeated. You sound so funny sometimes.

Now her camera was out again, and she was taking pictures of things: a close-up of the metal squares in the chain-link fence, the spot where the ceiling beam formed a trapezoid with another beam above them—shapes Max hadn't noticed before Billie focused on them. The way she looked at things so closely, Max wondered if maybe she saw something he couldn't. She held the focus, framed it, clicked it into place.

RIDING TO THE MALL WITH Pan and Billie was a mistake. Max knew it as soon as Pan slumped into the front seat of Billie's silver Civic. Pan was in a mood. The mood followed them into the mall, where Pan ripped blouses off the hangers, casually and without looking, from the department store displays they walked past. He watched the fabrics fall to the floor. A trail of rumpled clothes accumulated in their wake. Pan bought enamel buttons of skulls and anatomical hearts at the Dollar Shop. They walked through the food court and Pan made fun of fat people.

These are the people voting for our future. The mass-tards of Alabama, said Pan.

He kept trying to get Max to make fun of them, too.

Just let him be good, Billie reprimanded, even though she encouraged all of Pan's fun-making by laughing.

You got to loosen up, Sarah, said Pan. You're not Mother Teresa. You can say something bad about someone. Try it. Say something terrible about someone you don't like.

Max bought a soy hot dog from Dog King. He was starved and thought eating vegetarian would call back Pan's approval or at least undo the mocking. The three of them walked together through the mall's white, plastic stomach. Billie functioned as a kind of shield. Her girl presence made it easier to exist around Pan in public. Now they were just two boys and a girl. Weirdos but not fags. A trio but not a pair. Not a couple.

If he wasn't so cute, he'd be boring, huh? said Pan when they were back in Billie's car. But don't worry, you're easy on the eyes. We'll keep you around.

Billie laughed—like yeah, Max, *whattabore*. Or like yeah, Max, *socute*.

Pan turned and peered at him through the headrest. Max mouthed *stop*. Max shifted in his seat and stared at the pink clouds bound above them. The same strip of nothing stores collected below them. Same food-thrus. He watched the back of Pan's head—a perfect swirl of untamed hair. He wanted Pan to do better.

Careful not to smear your lipstick on the seat, said Billie. My mom freaks if the upholstery is even a bit dirty.

Pan's lipstick got everywhere—on his teeth, in the crease of his mouth, on his shirts, on Max's collars. Max appreciated knowing that small detail about Pan. *Intimacy*, he thought. He liked that he could find Pan's traces in places he no longer was. He was there even when he wasn't. Once, Max discovered one of Pan's contact lenses affixed to his bedside table. He had held it to his eye and looked through it, almost expecting the world to suddenly appear different.

Does that mean I can't smoke, said Pan, presenting a Virginia Slim. He adjusted the low V on the neck of his polyester tank. Shit, I'm showing way too much cleavage.

A hundred percent, said Billie.

So, you're saying I look like a slut? asked Pan. Offended!

What's wrong with being a slut? asked Billie.

Touché, baby, touché, said Pan. He flicked his eyes to the side mirror so that he could see Max, and Max could see him. So, is everyone in Germany as cold and distant as you?

Why are you being such a mean person? asked Max. Do you try to show it off?

Burn! said Billie. You are being a mean person.

Pan slouched down in the front seat.

I'm frigging curious, okay? I've never been to Europe. This could be an educational moment for me.

When I graduate, I'm going to Paris, and I'm going straight to Jim Morrison's grave, said Billie. I'll bring him a bouquet of black roses and place it over his heart.

They stopped at a red light and Billie toggled through the radio stations. She settled on something jumpy and electric with a head-nodding drumbeat.

I'll be twenty-seven when I die. Making sure of it. RIP rock 'n' roll, said Pan. I'm making it to twenty-seven then—

He drew his nail across his neck.

A wilted leaf rested on Billie's floorboard, right next to Max's foot. He stared at it—the dead edges. The brown heart. The stiff stem and the paper-soft body. Max sat on his hands. He'd already healed two tulips that morning. He needed moderation.

I just discovered this amazing band called the Who, said Pan. And I'm going to try to find them on my phone and play them for you.

I know the Who, said Max. My dad owns their records.

Your dad? said Pan, irritated. Whatever. They have an opera album that I'm like in love with.

You mean *Tommy*? Said Max. Their rock opera?

Pan sighed too loudly.

Billie laughed and said, Musical genius in the backseat.

Yes, I mean *Tommy*, Pan said. I guess you've heard it before.

It is a good album, said Max, remembering his home in Hamburg and the record player by the window.

Pan found the song on his phone and turned it up. He lit his Virginia Slim. Billie gave him the eye but let him smoke it. She even took a drag herself.

Max had heard this song a dozen times, but his English hadn't been as good then. He'd never listened to the words before. Its darkness revealed itself in a new way. It bumped against the sunny afternoon. Max enjoyed the contrast. *Like how sad songs make me happy.*

As if he were acting out the lyrics, Pan touched the lit end of his cigarette to the top of his hand and pressed it in. Pan held up his hand, so Max could watch the skin melt around the embers.

Do it to me, too, said Billie. She held out her arm for the burn. Oui oui.

You want one, too, Sarah? asked Pan. He turned in his seat to face Max again. He held the cigarette out to him, offering to burn him.

The song reminded Max of his father, of Hamburg, and of Nils. The record player spinning. The snow falling into the snow outside.

A clean quiet cold. Desire slid down Max's tongue. Max hated himself, a deep animal hate. *Where did the hate come from?* He didn't know. He looked down into his lap and back at Pan. The hate dissolved. Pan was a promise of something. Pan could be nice. He would be again.

No thanks, said Max.

Lights in his eyes. White stadium bright. Max was running and then he was hit. He braced toward the grass. The tackle came like a smack he should have expected. His head hummed. His joint snapped. He held up a broken finger. The pain panged, but he felt pride when he raised his hand to Coach on the sideline. His middle finger pointed back toward his chest. All wrong. *Here*, it seemed to say. *The outside to match the inside. All wrong.* Coach popped it back into place. Nothing else to do about a broken finger. Max knew. It wasn't the first one he'd snapped.

No doc needed, son, Coach said. Just make a splint when you get home. The only thing that'll fix it is time. You'll look at your hand in a year and think of this night. Just remember that, son.

Coach's face shone. Max studied the drenched seam of his hairline. Something inside him wanted out. *What is sweat before it leaves the body?* Max wondered. *Where does all that water come from?* Max watched a drop fall from Coach's nose. A mosquito landed on his forehead, and he must have sensed it land, because Coach caught the bug and crushed it. Killed it. Flicked it. Dead bug. Dead bug in the grass.

Max took his seat on the sideline bench. He had ruined a rare moment of playing time by getting tackled and breaking a minor bone. God's Way lost again. Later that night, Max stepped onto the bus that would take them home. Away games usually excited him, a chance to see other towns outside of Delilah, but that night he swept his excitement back. Max wanted to be home. He longed for the Sunshine smell of his sheets. He sat next to Wes. Wes, who kept his headphones in for the entire hour ride and stared out of the window, frustrated by the loss.

When Max walked into his living room, he was struck again by the size of his house. The tall ceilings and the sheer space of the entry-way. Their old cuckoo clock bleated at him from where it had been affixed to the wall. The peek-a-booing bird was one of the only orna-ments they'd taken from their house in Hamburg. His family had shared a single bathroom in Germany and never thought it peculiar. Here, Max could choose from three different toilets. A toilet for each member of his family. The picture of extravagance.

His mother greeted him at the door and kissed his swollen, bro-ken finger. Happy, maybe, that she could trace this broken bone to a knowable incident.

Max stood in the downstairs bathroom and texted Pan a picture of it. He waited and waited for a response. Maybe Pan would kiss it with the black heart of his favorite emoji 🖤. The kiss emoji 😘. The eggplant emoji 🍆. He would say something like *That looks like it hurts*. He might text a photo himself with his shirt pulled up to reveal his flat chest, his lips smashed into a duck face. But no text came. No text came until one a.m. The text said: I'm outside your door let me in.

There was Pan on the front steps. He wore butch clothes and no makeup. A blue and white striped shirt like a sailor, like he arrived on a ship. Max blushed. To see Pan dressed so plainly disarmed him. It was more intimate than seeing him naked. Max stepped aside and in came Pan. He instructed Max to lie down on the sofa. Max let Pan hold his hand up to the moonlight and examine it. He let him put it in his mouth even though it hurt. *Ouch*, he didn't say out loud. He wanted Pan to think each thing he did was the right thing. He wanted Pan to be proud of the way he tended to Max. Max would give him that.

I'm channeling my grandmama's ghost, said Pan.

Pan took Max's knuckle and rubbed it in. Pan kissed it all over. Then he curled up beside him in his sailor's shirt. He whispered into Max's ear.

I can't stay here. I'm going to go home.

Stay, Max said.

Can't stay, said Pan, drowsy, tired, and slow. I'm going home.

But he didn't move. He didn't go. Max clutched Pan's body with his hurt hand. They fell asleep like that and slept for hours, unmoved by the night. They slept like that until dawn came in pink and uncooked and placed herself on the floor beside them.

IT'S PROOF OF THE GREAT FLOOD, Davis said after Max explained that he and his family were going to visit Shark Tooth Creek.

Cool place. Real pretty. I reckon you'll find about thirty teeth if you look good.

The Great Flood? asked Max.

Davis pulled off his helmet and set it on the bench. He filled a paper cone with green Gatorade and handed it to Max.

C'mon, Germany, said Davis. Have you literally not read El Bible? The Great Flood. You know—Noah's flood. The one that covered Earth and wiped away every creature except the ones Noah saved with his ark. Two of each. A woman and a man so they could procreate. Save the world.

Oh, said Max, who had been told by his mother that the shark teeth found in the silt bottom of the creek were geological fossils. The shark teeth had been deposited there 40 million years ago when north Alabama was a barrier island, not a landlocked part of the state.

Forty million years! said Davis. You crazy, son. The world isn't more than ten thousand years old at best. That's right there in the Bible, too. I thought you knew better, man.

Davis shook his head like Max was something.

Max shrugged.

At Shark Tooth Creek, Max waded through the clear water. He bent down and ran his hand through the sludge: pebbles, the smooth edges of stones. A girl with wet hair spilling out of a scrunchie ran by him, her camo shirt soaked through, and her feet splashed water onto everyone she passed. She wore neoprene shoes and cut-off jean shorts. A kid chased her through the creek. They ran up on the sandy banks and crawled between the chaos of branches and vines. Trunks plunged upward from the sides of the water. Moss covered their knotted limbs. Max had never seen so many kinds of grass: brown and short, shagged and sparse. Tough tall tufts. Fallen trees were scattered along the creek banks, eroded by the wind and unstiffened by the water. People sat on the trees and counted the teeth in their palms.

Max's hand sifted through the wet clumps of earth until he found the hook edge of what he knew was a tooth. In his palm, it curved up in a cloudy black color. The tooth root took on a rough gray. He thought of the mouth it once lived in. The jaws that snapped together to make a body dead. The scales it tore and the muscles it cleaved. A tooth that had tasted blood. This was its own kind of weapon. Max put it in his mouth and pushed it against one of his own teeth. He spit it out.

TEXT MESSAGE FROM PAN: We got 2 do something with ur powers. Wasteful if u don't use them. Plz do more than pull up 💀 weeds
from the ground & hand me a bouquet of grass. (it's cute ok ok ok)
but we need bigger. Need 2 use them 4 real. Think big!

Max: I don't want it I wish I could just give it to u and u could
use it.

Pan: Don't say that. Mr. Sprinkles will get mad at U 🐐🐐🐐🐐🐐

Max: I don't want it.

Pan: Don't believe U. UR power is so much a part of U that U
wouldn't know who U even are w/o it.

Max: I'd feel normal.

Pan: U need to use it more really use it. U got a gift 🎁

Max: Ich don't want it ok!

Max: Sorry autocorrect been txting w my aunt.

Pan: Cuz I got an idea 💡

Max: What is it?

THE EVENING CAST A SHADOW over the woods outside Pan's trailer. Somewhere leaves were being burned. Max had a view of the yard from where he reclined, kicked back on Pan's mother's bed. Her purple curtains were parted just enough so he could see the first splat of stars through the open window.

Do you know where the word *glamour* comes from? Pan asked as he painted a color called Divine Streak onto his mouth.

Where? said Max.

Pan posed in front of his mother's full-length mirror with her dress unzipped down his back.

Glamour comes from witches, he said. It started as the name of a witch's spell. Glamour was what they called it when witches made reality bend in their favor, when they cast out an illusion to make something appear as it wasn't. Glamour affects the eyes of the one looking. It makes a thing seem more beautiful than it is.

Pan covered his bottom lip with color, pinker than a cat's paw, and examined the open tube.

To make yourself glamorous, said Pan, is to make magic.

A motorcycle thundered up the gravel road. The engine roared then cut to silence. The front door squealed open with an unoiled yelp. Then it slammed on its hinges. Heavy boots on the thin floor. The walls of the bedroom shook as the boots walked to the room adjacent. A man's voice mumbled to itself: Baconbaconbacon. Bringing home the bacon.

Who is here? Max wondered to himself.

Relax it, said Pan. It's just Quaid. He rolled his eyes. He's going through it. So, he's, like, staying here or something.

Pan smacked his lips to spread the color.

What is he going through?

Curiosity killed the cat, said Pan.

Max heard the metal skid of a skillet pulled from its drawer. The phlegm of a cough. He could piece together Quaid's movements from the sounds that echoed off them.

Are you mad at me or something? said Max. You have not been so nice this week.

Pardon moi, Pan said. I'm on my period. I'm not mad at you. Why would I be mad at you? Now do I look glamorous or what?

Max followed Pan into the kitchen, where Quaid fried up thick-cut Walmart bacon. Pan sashayed around the room, air-kissed no one, and said hola in Quaid's direction. Max hung back inside the door frame. The smell of fat sealed itself onto every surface. Quaid dipped his thumb into the hot oil of the pan and licked it.

Where does your momma keep the hot sauce, boy? Quaid asked Pan.

A stretched shirt hung from Quaid's shoulders. His slender frame was emphasized by his huge elbows and the swollen balls of knuckles he popped on his hands. A chain necklace with a copper cross was fastened just above his jugular notch. Something frightened Max about the way he fiddled with it like he might snap it off. The kitchen didn't feel big enough for the three of them.

Beats me, Pan said. I'm not a chef. Zip me up, Max.

Max moved the metal tab to the base of Pan's neck. He could almost see the orange-edged aura vibrating off Pan's body. He felt Quaid's stare and looked up to meet it.

Y'all cute for faggots, said Quaid. Pan, give your uncle a ciggy. My head's about to burst open, and you're fixing to see my brain ooze right out my ears if you don't share.

Max lifted his chin at the word *faggot*. He felt like he'd been spit on. Shame, his mother had told him once, was something done to you. No one was born with it. *Did Pan not feel it?* Max wondered. *Was Pan somehow immune to the shame?*

This is my last one, Pan said to Quaid. He tapped the cigarette perched behind his ear. We're fixing to get more. So, you'll have to wait. Want me to get you some Twizzlers or something while I'm out?

I'm off the sugar, sugar. Doc's orders.

The stippled bacon hissed in the skillet.

But I'm so damn famished I could eat a hog alive, said Quaid. I'd eat a damn brain raw from the skull. Swear to heaven.

Murderer, Pan said to him. He clucked his tongue.

Don't ever call me that again, you little shit, said Quaid, kicking out his hip and standing with a balled-up fist shoved against his heart. I am not a murderer and you know it.

Don't twist your panties, said Pan.

Sweat leaked down Quaid's temples. He raised his hand to wipe his brow and left a skid of bacon grease to glow on his forehead. As Max watched Quaid sweat, he began to sweat, too.

Max wanted to leave. He stuck his hands deep into the pockets of his khaki pants and tried to make his chest bigger. What was he afraid of anyway? Max wasn't sure. After all, he was bigger than Quaid, inches taller, many centimeters thicker in the biceps, though something inside Quaid seemed enormous and unpredictable. Pan took his time moving around the kitchen.

I'm trying to find my truth stone before we go, said Pan, as he searched for the leather clutch that held his crystals and charms.

Pan finally opened the drawer to the kitchen knives and discovered his clutch.

Almost ready, Sarah, Pan said.

Max walked toward the door.

Saw you at church, boy, said Quaid.

What, Max said.

Church. You were there. I saw. You like the music? Nice isn't it? Like a big ole hug right for your heart. Like a rock show. That's how they get you. Feels like pop, don't it?

Well, Lordy, continued Quaid. Speak up now.

I liked the music, yes, said Max.

He speaks, Quaid said. He speaks.

This cracked Quaid up, and he bent over in a fit of hysterics. Then he righted himself and smoothed down his hair with the fingers he had. Each nail bed was lined in a black grit.

That Judge sure has a thing for faggots, said Quaid. Pardon my français. He's my baby Pan's sugar daddy, isn't that right? You can thank your Uncle Quaid for that, son. You are so welcome.

The word *faggot* made Max shift again. His fists balled without meaning to.

Quaid picked up a white cowboy hat from the table and placed it on his head. The hat infused him with a kind of nobility. It looked like the one the Judge wore. Their sudden similarity struck Max, as if Quaid could be the Judge on another road, in another life.

Pan finished tying his clutch of charms around his neck.

Let's go, he said.

He wants to show you the light, boy, said Quaid. And the light, let me tell you, it can be beautiful. It can shine brighter than anything you've ever seen. I've seen the light, and the light is glorious. You been out to camp yet? Have you given it up to God?

Camp? Max said. You mean campaign rallies?

Oh, sure, son, a campaign rally. That'll set you free. That'll unshackle you.

The way he said *son* felt familiar.

C'mon, said Pan.

Bacon, bacon, bringinghometheback, Quaid muttered to the skillet.

Outside, Max could breathe again. The tied-up dog slept in the neighbor's yard under the nailed-up flag. Its legs moved like it was running in its dream.

You went to church? said Pan. You're a piece of work. You're keeping that from me? Why?

Pan rubbed at his arms.

Yes, Max said. I did go. I wanted to see.

Pan scoffed, but Max knew there was nothing he would do.

What does Quaid mean sugar daddy? said Max.

He means that the Judge pays my tuition at God's Way.

Max stopped walking.

He what? Why would he do that?

The red road unthreaded before them. It would soon turn into a gray road, parched and dusty, pebbles strewn along the loose top of it. October had brought most of the foliage to the ground, but some leaves still clung onto the branches and stayed there. Beneath the branches, kudzu climbed the trees as if to strangle them. The unmowed field to their right butted up against a scrawny, unkempt forest and its scrim of endless woods. To the left, wheat stalks shuddered amid pale grass and bushes grew round waxy leaves.

He would do that, said Pan, because he cares about Quaid, and Quaid is my uncle so he has to, in some twisted way, care about me. Or that's how the story goes. For the real story, you must dig deeper.

I would like the real story, said Max.

Pan started to walk again. Max hoped Pan would reach for his hand.

No shit, said Pan.

Will you tell me?

The Judge thinks that if he can keep Quaid subdued, keep his nephew—that's moi—in school, that Quaid will keep his secrets and protect him.

Pan cupped his hand around his last Virginia Slim and lit it.

That's where you'll end up if you stay with the Judge, said Pan. Blackmailed and brain-dead.

I am not follow, said Max.

They were headed for a gas station a mile away that was owned by a man named Josef who let Pan buy cigarettes and wine coolers. Max wished he could enjoy this rare moment of being able to walk anywhere, but he couldn't. An eeriness had settled in the silence around them. Behind the silence was the ambient crick of crickets. The occasional rustle of a rodent. The cry of a frog in a creek. A pinecone plummeting into a nest of needles. Pan's hand hung by his hip. Max reached out to hold it. Pan squeezed him and then pulled away.

Not here, honey, he said.

Max nodded, Yeah. Of course.

Quaid's drunk poison for years, said Pan. But he drank too much finally. Now his brain is gone, and the Judge can't trust him. He is no longer stable or sane. The Judge thinks he needs to be monitored.

What is poison having to do with this? asked Max.

Max worried his tongue over a rough chap on his lip. He didn't want Quaid to know a thing about him.

I have to tell you something now, said Pan.

You haven't told Quaid about my powers? interrupted Max. The thought seeded in his stomach. He felt sick. He might vomit. Have you? Please, if you have, tell me.

Don't worry, said Pan. No. I haven't. What I need to tell you has nothing to do with you. But I do need you to listen. I need to tell you something. I need to tell you about the plan.

Pan took a crystal from the satchel around his neck and heaved it out in front of him. He froze in place with his arms out like that, like he'd been turned to stone, and for a moment, in Max's mind, they were sealed together like that in the woods, becoming stone statues that stood side by side forever while the forest lived and died with the seasons.

Syndricadaba, Pan said. His face scrunched when he hissed his word. That's for the truth, he said. This is the stone of truth.

Pan thrust the pink rock to Max's face. A deep groove ran through its center like it was meant to be two.

Hold it while I tell you.

You are scaring me out, Max said. You're scaring me a little.

Kiss it, said Pan. Kiss the truth stone. Kiss and know the truth.

Pan pressed the cold object against Max's lips. It was the size of an egg. He shoved it into Max's mouth with such force that it knocked against his teeth. He thought for a moment Pan might push it down his throat.

Ouch, said Max, and he spit the stone into his hands.

I hope you're going to trust me. Because this here is real doozy woo, said Pan, and though he tried to sound lighthearted, Max could sense Pan's fear. I always knew the Judge was wicked. Tying up Lorne like that. Speaking hate on whatever stage you give him. But now I have the certainty to bring the wrath upon him. Now I know he's killed.

Maybe Max could have said *don't tell me*. He only wanted to walk to the gas station where the overhead lights buzzed like mosquitoes, and the wall of freezers hummed their cool blue breath onto the slick tiles. He wanted to sit on the curb outside and eat ranch-flavored chips while Pan smoked with his LIFE hand and talked about outer space. He wanted to share a Styrofoam cup of diet cola. He wanted Josef to walk out and stand in front of them, his jeans slung low on his hips, and his mouth moving a mile a minute while the television inside flickered. Josef would tell them how his brother just got a job as a trucker and had seen the entire Southeast, had driven a rig filled with safety pins for seventy-two hours without stopping, living solely on the meat of cashew nuts, candied peppermint, and the hydrating elixir of a vitamin water called IQ.

But Max could not say no. It was the look in Pan's eye. Scared. Pan looked more unguarded than Max had seen him. His eyes wide and scattering. The rawness of his expression drew an ache in Max. Whatever Pan said was going to put them on a new course. He felt defenseless. He would not leave Pan alone in his feeling. Any wall that had stood between them had been chipped away. Pan could step right into him. He put his index finger to Max's lips.

I'm talking, said Pan. Mind be still. Quiet your Ping-Pong balls.

Pan tapped his forehead, as if telling Max's mind to listen.

It sounds crazy, I know, said Pan. But the Judge is making people drink poison to prove they believe in Jesus. And he is watching them die. Letting them die. They're dying.

A stick snapped in the way back. Max fought the urge to look over his shoulder. They rounded a bend in the road, and Max half expected the Judge to be there. Grand cowboy hat atop his head, arms crossed, conjured from thin air by the invocation of his name. But no Judge stood in the woods anticipating them. There was only a garden snake, whipping across the path far up in front, almost invisible in the night.

Why would he do that? asked Max. *Rat magic*, said his mind. The shine of the moon. He saw Knox crawling in the grass of the field. Thought of the flask passed around at the river. *Not yours yet, Germany.*

So he knows he can trust them, said Pan. That's why he gets them to drink. It's all about his origin story. He drank poison and saw God. Now he thinks it's a test. If you have God inside and drink poison, then you get stronger and enlightened. If you don't have him in you, when you drink, you die.

I cannot even fathom this to be true, said Max.

Now the snake was gone. Now the path held no memory of it. It might never have been there at all.

The Judge is testing people. Seeing if the Holy Spirit is living in them. If they pick up a copperhead and get bitten and die or drink the poison and die, then he knows they aren't right with God. If they live, they can join his Christian army.

You are nonsense, Max said.

I wish I was, said Pan. But nonsense I am not.

Pan was acting strange. His breath was short and shallow. Pan bent over, hands on his knees, spine arched and tried to catch air. He stood again. He swayed as if he were light-headed. Max placed a hand on Pan's chest to ground and center him. A trick his mom had done when he was having his nerve attacks in Germany. But Pan stepped away from his hand.

If you can drink poison and not die, Pan said. He pointed at Max. Poked him with each word, smacking the emphasis. REAL. LIFE. That means the Holy Spirit is in you. It's an old trick. Comes from the Bible. It's a way of testing one's faith in the Lord.

Pan looked at Max as though he wanted to extract something from within him. Pan started to speak again, slow and even. The voice of an expert in control of the facts.

The Judge only surrounds himself with people who have the Holy Spirit in them. And he's a paranoid. Won't trust anyone. So, he tests them first. Plain as that.

With poison? asked Max.

Where do you think Quaid's fingers went? I told you. Taken off by the mouth of copperhead.

Stop, said Max, forcing himself to laugh. This is crazy talking.

But Pan wouldn't stop.

Max thought, *Some kind of rat magic.*

Pan told Max how the Judge and Quaid had grown up together. Quaid had been with the Judge the night he went missing and fell from the cliff. The others had given up and gone home, but Quaid had searched for the Judge all night and for days after. He didn't stop searching until the Judge had driven back to town, safe and sound. Quaid's love and loyalty had moved the Judge. That kind of loyalty was not something he would ever forget. The Judge had always been open about his conversion story. He told it when he ran for district attorney and later for his judicial position. What he did not tell people was that he still drank poison. He had with him a small circle of men. Their secret congregation was built on the idea that you had to radically trust in the love of God and give yourself over to him entirely or else perish with the sin of the world. You had to test yourself and others by walking to the edge of death. If God kept you safe, it was because you trusted him. It was because you really believed. If he did not keep you safe, it was a sign that you had let the devil in.

Are you listening to me? said Pan. He looked scared. His shoulders were up by his ears, making his body seem smaller. Are you listening?

Yes, said Max.

The wages of sin is death.

Pan said he and Lorne used to go with the Judge and Quaid to the services—not normal Sunday services like Max had attended but nighttime ones behind the Judge's lake house. Lorne and Pan would sit in the back and play Pogs. They were too young to drink the poison then, but they had been baptized in the black water and saved and one day they would be asked to drink, too. They would watch the men lift the jugs to their lips, dance with water moccasins on their shoulders. When the Judge began to run for office, they had to become careful about those meetings because they knew it could scare people. And then Quaid began to lose his mind, slowly at first and then fast, and the Judge took it as a sign of his moral deterioration and began to distance himself. The distance nearly killed Quaid. Sent him further into madness. Then the Judge had his vision of Pan and Lorne and banned them from seeing each other, but still the Judge paid for Pan's education as a gesture of his love for Quaid. Though Quaid could no longer be trusted, he could still be loved.

You have lost it, said Max. Sounds like you are the one who has lost it.

Max saw a tantrum gathering speed. But Pan remained calm, a reed blowing gently in the wind. He breathed in his Virginia Slim. Smoke swirled around his yellow crooked teeth as he talked.

I am not allowed to go to the services anymore, and neither is Quaid on account of his deterioration. But he snuck out to one of the gatherings recently, and he told me something.

You are not very right in your head, said Max. That's what you aren't.

Pan flinched when Max said that, and Max told himself, *Be nicer.*

Last month, when Quaid went, he said the lake house was filled with doctors, lawyers, business owners, all these powerful people, said Pan. People who would have never come to join the lake before, not before the Judge became someone with power. Quaid said some of the men were wearing masks or hoods over their faces. It was three times larger than he'd ever seen it. The man who owns the biggest used car lot in town walked to the front of the barn and drank a whole bottle of rat poison. Quaid said the man just froze and his muscles went stiff. They dragged him away to the corner and the Judge prayed over him. He raised up his hands, spoke in Judge-tongue, set crosses on his body. Then he proclaimed that the man was not a believer and dead.

Serious? said Max.

And guess what? said Pan. The next day the TV said that this same man died of a brain aneurysm. You know what this means? The Judge is poisoning people, and it's covered up for him. Doctors are covering it up. Doctors are on his side. The whole damn state. You get poison! You get poison! You get poison!

Pan pointed to the trees around them, shrieking off his proclamation. *Yougetpoison!*

Then go tell the police, said Max. If it's real like you say.

I mean people used to die once in a blue moon, but now Quaid says they're dropping like flies.

Max pushed back the memory of the man falling over in the aisle talking nonsense with his eyes rolled back in his skull. Mouth froth. Quaid had drifted through the Sunday crowd. Quaid had fit in so well Max couldn't find him. The cowboy hat and the cross. Max didn't know what to believe.

Fear was what he should feel, but fear toward what, he didn't know. Fear toward Pan who understood so much about him, who might even love him, and who seemed like a broken door slamming against its own hinges? Fear toward the powerful Judge his mother hated but whose presence could captivate a room, a city, a state? Fear at the God in the sky who might be there, might not? Fear at the sin inside of him?

Pan touched Max's forearm.

Will you help me? Please.

Max wanted to say no. He would not help because there was nothing to help, because Pan had made up a story and the story was not real. There it was pulsing two-lettered in his brain. N-O. But how could he not help him? Pan had set up this choice and made it impossible to turn away. He did it on purpose. He wanted to make him choose.

Max heard himself say: Yes.

Before Pan could respond, a white man in a red Durango slowed down as he passed them and threw a plate of beef nachos at Pan. Pan screamed and so did Max, shocked as he was by the hot cheese that splattered against his face.

I'm going to rip that dress off you, bitch! screamed the man. Then he sped off.

Pan dropped his cigarette and sprinted after the SUV yelling. He jabbed his middle fingers into the air in front of him as he chased it, but the Durango was long gone. It coughed out a black stream of gas and left skids on the pavement and the two of them running down an unlit gravel road as if toward nothing.

THE WEEKEND PASSED WITHOUT A text from Pan. Max checked his phone compulsively. The less he heard from Pan, the more space he took up. Worry followed him like a dog. Worry scratched at his leg and howled.

Pan was everywhere Max looked. Pan was Kurt Cobain's pout, sulking above his bed. Pan was the iris inside the tiger eye. Pan was the protection scissors that had fallen from the ceiling and lay, jaws open, on the carpet for anyone to step on. He was the one who'd said *You're gorgeous, Max, and I think that even when I don't say it.* Pan was the shark tooth he'd never given him.

One text could dispel all the worry, Max was sure. But one text did not come. It did not come as he brushed his tongue, peed in the toilet, poured his orange juice, did a hundred jumping jacks, campaigned at the Judge's office.

When Max closed his eyes, Pan was in bed, pressed against the length of him. When Max ran his tongue across the roof of his mouth, he tasted the clove of garlic Pan had eaten for lunch. When he opened his eyes, Max was standing alone in front of the Judge's HQ.

Davis was already through his fourth Dr. Fizz when Max walked in. He belched a greeting. Lorne mumbled on the phone in the corner where he sat proselytizing for his father. Max could hardly look at him.

He slouched to his desk and collapsed into his chair.

A name stared up at him from the list.

A number beside it.

The script he'd memorized by now.

The phone rang.

Had he dialed it?

The phone was at his ear.

A man picked up after three rings.

Hello howdy hi, said the answerer.

The man's voice sounded bright and Southern.

Hello, sir, said Max, and he began his spiel. *I'm calling from the Judge's office blah blah blah.* Then he stopped himself, because he felt the energy on the line shift.

Son, the voice said, steady and sure. Son, can I ask your age? If you don't mind.

Max liked how this man spoke. Slow and thoughtful. A man in a cardigan, maybe smoking a pipe. A man propped up against a wall of bound books.

I'm sixteen, said Max.

Sixteen, said the man, as if that were something. Sixteen, he repeated. Ah. The age of change.

Max sat up straighter.

Odd fellow.

Sixteen, said the man. You can make your mistakes at sixteen. But do I detect something in your voice? Are you feeling sad, son? I hear something in the way you speak.

Sad? asked Max. I am just from Germany.

That was off script, and it caught Lorne's attention. He turned his face toward Max and mouthed *What.*

Son, I don't mean to pry, which is certainly the point of what you're doing over there for the Judge. But I hope you've given thought to what you're doing on behalf of that man. That's not a good man, son. That's not a good man. Do you listen, truly, to what he says? Have you thought about what you want to stand for?

Um, said Max.

Son. You're the one who called me. Otherwise I wouldn't be so forward. But I work down at the university. In the Sociology Department. You come see me sometime. We'll have a Coke. Go for a walk.

Max hung up. Davis and Lorne stood in front of his desk now, heads cocked, eyes thin questioning lines.

Hey, fellows, said Max. He felt out of breath, like he'd just gone on a run.

You all right? asked Davis.

Yeah, said Max. Looney Tune on the line. So, I hung it up just now.

All right, said Davis.

But Lorne stood there, skeptical. Freckles ran up his neck.

He's got freckles everywhere.

Keep to the script, Germany, Lorne said. Keep to the script.

MAX TYPED INTO HIS PHONE: *Poison drinking Alabama.*

He reclined in the giant armchair of the living room. He sank into the cushions, shifting slightly against the lumbar pillow propped up behind him, the one that said *Joy!* Another flourish of décor that had come with the house. His mother usually positioned it backward, so that the script faced the fabric of the chair and not the living room. His parents sat together on the sofa. His mother sketched in her notebook. She was dressed in all black, her usual uniform. By dressing in one color, she could eliminate one decision from her day. CNN talked at them from the massive screen that sat on the console. After-dinner tea steeped on the coffee table. Beside it a plate of cake.

The first thing Google presented to Max was an article about a war criminal who drank poison in court.

As he scrolled through the Google image results, he saw a refrigerator packed with soda cans. A lineman in a crimson red jersey. A man with his face down on a bar. The Judge standing at the pulpit. No poison. No snakes.

Who are you texting? his mother asked. You can invite Pan over if you want.

No one, he said. He put his phone down. He pretended to watch the TV.

Honey, she said. Want some popcorn? I can make some.

No thanks.

Really? No popcorn? But that's your favorite.

Not hungry, said Max.

You got a headache again, son? said his father. Maybe you can call your friends and go toss the football.

They're busy, said Max. And it's dark out.

You know, said Max's mother. She rearranged herself on the sofa, which meant she was about to say something serious. She placed her notebook on the coffee table. We've been talking. We don't think it's a good idea for you to go to church again without us.

You are banning me from church?

No, said his father. We're just saying we'd like to go with you. Check it out.

I don't think you'd like it, said Max.

Why's that? his father said.

If we don't go, you don't go, his mother said.

She said it with the kind of control that came from practice. She must have repeated that phrase countless times until it sounded both strict and certain. She lifted her eyebrows like—got it?

Already you've grown so distant, his mother said.

And we don't know about all this religion, said his father.

You know, said Max. Most people's parents would be happy their son was going to church.

Well, I'm not most people's parents, said his mother. I'm yours.

Max stared at his nails. Clean, scrubbed squares.

I just want to come next time, said his mother. To the service. See what they do there.

Max could not picture his mother in church. Her closed, judgmental gaze. It would be like bringing in a spy. With her there, he would have to look at it through her eyes, and already he knew he didn't want to subject himself to that. What if someone fell to the floor and shook? What if someone stepped into the aisle and sung in a language no one else knew? His mother could not open herself to mystery. She didn't believe in magic. To her, science was wonder. A data sheet expertly executed. A drawing rendered with exact precision.

He felt cold. The need for a sweatshirt overcame him. How could all of those people be wrong? His mother would never open her mind enough to let even the possibility of God in.

This is mine. Can't I have something that's mine? he said. You would hate it anyway. It would bore you. You would judge and make me feel stupid.

No one is trying to make you feel stupid. And you have many things that are yours already, said his mother. I know I'd hate it, but that's not the point.

Max wondered what his father really thought about all of this. Nothing, probably, as long as Max didn't stay inside the house with a headache. *Lazy.* His father hated lazy people. He hated it when his son seemed lazy. Lazy as in sloth. Sloth as in sin. If his father had grown up in Alabama, Max knew he'd be like the other men here. He'd be in the woods worshipping God, drinking magic, tackling a man on a field. He was a product of his environment. A good German engineer with nice German hair and a flat German stomach who ate squares of German cake. He did what he was told. Max admired that: the ability to fit into the mold put before you. Max wished he could see a mold and know how to fit it.

Max was doing push-ups at the foot of his bed when the phone rang. He sprang for it, desperate, and yes, it was Pan.

He wanted to sound casual.

How did casual sound?

Let's work on the plan, said Pan, exuding a level of ease that Max envied.

I cannot, Max heard himself say, do the plan.

He sprawled out on his stomach and rubbed his chin into the carpet. It felt like stubble.

You haven't even heard the plan yet!

I cannot anyway.

Oh, come on. Are you mad at me for not calling?

No, said Max. I was not ever mad.

Liar. Don't lie.

Where have you been? asked Max. Why did you not want to call?

Max could hear Pan shrug.

Nowhere, buttercup. I just wanted to give you time to think. Think about what you want.

I want you, said Max, without thinking.

Well, good, said Pan. Because I've got a plan. Tell me you're not tempted. Bring your fingers, they're part of the ingredients.

What kind of plan? said Max.

I've discovered a spell that will let you transfer part of your power to me.

My curse, you mean?

Your power. Just come. Just trust me for once.

FOR A MOMENT, THE WORLD seemed carefree and completely unmagical, like Max had nothing to do but this, walk his body along the beach of a lake and through the night. He followed Pan up a rough sandbank until they located a place to cast the spell. Water ran up to touch his ankles. The lake looked solid enough to walk on.

Pan presented a swath of paper with instructions rolled into a scroll. He unfurled it.

<u>Needed for spell</u>
6 fingernail clippings from Max
1 shaving of callus
Eye of an animal
Leaf
Candle for burning
Sliver of a moon
Thimble of lake

Pan waved a sanded-down stick like a wand. He lit a candle that he unloaded from his purse and recited a spell.

Use this water to draw out his power
Let the moon do its glow
Seed magic in me and watch it grow
Take it from Max and let him go.

Pan bowed his head. The candle had an itchy, ragged smell that made Max cough. Pan leaned in like a suggestion. Closer. Lined red lips, lined green lids. Makeup smeared and dripping. His Adam's apple pushed at his throat like a Gordian knot. Max saw how far Pan's wanting went.

Any second now, said Pan.

They reclined on the beach, which was just a patch of wet loamy dirt. Pan bent down to touch his lips to Max's hip. They sprawled out for a while on the rough earth and talked. The constellations that pressed into the asphalt of sky looked like they were frozen specifically there, right above Alabama. It amazed Max to think these were the same stars that had shone on him in Germany, which felt so far away it might not even be a real place anymore.

Pan talked about pictures he'd seen of the earth from outer space and how beautiful the photographs were and how blue.

There's nothing more than a thin line of sky that's holding us here, said Pan.

I guess that is right, said Max.

It is right, said Pan. I heard Al Gore say it on NPR.

I think it is time, Pan went on. He pushed Max off him. I feel something in my third eye.

Okay, said Max. Go test it.

But Max knew the spell hadn't worked.

Pan retrieved the bag he brought with the dead kitten in it. He removed the stiff, lifeless creature with its matted fur and static eyes.

Damn, Pan said after massaging the body, stroking it.

Nothing happened. The cat stayed dead.

Maybe you need to start with something smaller, Max offered.

Max took the kitten in his lap, and it began to purr. He stoked the cat's head and scratched its belly. Bubblegum flavored. The cat induced the taste of candy. He closed his eyes and sought the headache.

Pan did not tantrum. Instead, he sang.

Dig them up, dig them up. We're going to dig the bodies up and bring them back to life. Dig them up. Dig them up. We're going to dig the bodies up.

Dig them up.

Dig them up.

Dig them up.

Dig them up.

Dig them up.

That's what Max heard for the next hour, for the next day, for the next week. It was like a mantra that he didn't want to know. It rang through his head like a bell. Max wished the plan wasn't what brought Pan back to him. He wished Pan had no other intention than to see him, spend time with him, to stretch out their bodies in the sand side by side, and be absolutely nowhere else.

MAX STEPPED DOWN FROM DAVIS'S TRUCK. Waved a hand like thank you as Davis left him by his mailbox. Max balanced his feet on the curb where leaves accumulated. Autumnal colors. Death's season drew near. All things would wither. Max would need to resist the impulse to give the camellias and crepe myrtles an early spring. He held the straps of his backpack. He had healed the cat at the beach the night before last. He'd need another resurrection by the end of the day if he wanted to keep his reserves regulated and curb his cravings. He remembered the dying tulip in the kitchen vase. Pan had given him small baggies of sugar to ingest between healings, if his cravings got too bad. He touched the bag in his pocket. Not yet needed. Across the street a neighbor boy tossed a basketball toward a hoop above his garage. He missed again and again.

Honey! He turned to locate Miss Jean's voice on her porch, her arm waving.

Honey, said Miss Jean when he reached her. Your nose! Did you break it?

Max touched his nose. The sting was there. Helmetless during warm-up, Max had caught Wes's throw with his face.

No, ma'am, he said. I hurt it during the practice, but I think it will be fine.

The truth was it felt broken. The pain nagged. It distracted, which was nice.

Honey, said Miss Jean. It looks awful. Purple at the edges already. You can't see it but it's going to leave a big ole bruise. I'm fixing to grab you a bag of ice from the freezer. Hang on a second.

Miss Jean disappeared inside. Her cat, Puss, came out and rubbed itself against his shin, purring. He felt the vibrations and knelt down to scratch it behind the ear. Animals loved Max. Mr. Sprinkles came meowing each time he was at Pan's.

Puss, he said. What do you think of it here? You like it?

Miss Jean had a living room on her porch: couch, rattan recliners, rocking chair, side table, the whole shebang. Beside the porch, marigolds, Russian sage, purple cabbage, and pansies bloomed in a raised bed. Miss Jean liked to sit outside rocking and pouring cups of sweet tea from her pitcher into an insulated tumbler filled with ice and stickered with Alabama A's.

Here you go, sweetness, said Miss Jean.

She handed Max a washcloth tied around a handful of frozen peas. He pressed it into his nose. His face throbbed. A sharpness streaked into his eyes.

Now I need a favor from you, she said.

Okay, sure, ma'am, said Max. He loved any opportunity to say the words *ma'am* and *sure*.

Can you get me a yard sign for the Judge? They were out at the campaign office. Can you believe it? But now, I think you might have insider access. Isn't that right?

Max grinned from behind his ice pack.

Yes. I do, he said. I can, I am sure, get one for you.

Can you get me one of those that say RISE UP, ALABAMA?

Think I can, said Max. Lorne has them, I think, at his house.

Lorne! Look at you on a first-name basis with Southern royalty. Now that's a good boy, she said. I knew it. I knew you'd find the right crowd quick as sin. I had a good feeling about you right way. Minute I saw you. I thought: this one is special.

You did? he asked.

Sure, I did, honey! Now you go ahead and take that washcloth with you. You can return it when you bring me my sign. And keep that nose iced for at least twenty minutes to cut down on the swelling and bruise.

PAN'S PLAN. MAX MASSAGED HIS temples when he thought of it. He hoped Pan would forget it. Put it off perpetually. A fantasy. But Pan was obsessed.

It would happen in the town cemetery. It would happen in the middle of the night. *The witching hour.* They would go to the graves of the people the Judge had supposedly poisoned, and Max would raise them up. One by one. An undead army. Pan had made a list of where each person had been buried. The list made Max nauseated. *Twelve names.* Max had held the list up to the light in his kitchen. *Had the Judge poisoned twelve people? Had he poisoned anyone at all?* In Pan's plan, they'd dig the holes, unseal the caskets, and Max would place his hands on the cold skin of each dead person. *We'll clamp our noses with clothespins to protect from the smell,* Pan had said. *We'll strap masks over our faces to protect us from their eyes. They won't know who brought them back. They'll think we're angels. We'll wear wings.*

In Pan's plan, the risen dead would be seen as a miracle, returned to life by angels and the will of Jesus. The risen would report what the Judge had done to them. They would explain that they had been poisoned. It would bring the Judge's demise. It would be a reckoning.

Why did Pan hate him so much? Max wondered. But in his heart, he knew the answer and the answer was Lorne. The Judge had taken Lorne from him. The Judge had taken Quaid, too. When Pan talked about the plan, Max felt like he was listening to someone recount a bad dream. Pan sounded too crazy to be serious, which was what allowed Max to go along with it, to load shovels into the car, to mold papier-mâché wings, to buy ski masks from Walmart and try them on in the mirror.

It felt like a game of chicken, and Max wouldn't swerve first. He couldn't. He knew that as soon as he said no to Pan, as soon as he challenged him on this, he would lose him.

The middle of the night at Pan's house and noises crept through the walls. Max heard every rattle the wind made. Music crooned from a truck that idled somewhere in the dark. Max rolled and turned and tossed in bed. The sheets bunched up under him, and Pan boiled. It was just like Nils. Fever dreams and pillow talk and desire that ran from nose tip to toe.

Max got up from bed to pour himself a glass of grape juice. He walked in circles through the living room and kitchen. He pushed at his nose. It still throbbed.

During the day, the living area looked neat and vacant as a waiting area, but now, the shadows turned every corner foreboding. The furniture leaned toward the center of the room. Anyone could come through the door at any minute. It was just a thing that could open. Max walked to the stove.

Tacked to the fridge was a class picture of Pan from third grade. That same pout, angled-in eyebrows, pointed teeth sitting on his lower lip. So completely normal-looking. A bit angry, but a regular boy. Max wanted to understand Pan's transformation. He grew up with the boys here. They went to elementary school together. When they hung out together, it felt comfortable. Pan knew their language. They did not prank or haze him the way they did the others at school whose ears they penetrated with candy bars and whose homes they ruined with raw eggs and whose cars they keyed. Max figured Pan wanted to pretend he tumbled from the ether a fully formed weirdo, but that wasn't the case. Everyone got to be who they were in some way or another.

He thinks he's a princess.

Pan stuck his head out of the bedroom door.

Ready? he whispered.

Sure, said Max even though he wasn't.

Shh, Pan said. The mother doth sleep.

Pan drove the car through the damp night, down that rutted-up road with not a soul on it. Piles of red dirt were stacked on either side. Pan fidgeted in the driver's seat. Max could feel the excitement coming off him in waves. Max couldn't tell the difference between fear and intuition. But one of those feelings pawed at him. It ran knuckles down his spine. Around them, forests unspooled and solidified. So much land with no one watching it.

Davis had asked Max once: What's the worst thing you could find walking alone through the woods, way far out with no a gun or nothing?

I do not know, said Max. A bear? A rabid wolf?

Another person, said Davis.

Max leaned into the passenger door and thought: *anotherperson-anotherpersonanotherperson.* Pan explained where they would turn, pointed his painted nail, glossy and black for the night's occasion.

As Pan sped the sedan toward town with the velocity of two boys on a mission, Max knew he wouldn't do it. He heard the shovels clink in the trunk. He winced each time they clamored against one another. He knew he wouldn't slip the ski mask over his eyes. He wouldn't undead the bodies the Judge had let die in the name of Jesus. But he couldn't tell Pan this. Not yet, not until after Pan flipped off the car, stepped onto the wet cement of the cemetery parking lot.

Then there they were. Headlights cut. Night unlit. Trunk open and empty. Leaves shook in the trees above them. A shivering came from somewhere deep inside Max.

He turned to Pan, who held a shovel in his hands. Dirt still on the spades. The boys stood on either side of the car's hood, and Max was glad there was something between them. Pan looked older, looked like the person he might grow into. Pan was not a witch. He was only a boy, and both of them knew it. The magic Pan possessed was a different magic. He believed in Max just as much as he believed in Quaid's story. His belief was going to dig those holes, raise those bodies, throw the Judge in jail. And if Max let him, if Max would take the next step with him, then maybe, Pan's belief would have been magic enough to make it true.

I can't do it, Max heard himself say.

Pan stared out at the graveyard. His jaw quivered, but Pan must have known already, because he only nodded underneath his wings.

You believe in the wrong things, said Pan.

His voice caught. It was a note that wanted to break but couldn't.

Let's just be us, said Max. Let's go back to the lake.

We're never going back to the lake, said Pan.

On the drive home, Max knew not to reach over and place his hand on Pan's thigh, which felt far away and no longer his at all.

PART 3

AUTUMN IN ALABAMA WAS BEAUTIFUL. The pavement was no longer too scalding to walk across in bare feet. The lakes were no longer the temperature of drawn bathwater. In the evenings, it was pleasant. The boys took sweatshirts with them that they would pull over their shoulders when the sun went down. Piles of leaves smoldered under naked trees. Their burning lit whole neighborhoods with the smell of sweet smoke.

The boy across the street from Max's house roamed the yard with his friend, their mouths smeared with BBQ sauce and their hands dusted Cheeto orange. They pointed BB guns at squirrels that ran under the shrubs, at Miss Jean's cat, and at the three-legged dog that everyone on the street fed scraps to.

Pan had stayed away from Max for weeks, and Max understood. *Space*. He needed space. He'd driven Max back to his house without talking. Max had seen Pan's tearstained face reflected in the glass and that's when he knew how much he'd let him down.

Distractions helped, like football. Max did not want to be alone. He went home with Knox after practice and ate hot dogs stuffed with Velveeta cheese. He raked Miss Jean's yard. She made him chicken and dumplings. He joined his mother at the arboretum and hiked through the piles of auburn crunch. Max saw Pan only during Physics, where they used foam tubing to construct a roller coaster in the hallway that carried ball bearings down loops and around hard turns. They timed the ball bearings at certain distances to measure their speed.

MAX PRESENTED A BASKET OF Kinder Chocolate to a convoy of ghouls. Sheets cascaded over their bodies. Holes had been cut into the fabric, so they could see. Blue eyes blinked into the dark. Young girls in tutus waved wands. Girls with whiskers drawn across their cheeks meowed at him, then hissed. They bared human teeth.

A fleet of ghosts ran down the street. Witches descended in tall black hats. They skidded from block to block on brooms. Robots walked the hills and dropped candy corn into the flowers. Silver wrappers glinted against the moonlight.

The Judge warned against Halloween. He said it taught children to beg for handouts. He disapproved of dressing up as the dead, as ghosts, as devils. Max gave candy to a devil. Red horns perched in a boy's blond curls, tied down with barrettes.

Trick or treat.

What are you?

Oh, a skeleton.

Oh, a scarecrow.

His mother loved the girl dressed as a black sheep. Her shoes looked like hooves. She had a fluff of a tail, a red nose, and a small, thrusting mouth.

It was custom before the last game of the season for the boys to spend the night in the abandoned insane asylum. Wes told Max how they had crushed cans of beer against the rusted red walls and blood poured out, how they had dared one another to spend an entire night in a ward where human brains had been lobotomized. The boys had woken up with their underwear gone. He told him they had seen an absolutely real ghost stare back at them from the bathroom mirror on the ground floor. He said a homeless man without a face had jumped at them and tried to piss on their feet. The boys knew for sure that a family of spirits lived on level five, and there was a patch of air cold as a refrigerator in the attic that was the soul of a murdered girl.

Doctors used to have to trim the bottom of magnolia trees because patients would sneak under the branches that reached to the grass and have sex with each other, said Cole.

He laughed like this was hilarious. Wes was sitting next to him in the backseat of Lorne's truck, and he laughed, too.

It was bad here in the day, said Davis. People from the government had to come to the state in person to shut it down. The docs treated these people like garbage. We're fixing to show you some gnarly stuff.

Alabama, Wes said, is full of places with ghosts trapped, and they can't leave.

Why? Max asked.

Cause their stories never got finished, said Cole.

The building's chipped paint and broken windows and grand porch came into view. It had the look of something that was once magnificent. Lorne pulled the truck around the circular driveway, but Davis said, Park away from the road, stupid.

The driveway's long enough, Lorne said. I parked here before and you can't see balls from the highway.

Max looked in the direction of the highway. In between the truck and the road rolled a lawn where patients once roamed in hospital robes. He tried not to think about the psychiatric practices from the past. Davis won the argument and Lorne drove a little way down a dirt road and into a thicket, where they hid the vehicle, parking it near a wilting gardener's shed. They'd have to walk back to the asylum through a wooded path that crisscrossed the old hospital grounds.

The boys stepped out into the night. They slammed the doors to the truck and announced their arrival to the great wide fields. The wind smelled like bad vegetables. Someone had spray-painted the shed's exterior. Cock Suck Piss dripped in red paint. A water tower watched them from the distance.

It's healthy to give yourself a good scare, Cole said. Freak the daylights out of yourself. Keep your heart healthy.

Lorne flung his arm around Max's shoulder. His hair frizzed with humidity. A zit tipped his nose. He dialed his eyes onto Max's lips. Max held his breath. He felt connected to Pan in this moment. He didn't know if what he felt was jealousy or desire. Maybe one could spawn the other. Maybe they could be the same. Lorne had a boy's beauty. He had a mouth that always hung open. Pan knew how those lips tasted, that mouth. Heat spread across Max's chest. His heart would never beat like this for Billie and her macramé bracelets.

He was my first husband. And I was his first wife.

You've heard the story of Henry, said Lorne.

He kept his arms around Max's shoulder. Max decided to fling his arm around Lorne's shoulder, too. He shook his head no. Shake, shake.

Henry was a ghost that haunted a girl. He walked through her house and knocked things off the counters and scared the daylights out of her. Like she seriously couldn't sleep a minute. She'd go into the room after something fell and say *Hello*. Nothing. No one was there. One night she took a picture of herself after she'd tried to say *Hello, Henry, come out*. That's what she called him. And guess what? Guess who's just sitting there smiling smug as hell in the picture once it was developed?

Lorne's lips were close to Max's ear, tickling it.

Henry was there. But you can't see him unless you take a picture of him first.

Really? Max said.

Really, said Lorne. How about that, huh?

Davis walked up beside them carrying the sleeping sacks.

Check out how scared shitless Germany looks, said Davis. He laughed and began to run.

Max let his eyes widen as Wes told him about the asbestos that was spread across the floorboards like snow. Cole told him they'd say a prayer to Jesus. Jesus would put a protective force around them that kept them safe from the devil, if the devil lived in the asylum, which the boys said he probably did.

After they passed torn-up and falling lean-tos, the giant building stood before them, six stories of dark windows. Only half of its front columns remained intact. The boys claimed they would show Max the ward where the criminally insane used to live. They swore to God that old medical records were scattered all over the ground.

There's one dude who lived in here, said Cole. He chopped whole families into bits with scissors because he thought they were aliens and he hid their body parts in a golf course. That's true. Swear on my mom's grave.

Some of it is going to make you feel a little sick, Germany, said Lorne.

Yeah, don't pee yourself okay, you dumb Nazi? Davis said.

They walked up a wrought-iron stairway. Humans had been there and signed their names as proof. Beer cans littered the front porch. A giant swastika had been carved into the front door. Slurs ruined the walls inside. They passed under archways flanked by windows that would stream in sun if it was daytime. The boys talked loudly, as if to prove they weren't afraid. Covering the floor underneath them: dust, bent wires, cracked glass, dry newspapers, a bent hypodermic needle. Laughter ran from the children's ward and into Max's ears. He was alert to every creak that careened down the vacant, crumbling hallways. On the third story, murals of stone-eyed elephants stared down.

They walked in a huddle. Max squished into the middle, the protected, sacred center. They swung the arc of their flashlights down dark halls and turned slowly to check behind their backs when the wind blew. They decided against sleeping in the criminally insane ward and walked up to the roof. It was less scary up there, and Max was relieved to be outside again.

Pan would love it here. Maybe he'd even been. Maybe Lorne had taken him.

From the roof, Max gazed over the pointed heads of pine trees. A car traveled down the highway. The perspective soothed Max. Lights from Delilah smoldered in the distance.

Father God, Davis's voice boomed out into the cool night. Banish all evil spirits from our presence. Make this place holy for you. Keep us safe from the devil if he lurks here, which we know he does!

Davis's fly was unzipped, his flaccid penis pissed the perimeter of the roof as Davis walked it. When he was done baptizing the place, he turned to them and shook some drips off the head and pinched it.

The roof had been slept on before. Max knew because someone had scrawled I Was Slept Here in red paint above the outline of a body. Lorne laughed like it was a joke. He was genuinely not scared, but the others seemed uneasy, even Davis.

Cole said, Countdown to camp has begun, fellas.

Davis stretched his arms above him. Cannot even wait. Holy God, knight me already.

What's camp? asked Max.

Camp can only be experienced, said Davis. Never explained.

That's why I don't get it, said Wes. My mom won't ever let me go.

You got to just sneak out and come with us this time, said Boone. Lie and say you're staying at my house. This year will be a big year. It's right before the election.

My mom is a literal psychic, said Wes. And my sister would tell on me. I can't go.

What Glory don't know, don't hurt her, said Boone.

Then you never met Glory, said Wes. Cause that girl knows everything and all.

I'd like to go to a camp, said Max.

Davis said, Yeah, duh, Germany. You are coming. No doubts in the mind.

Guess who I brought? Lorne said.

He extracted a flask from the pocket of his coat. He held it up and winked. Davis revealed a fifth of whiskey from his bag. They clicked the edges together. *Cheers.*

Max did not want to get drunk around the boys. He still never had. He would usually sip his beers slow and pour them into the sink or into the grass when no one watched. He didn't care to be out of his mind. He didn't know himself enough to trust what he would do or say around them. He remembered waking up in Pan's bed with red nails and an empty head.

But that night on the roof, he consumed so much whiskey that he curled into the shape of a snail right on the scrawled outline of the body that a stranger had drawn. The boys wanted to make sure Max didn't fall off the roof, so they lorded over him and drew boobs on his back and wrote the words *broken angel* on his chest and *beer*. They made sure he drank water, and thought it was hilarious when he vomited into a neat little puddle. Lorne had two paper bags of miniature hamburgers from Shakes & Stuff. He tried to stuff one in Max's mouth to sober him up, but the burger just came right back up. Max dropped his head in Lorne's lap and moaned into his jeans. Lorne pushed more bits of hamburger into Max's mouth, then wiped away his dribble with the back of his red-haired hand.

Price shared some of Knox's moonshine, and Davis drank so much that he began to howl and chant.

You sound like a madwoman, said Lorne.

Like a tater tot, said Boone.

Rat magic? Max tried to say, but it came out as a mumble into Lorne's thigh, where his head still rested. Poison?

What's that? asked Lorne. A hand in Max's hair. Small pets. Shhh.

Look, fellas, said Davis. He stumbled toward them with his arm outstretched. A small black snake dangled from the pinch of his hand.

A serpent, said Davis.

Davis began to dance. He lifted the snake above his head. While they watched, Lorne stroked Max's hair, almost sweetly. Davis began to sing and held the snake toward the stars. He brought it right in front of his nose and stared into its face. Then Davis bit the snake's head off.

Fuck, said Boone. You are fucking crazy!

Davis spit the head off the roof and threw its body after it. The head and body blended into the black night and disappeared.

Max moaned into Lorne's leg.

Shhh, said Lorne. It's only a snake.

That night, Max dreamt that Lorne dragged his body to the other side of the roof. Max felt Lorne's bulking arms around his torso and the labored breath on his neck. *Ow,* Max said in his dream when his knee collided with something metal. Max stepped outside of his body and climbed into an oak tree that reached above the roof. He sat on a branch and watched from his dream. He watched Lorne struggle to move him. He watched himself sleep. He batted at his face in the tree and his hand smacked Lorne's chin on the roof. Nothing made sense. A headless black snake circled them and left a trail of blood. He found the snake head and put it in his mouth. He wanted to chew the snake head. He was so hungry. But even in his dream, he told himself no. Just swallow it whole. Just swallow the snake.

Lorne's arms tightened around Max's chest. It was a threat and not a hug.

Quiet, Lorne muttered, because maybe Max tried to slur out a word. Maybe he had tried to ask a question.

What are you doing?

Lorne dropped Max. He'd found his place. Max stretched out on his stomach. *Sleep. Finally sleep.* Then hands were on his belt. The leather slithered as it left the loops. The belt hit the floor. Lorne's palms dampened his sides. They ran up and down. Lorne jerked Max's shorts to his knees. With one hand, he pressed Max's face into the roof and into the filth and pine needles.

In the dream, Max tried to turn off his mind and just let Lorne do whatever he wanted. After all, it was just a dream. Pan had done it. This is what Pan had done. For a moment, Max imagined he was Pan. This was what it felt like to be Pan. Maybe he had fallen into Pan's dream, and this was exactly what he wanted. But when the morning stretched across the new sky and pried Max's eyes open with her hot fingers, his shorts were unbuckled and his boxers were muddy. He was far away from the others who were asleep on the other side of the roof. Max's palms were torn as if he'd been dragged. His belt was looped in a pile, and his mouth tasted like he'd sucked on a star.

THE STADIUM LIGHTS BLOTTED OUT the faces in the stands. They pounded down fake brightness, turned the boys into celebrities. Max felt like a celebrity. He was one of them, at last. He was called into the game late in the fourth quarter. Max took his spot against the opposing team, St. Paul's Angels. On every passing play, Wes was hit hard by the Angels' blitzes. It was getting worse as the night wore on. Wes's teammates helped him up each time, but the impacts accumulated. Before each play, Wes scanned the defensive line to try to figure out where the next hit might come.

Coach hulked up and down the sideline.

You boys tired? You're looking tired! Wake up, Davis. Wake up!

With less than two minutes left in the game, God's Way was down by four points, but they had the ball at midfield with two time-outs left. The ball flew sharply through the air, and Max stretched his hands out to snatch it between two defenders.

Cheers erupted from the stands.

Max sensed his father's pride, even though he couldn't see him. He pictured him clamor to his feet and yell *run* in German. Max thought—*You do like it here*. Max turned on his heels and sprinted as fast as he knew how. Adrenaline was a real thing. It flamed up, burned through his muscles, and edged him on. Max clenched his mouthguard between his teeth as a player from the other team flew at him—helmet, shoulder pads, and arms like one hard missile. Max fixed the ball high against his chest like the wide receiver coach had taught him. He stuck his other hand out and used a stiff arm to push away the tackle. His head pounded, and his knee felt sore.

God's Way quickly got back into formation as the clock ticked. Thirty seconds left. Thirty yards to go. Again, Max caught the ball, and this time he had a wide-open sprint to the end zone. A player dove for his legs and tripped him up. Max started to fall but reached the ball over the goal line before his knees touched the ground.

Pain sung through his skull, but Max sprang up and stood staring at the scoreboard as people yelled. No one had ever cheered for Max like this, like he was the hero, like he was the one to be proud of. He extended his open palm to the player who tackled him. The crowd watched Max pull him up. They watched his gesture and thought: *Isn't he a good, good boy?*

The team dumped the icy contents of a watercooler over Coach's head. He yelped, delighted. Their fists flew up and punched with something fierce and free.

In the locker room, Coach called Max over and presented him with a tiny gold cross. Max blinked. His eyes were filled with streaks. He blinked again. Still there. He had just showered, and a towel was tucked around his waist. Coach dropped the chain into his open hand.

Just tuck it under your shirt, said Coach. And you got him right there always.

Him?

Christ, said Coach. You got Christ there wherever you go. He's going to look after you. Make sure you're protected.

Max stared at the necklace. Tiny nails fastened the small body to the small cross. The head hung down in what Max assumed was anguish. Max felt like the body on the cross. Pinned to the post. He wanted to feel the anguish against his chest, driven through the meat of his palms and into the bones of his feet. The Judge wore a cross just like this one. Quaid wore one just like it, too. Lorne, too, wore one. And it had swung from his neck in Max's dream.

Max wondered if the Judge felt the cross bounce against his clavicle when he walked, if the cross lifted off his body and fell back with each stride. Maybe the motion reminded him that life is winning. Max secured the clasp at the back of his neck and it settled against his skin. He looked Coach right in his eyes.

Thank you, Max said.

PAN HAD CALLED FOOTBALL BARBARIC, but Max still thought it was romantic. He thought of the romance as he dressed by his locker, as he pulled on his light blue shirt and buttoned his wrinkled jeans. Football still reminded him of the Romans and their Colosseum, all those people looking on at the spectacle, all those people watching what a body could do to another body. The boys had left for the party already. The metal lockers underscored the emptiness of the room and its four tall corners and its firm flat benches. A light overhead sputtered as if it, too, were done and wanted Max to leave, turn it off, and go.

The night was crisp and clean, and Pan was in the parking lot waiting. He wore a pink skullcap over his hair. His lips were painted blue, as if an ode to winter. He nodded when he saw Max, like it hadn't been long since they'd talked outside of school. Pan looked skinnier, as though his bones had sucked the skin in. Somehow, Max knew Pan would be waiting. He had felt the waiting. *Intuition*, Max thought.

We won, he said.

Ain't that something, Pan said. I saw.

You saw?

Pan looked like he might not be angry anymore, and Max thought maybe this would be the night they made up for good.

Did he want that?

So, Pan said. You know. Hi.

Hi, Max said.

He scrapped his vocabulary for another word. Any other word.

Guess you're going to be at Davis's tonight, said Pan.

Max tightened the grip on his gym bag and said, Yes? And you—?

Let's ride together, said Pan.

You're going? Max said, confused. I thought those parties were beneath you.

To this Pan only shrugged.

They shared the sidewalk for almost a minute as Pan finished a cigarette. He crushed his Virginia Slim into the ground with the toe of his boot and adjusted his blouse.

Cute necklace, said Pan. I love how in vogue dead bodies are around here.

Pan avoided the main streets and took back roads. Maybe he wanted privacy. Whatever the reason, Max appreciated it, because he didn't want to share Pan. Or maybe he didn't want to be seen with him. They rode down a quiet road, and Pan pulled onto the side. He reached over and unzipped Max's fly. Pan bent his head down and took Max into his mouth. Max watched the oily crown of his head move up and down. The cast-off pink skullcap stared at him from the floorboard. It looked suggestive, like a discarded thong. They pulled back onto the road and drove a little farther until Max found himself in the same parking lot where they had once slurped down ice cream cones and wished to life every dead bug on the windshield. The parking lot looked different to Max now, less exotic and almost sad.

Max touched his face to the furless skin of Pan's stomach. How he missed that stomach. He shoved his nose into the space between his ribs and inhaled. He smelled like a root. Pan spit in his eye. Max blinked it out like a tear. They gasped at the air like someone was drowning them and drove the rest of the way to Davis's house in silence, with Pan's hand resting on Max's thigh.

PAN PARKED AT THE END of the cul-de-sac. They stepped out of the car. Max itched for something else. The yards here told the same stories with their shimmering shrubs and pompoms of hydrangeas. They said happy families inside.

No trespassing.

Guard dog on watch.

Enter at your own risk.

They heard rap music as they approached Davis's house. Pan twerked for a moment on the sidewalk, then moonwalked past the elephant ears, those thick palms of green plant. Max thought about asking Pan if he wanted to just leave. They could go somewhere, the two of them. But Pan seemed eager to keep moving.

A boy from Max's team greeted them at the door. He held the two of them together side by side in his mind. Max knew this boy not so well. The boy's shoulders hung up around his ears, and he moved with the slow, swollen movements of someone who had ingested large quantities of steroids.

Max translated the knit brow and guarded gaze as suspicion. Like—*Who brought the witch?*

Going to let me in or what? said Pan.

Pan took off his leather jacket in the freshly painted foyer and hung it on a peg beside a row of identical fleeces. He turned to Max.

Toodaloo.

Pan walked past a window framed by tacky floral drapes and across a carpet already gathering mud from the boots the boys failed to leave by the door. In Germany, shoes by the door was a necessity. One rich kid elbowed another when Pan passed. They lifted the rims of their Solo cups to hide their smirks. The rich kid with Chiclet teeth and a greasy bowl cut laughed the loudest. He was neither attractive nor funny nor particularly smart nor kind.

Max had half a mind to follow Pan up the stairs but then what? Pan was on his way to Lorne. He knew it. And Pan wanted him to know it. His intuition hummed.

Dozens of guys lounged around the house. They outnumbered the girls almost two to one. They sat on counters and cast their large limbs over furniture. The girls danced with one another, swinging their arms by their sides, throwing them in the air, and shimmying their bodies to the slow beat of the bass. Max let his eyes linger on Hayes, sore-muscled, freshly showered, doe-eyed, and draped across the couch.

On the back porch, Max dug through a chest of crushed ice until he uncovered a canned beer. He did not want the beer. He wanted to hurl the beer through the upstairs window where he imagined Pan was talking to Lorne. Max thought of his dream: Lorne had not been gentle. Max fumed beside a game of beer pong and watched boys attempt to flick weightless celluloid balls into plastic cups. Behind them, taxidermy deer heads protruded from the wall. Maybe one day Max would hold a rifle to his eye and life wouldn't win.

That's a whitetail, said Davis. He tipped a beer in the direction of two more. And that one is a buck and doe pair. Cute, ain't she?

Sure, said Max.

Hey, buddy, said Davis. He touched his arm. You all right? Something gotten into you?

I am fine, said Max, and he took a swig from the beer he'd poured into a cup. Buddy.

Max looked over at Wes, who seemed sober.

You ever been hunting, Max asked him.

Nah, not really, said Wes. Not really my speed.

I love to hunt, said Max. I am starting to pick it up like a new hobby. I maybe even buy a gun. Max positioned his arms like they held one and pointed it at the wall. He tilted up his empty arms as if firing a shot at the space between the girl deer's eyes.

Right, right, said Wes. It's good to have a hobby.

Beer pong progressed. The boys called for a group of girls, and the girls appeared on thin, thigh-gapped legs, sipping vodka and Gatorade. One guy stumbled to the stereo and wrenched the volume dial all the way up until the rap music was inside Max's brain.

Wes! Wes! The boy with the hunched-up shoulders called for Wes and tried to get him to dance for them. The spectacle embarrassed Max, the way they pulled Wes into the middle of their circle and clapped wildly. But Max did nothing. Couldn't fathom intervening even if he'd known how. They pulled Wes back into the center of the circle each time he tried to sit down.

Pan's body appeared on the back porch with Lorne. Max watched through the sliding glass door as Lorne lit Pan's cigarette for him, something Max had never done. Seeing Lorne made him uneasy and scared. He thought of the roof. Maybe it was only a dream. It might have only been a dream. Their boots pointed toward one another. Cowboy and army. Max shivered. A knot knit in his gut. Pan reached out to light Lorne's cigarette for him, too. It was a tender gesture, and Max encased it in amber. Then someone said: *Hey, Max.* When he looked again, Pan and Lorne were gone. It felt almost like he'd made it up. He bit his empty cup open at the top and then slowly ripped the red plastic in half. *What was Pan up to?* He imagined Pan telling Lorne about Max and his power. *Satanic.* Lorne might call it. *Sin.* He imagined Pan saying *faggot* just like Quaid had said.

Party's lame, said Boone. Let's go find more chicks.

Max couldn't stand to be in the house a second longer, so he left with Boone. They climbed into Boone's truck and headed out to Cole's father's field. Max surfed his hand through the thick air and closed his eyes. Boone took advantage of the solitude on the highway and broke 110 miles per hour. The truck shook. Gears whirred. The engine ground out the strange noise of something being pushed past its limits.

Truth or dare, said Boone.

Uh, said Max. Truth.

That's no fun.

Should I dare then?

Naw, you already said truth. Lemme think.

Boone squished his face like he was searching.

Got it, he said.

Max waited.

Tell the truth.

He set his jaw and rolled an eye at Max like he was watching to make sure he would follow through.

Did whatshername give you a taste of those DSLs yet?

Max was surprised by the question. Billie?

Mmm-hmm.

Uh. Yes. Uh. Yes, she did do that.

Yeah, that's what's up. Boone stuck a fist in his direction and waited for him to bump it.

Boone blinked at the dirt road rushing toward them. He brought the tip of his Coke bottle to his lips and spit something black down its plastic neck. He lifted his butt and adjusted the denim around his crotch. Even this simple motion formed a pit in Max's stomach. A song about forgiveness streamed from the speakers. It ended. A song about fishing replaced the sad melody with an even sadder one. Max never knew catching fish could stir up such melancholy in a person. But the gruff voice that flowed from the speaker made waiting for a fish sound unbearable.

The truck slowed. Boone pulled over behind a convertible jeep. The sound was a great groaning wind. Somewhere a low laughter rumbled and gathered like a storm. Boone used the flashlight on his phone to light the path toward the laughter. They walked through a patch of dark air concentrated with mosquitoes. Max wasn't nervous coming out here anymore. He'd been back during the day and seen how alive the fields were. A clearing appeared before them, but no Pan. He was back at the house with Lorne. *Lorne, his first husband.* The alcohol turned Max's mind into a slow-moving thing. He swayed between anger and hunger. Billie brooded near the fire, smoking, staring into the flames. Guilt edged at him.

Max walked right up to her and said, Want to take a walk?

Oh shit, said Boone. Go on.

Billie did not move her eyes from the fire. Sure, she said. As long as you don't take me cow-tipping.

In the tall stalks of the field, Max and Billie walked side by side, awkward as two people who'd only just met. She moved with a lightness. Those same macramé bracelets choked the columns of her wrists. Copper charms hung from them. The paleness of her arms repelled him. He wondered what it would be like to take her hand. He wouldn't know what that kind of desire would feel like. But he wanted to know. If he were a girl, he'd like Billie.

What's that say? he asked, surprising himself by how gruff his voice sounded.

The beer had done it. He pointed to a line of Magic Marker scrawled on her forearm.

Lyric from a Bikini Kill song, she said.

He didn't like her tone. No attention for him. Not even a smile.

What's wrong with you tonight anyway? Max asked. Everyone's in a bad mood. Pisses me right off.

Nothing. Everything's freaking grand. A real ball.

They walked toward a pond. He took the truth stone from his pocket, the one Pan had given him on their walk that night, and hurled it into the field. He remembered the shark tooth in his wallet. Maybe he'd give it to Billie. They could use it to carve their initials into a slab of stone like people did when they loved each other and wanted the love to be remembered.

Hey, he said. Truth or dare.

Truth, she said.

Boring, he said, but that's what he wanted her to pick.

Billie wore a black spaghetti-strap tank even though it was cold. He liked her white T-shirt better than this one that showed off her cleavage. What would Internet Boyfriend think if he could see her now, wandering the fields with him, her breasts shoved into a perfect V for him to admire? If Max were her boyfriend, he'd let her do whatever she wanted with her cleavage. He wouldn't care. He thought he could smell her vagina, though maybe he made that up. Something smelled like tuna and he knew that's how vaginas were supposed to smell. *Davis likes the smell*, thought Max. *A good smell*. Pheromones. Her biology should talk to his biology and say: desire.

Whatever, she said. Truth anyway.

Fine, he said. Tell me about Pan. What do you think went wrong with him?

Billie looked confused.

Why, she said. What'd Pan do to you?

Her tone was accusatory and protective.

I mean, said Max. Nothing. He did nothing to me.

Why then? she said. You in the market for some fishnet stockings or something?

No, Max said, bumping up against anger again. She was making this difficult for him. *Make it easy.*

I thought you were friends with him, he said. I thought maybe you had some insight. I just want to know how he got weird. When he became witch.

Are you trying to figure out how to ride a broomstick? she said. Or where to get a discount cauldron?

You are making fun, he said.

Don't try to fuck with him, she said. He's harmless. You've got nothing to worry about.

Max held up his hands like people do when they want to prove they don't have a gun.

I am not the one trying to fuck with him, said Max. Maybe he is the one trying to fuck with me.

Ah, said Billie. She lifted her hands to her face. Took them away. Made an expression that meant *unbelievable.* Okay. Her tone dropped. I get it. She sighed like a lightbulb had been pulled above her head. I get it.

Get what? Max asked.

She mouthed the word *wow.*

I'm an idiot I did not see it sooner. That's what Pan meant.

Meant when? Asked Max. When?

Pan, that sweet nugget. You're crushing. You are. I get it, she said. Just don't get too sweet on him or Lorne will kill you.

Billie stooped down and ripped a flower right out of the earth. Yellow roots dangled from the green stem. Max watched her just kill things. Just like that. She shoved the dead flower into one of her frizzy braids.

Lorne?

Billie looked at him and laughed, Yes. *Lorne*. Did I stutter?

I don't crush on him, said Max in his most serious tone.

Max stopped walking. A firefly flicked through the air between them. He could hear yelling in the distance. It was the kind of ambient scream that might be laughter or might be a threat.

It's so obvious though, she said. Now it really is. So, so painfully obvious, wow. It's like once you see a thing you just see it. Boy. I was actually quite wrong about you.

She looked at him like she knew him, like she knew how he was. He watched how her ugly little ears wiggled as she laughed.

Don't laugh at me, he said. Don't laugh.

But this only made her laugh more. She laughed with a cruelty he did not know belonged to her. Her laughter was at him and not with him. This was not the Billie he knew from Davis's house or from the dugout or from the mall. She looked at him like she saw the sin inside of him. He wanted to stop that nasty laugh as if that could stop her knowing. Her face crumpled into a twist of snout and cheek and brow. A pig girl.

Stop, he said.

He grabbed her shoulders and held her away from him. He wished he wanted her even a little. He tried to scrape his body for a shred of lust. He willed his crotch to grow. Max wanted to do something to her that would prove something to them both. But he couldn't summon it. More power existed in the clumps of grass on the road than in him. He tightened his grip and shook her, but not hard.

Get your hands off of me, she said, and tried to wrench herself away. But Max held on. He stumbled toward her as she struggled to free herself.

Max grabbed her again. This time he wrapped his arms around her soft girl waist and held his face right against the warm dough of hers. Her cheek had the same makeup film as Pan. He smelled her fishy little mouth. *She doesn't get it. Billie doesn't get it.* She didn't understand what he was asking her, what he wanted, but neither did he. He felt rot and salt, brine rising up inside of him, slipping over his edges.

Can I kiss you? he heard himself mutter into her cheek.

CanIkissyou, he whispered into her stupid braids.

She tried to pull away from him again. Her nails dug at his forearms, the forearms that could crush her. The forearms that no matter how completely they could hurt her could still bring her back to life. Maybe he should show her.

Don't leave, he said, as Billie thrashed against him. I'm not going to hurt you. I just want to kiss you.

I'm not fucking kissing you, she said.

He released his grip, and she stumbled back, but she didn't run away. She stood there looking at him. She looked like she felt sorry for him.

Please, he said.

Maybe that would be all it took. Maybe he just needed to kiss this one girl. *What was he doing?* He felt suddenly small.

Fuck you for saying that, she said. For saying you want to kiss me.

She drew her arm back like she might punch him.

Do it, he said. Punch me. Please. Punch.

Billie looked tough. She was more boy than he was, and he liked that about her and envied it.

Fuck you for saying you want to kiss me, she said again. Fuck you for being like them.

She dropped her arm to her side. She spit at him, and the glob landed at his foot and bubbled.

Hit me, he said. Please.

You're just a sad boy who deserves no punches.

Her forehead glistened. She pulled a cigarette from the metal canister she'd used in the dugout. Her hands trembled. She had been afraid. He saw it clear as he saw the spit before him. That's what she'd been. He covered his face with his hands and tried to rub away the moment.

Here I was thinking you were different, she said. Here I was thinking that.

MAX WALKED TO THE POND ALONE. It must have been polluted, because the fish that once lived inside it had bobbed to the top. Max tried to skip a stone across the algae-scabbed surface. It took a few tries and then he did it. He skipped the stone three times. He picked up a rock. It reminded him of the Jesus toes at the church in Spain, gone smooth from something moving over them again and again. Max tried to hit one of the dead fish, but he missed. He could smell honeysuckle. The wind hurled itself with such sound. Shiver and sweat at the same time was something he had begun to love about Alabama.

Boys screamed somewhere in the distance. They drew beams through the night with their flashlights, hunting for cows to tip. Cows slept standing up, Max had been told, so it was possible to give them a shove and their powerful thighs would buckle right to the ground. Someone hollered when he came upon a cow. He whooped for others to join them. The cow would fall, and they would celebrate. Their joy would last until the time it took to find a second cow. Then their joy would repeat. It was simple.

Max walked into the pond. He continued to sweat even when he was hip high in the water, water that smelled nasty and of egg. He waded into it anyway. He needed the water. Above him, a plane blinked red lights. It might have been going anywhere, shrinking the vast space between continents down to a few hours. At the deepest point in the pond, the water touched his nipples. The water circled his hips and stomach and chest and lifted up the fabric of his jeans, his cotton shirt. What's on the bottom, he wondered as he trudged over the slick muck. Nails? Rusted tractor parts? Dead dog? Something that looked like a wig danced in stringy patches off the rocks beside the water.

Billie's face floated in the air in front of him. He held her face and kissed it. He heard another whoop, and it sounded like her.

Why did Pan go to Lorne? What did he tell him? What would Lorne do to him? He shivered in the water. *I'll lie,* thought Max. *I'll just lie. They'll believe me.* Fear tightened his neck, tightened his tendons into metal wires. He didn't want to be tied to a tree in the forest, left there all night wrapped in his own fear.

The fish squirmed. Their scales shimmered. They slipped from his hands and spilled sugar down his throat. They flipped themselves into the air, absorbed the night, and swam away from him. Even as he healed them, he knew they were only going to die again in this polluted pond. But he needed to do something good. He would heal this one thing, this last thing, then he would lie.

MAX WAS AMONG THE HANDFUL summoned to the Judge's campaign office. It looked how it always looked. Stacks of neatly cornered papers covered the desks. A hand-stitched biblical saying from Proverbs was framed above the fireplace:

In the LORD's hand the king's heart is a stream of water that he channels toward all who please him.

The heating rumbled and heaved as if sick. The building was too hot, and condensation rained down the windows. It was still too warm for indoor heating, but people in Alabama could not stand any cold. Max touched the wallpaper where it peeled. Pictures hung from the walls. Photographs mixed together with spiritual sayings and campaign slogans. Max had passed them a dozen times, but tonight they seemed new. What drew him toward them, he didn't know, but something whispered, C'mon here. C'mon here and *look*.

The other boys assembled chairs in the biggest room in the office, the one where they made the phone calls. But Max loitered in front of the photos. He slipped his hands under his shirt and rubbed the squares of muscle on his stomach. His own stomach impressed him. Max amazed himself sometimes. He was such a boy, even when he felt otherwise.

He leaned in to look at a picture where a man held a young Lorne on his lap. The man looked familiar, but it took Max a second to realize the man was Quaid. Part of him hadn't truly believed the connection between Quaid and the Judge, but here was proof. Even though Quaid was hardly Quaid in this picture. His body was varnished with a healthy, luminous tan. His hand was full fingered. On the table before Quaid and Lorne a fish had been licked down to its bones. Its ribs curled up from the sucked-white spine and ended in tight, menacing points.

It unnerved Max the way years had snatched color from Quaid's skin, fat from his limbs, life from those eyes. *Poisoned.* Maybe it was true. Quaid's eyes slid toward him and seemed to wink. The hat Lorne wore said VOTE FOR YOUR JUDGE! Lorne's freckled legs were splayed over Quaid's lap. His body was cocked to the side like a ventriloquist doll.

You done yet? said Lorne. He was propped against the door frame, the one that led to the hall that would take them to the big room. We're waiting on you.

Max flinched at the sound of Lorne's voice. He followed Lorne, lead-legged, as if on a leash. As if made to. Max remembered how Lorne had cradled his head in his lap, how he had shoved the hamburger into his mouth and moved his jaw to help him chew the meat. In Max's nostrils, the scent stayed, like an onion skinned and sliced. He heard the slap of his belt hit the floor. He was back on the roof of the asylum. He felt the hot hair of Lorne's calves hook onto his own. Dirt and pebbles embedded in his chin and the caps of his knees. He'd heard a thud as one of Lorne's palms then the other hit the roof beside his shoulders.

You, all right? asked Lorne. You're sweating like a pig going to slaughter.

It is okay, said Max, but his voice shook.

He looked at the back of his hand where a hive had formed. A red welt shaped like a halo.

Lorne and Max joined the boys drinking chocolate milk in the room. A man with a blond beard would tell them about camp.

Max placed his shaking, hive hand in his pocket, where it continued to sweat.

Where's the Judge? Max asked Davis.

Busy, busy, said Davis.

The man in front of them talked about how his life had once been difficult and bad. He did things of the unspeakable variety. The devil took him and made him his own.

Porn addict, whispered Cole, who sat next to Max. Rehabilitated.

The man said, And you know where I was saved? I mean truly, really saved?

That's when the flyers came out. Flyers for camp. A weekend away in the woods.

Give those to your parents if they ask about where you're going, said the man.

Boys, we're about to go to the deep mountains, said Price.

Jesus, said the man. Jesus is there. I can attest to it. Just wait. The Holy Spirit is there. The great Spirit of the Lord.

I'm going, said Cole to Max. You going?

Uh, Max said.

He eyed Lorne.

The team is going, Lorne said. You're going.

A STORM WAS COMING. A hot day had wriggled into the middle of a cold week and the clouds thickened and the air hung still. Even the ozone felt sucked at and inward. No wind. Max stepped off his porch. He watched tadpoles sliver through sludge of a sewage drain in his yard, then started off on a walk.

Miss Jean stepped onto her lawn in full makeup and a bathrobe. Puss the cat ran toward the road. A man brought his dog to shit on the curb. The shit steamed. *Didn't they care it would storm? Couldn't they feel that a strangeness had seized the air?* Max walked past a dead patch of weeds. A mower had severed the necks of winter flowers. Their blooms had turned brain-gray. Max picked them up and the flowers burst back to life. *Ka-pow.* Vanilla. *Boom.* The lilac crunch. Max tried to conjure words for his feeling.

Another smell fumed through the streets. *What was it?* Like a match lit to mildew. Like wetness at the center of a glove. The clouds in the distant hung low and green. A billboard asked—GOT INSURANCE? Max imagined Pan next to him. He tightened his grip around an invisible Pan. There was something easy about Pan's mascara, and the imprint it made on his white sleeve: two crows silhouetted in the sky. It felt good, and it felt temporary. *A cut bouquet.* A knot released in his neck. His jaw loosened for the first time in a week. It smelled like it had already rained. The soil did that. The soil reached out for the rain. Max's chest ached. The muscles around his heart felt sore.

The night before, Max had had a nightmare. In the nightmare, he saw thousands of bodies, purple-skinned and starved, rise from the red Alabama clay and climb down from the trees. Their arms had been tattooed with numbers like the concentration camps in Germany. The bodies filled the entire town. They stood in the middle of roads. They sat on benches. They let their legs dangle from the billboards. Maybe these were the bodies he had never risen. Maybe these were the bodies he had. Max wanted to run from the bodies, but they were everywhere.

One of them crawled down from the roof of the Chicken Shop. It was a football boy. Max felt relieved. Just a football boy. Then there were dozens of football boys. They surrounded him. Then he noticed their faces. Scratched-out mounds of keloid tissue covered the sockets where their eyes had been. Other than their torn-out eyes, the boys seemed fine. They carried on with their days as if they could see fine. They threw the football. They ripped guts from the throat of deer in the field. They aimed their shotguns at the horizon. *Dove,* they said, looking at the earth and not where they fired. Dove. Bang. Dove. Bang.

Max's hand made a gun. His index finger extended and cocked like a trigger. Then the bodies were gone. He touched his own face and felt the slick clump of scars piled up across his eyes, too. He shot up in bed thirsty and scared he was blind.

Now, Max was trying to walk off the feeling, but it struck him. He felt like he was walking over a grave. A thousand graves. A million graves. The trees, even the trees, felt like graves.

Pan had told Max he was scared of his own power, and he was right. Max didn't want to know if he could raise a human from the dead. How could he live with himself? All that responsibility. All that guilt. He couldn't. He needed to believe his abilities had horizons. Max tried to fight off the memories again, but they came for him anyway. Nils died a slow, second death alone inside the earth's crust, his nostrils filling with the smell of soil. His throat raw from screaming. Perhaps he would have torn his vocal cords open from all the screaming. Max saw Nils start to eat himself to survive, gnaw at his own arms until the flesh was hot pulp, hoping that someone would dig him out. What would have killed him first? Hunger or suffocation? Could fear have killed him? Could one die of fear alone? Max had laid his ear to the grass near Nils's tombstone and tried to listen for the screams. He had thought, maybe, he heard a moan come through. Terror had straightened his legs to standing.

But Max had known, even then, that if he told someone his fear, if he dug Nils up himself, all they would find was a dead boy. No drama. No second death. He would have discovered a Nils who died one time in the sterile hospital bed and never came back again.

MAX HAD TO BARGAIN with his mother to allow him to go to camp. He told her he would let her come to church with him when he got back. All she had to do was let him go. His mother studied his face when she dropped him off at the bus. She looked at him as if she were seeing him for the last time. It made Max uneasy, but he hugged her and felt himself age as he comforted her.

It's okay, Mom, he said. Everything is fine.

He towered over her as they stood by the car. Her band of white hair was pinned back into a nest of black with a moonstone barrette. Max watched over her shoulder as the boys filed into the bus across the street. Max had never felt bigger than his mother, but he did then. His parents had never been good at enforcing rules because they never had to. Max had always followed them.

You know, we only want to go to church with you because we love you, his mother said.

When you say we, you mean you, Max said. Dad doesn't care.

Okay. I mean me then.

What if I want something for myself, Max asked. Something that's just mine? Like I said. I tried to explain that.

You sound like a grown-up, said his mother. Almost. I don't know. What if?

That's what I want, said Max.

A cockroach was next to his shoe. It was on its back with its legs curled in. Unalive. Max wondered if he'd ever tell his mother about his power. His curse. He didn't know what to call it in his head. Maybe one day when she was old, he'd tell her. She'd die, and he'd save her and that's how he'd tell her. He could have shown her then. He could have picked up the bug, and she could have watched it crawl up his arm. What stopped him from doing it? She would continue to love him. Her love would reach out to cover him even after everyone else's had receded. But no, Max needed something that was his, like he'd told her.

He watched the dead cockroach. Liquid brown shell. Eyelashes for legs. Why did everyone hate those creatures? Something so little and defenseless. It was so like the world to kill cockroaches.

You think I don't understand what you're going through, his mother said.

She reached out and cupped the back of his neck. She placed her thumb on the swirl of hair at his nape. He flinched her away.

How can you understand? Max asked.

He knew he sounded stupid.

You want your church? she said. Go have your church.

I don't believe in God, Max said, but after he said it, he realized he might.

Just don't lie to yourself, she said. Okay? Promise you'll be truthful with yourself of all people.

She rubbed her temples. Crows landed on either side of her eyes. She, too, suffered from headaches. He placed a hand on her shoulder and let her smile. As the bus pulled out of the parking lot, his mother stayed by her car, watching. She would not leave until he was gone. Out of sight. His watcher. Max turned and saw her diminish through the glass. Her watcher. She receded into the distance, framed by the window. A miniature mother. No bigger than a drawing in a book. A paper dress of a person.

ON THE DRIVE TO CHURCH CAMP, tires kicked up clouds of red dust. The man with the blond beard from the campaign office walked up and down the center aisle of the bus and led them in song. His fingers waved through the air, but he waved out of tune. The song was about dry bones and dead hearts coming back to life. It was about how God's love could find what was dead and call it all back.

Max had trouble singing. He stared out the window instead. The trees on the side of the road looked starved of water even though it had stormed that week. There were miles of dead trees. Their naked branches curled through the air. Their trunks sloughed off long pieces of bark, which were littered like brown ribbons across the swollen roots.

In the middle of the chorus, Max nudged the boy next to him.

What's with all the dead forests? he asked.

The what? the boy said.

The trees. They're dead.

Beats me, he said, then turned back to the game on his phone, his mouth moving around the words:

We call out to dry bones.

Come alive.

Max searched the seats for Wes, but he was not on the bus. He had hoped he would be. They could experience camp for the first time together. Nerves swarmed his stomach. He could not pin down the origin of his nerves. Anxiety or excitement. Maybe both. Lorne sat a few seats ahead, an Alabama cap pulled down over his face. He didn't sing. Each time the boys yelled for the dead souls to come to life, which was often, Max shuddered. Nils in the casket. The poisoned men and women in their caskets. *Dry bones.* He'd never thought of it like that: that this religion was about the dead rising up and coming to life. He wondered if Jesus had known he was going to come back or if it startled him to wake up with his limbs wrapped like a mummy in a dark cave. Maybe he hadn't meant to be a miracle. Sometimes crazy stuff just happened to people. With no good explanation at all.

THE LEAVES IN THE HILL town were devil red. When the bus rolled into camp, the sky tore open and rays shot down as if Jesus were trying to speak to them. That's what the man from the campaign office said; he said, Sweet Jesus knows we're coming down the mountain.

Amen.

The foothills of the Appalachians crammed together in a vague smoky blue. Max followed the way toward a wooden structure. Cole walked in front of him. What he saw: just a brown barn and a couple of two-story cabins and a fire that raged by a river and a still black lake.

Max watched Davis's spine against his thin white sweater as he led the way to the cabin. Once inside, Davis dropped his army duffel and jumped onto his mattress, dirty sneakers still on. He picked the only single that wasn't part of a bunk bed. He jumped a few times in preparation and then did a backflip. He landed on his knees, crooning.

I'm going to land it perfect soon, Germany. Just you wait.

I believe, said Max.

Max threw his backpack onto a bed made with sheets covered in illustrations of praying angels. He'd chosen the top.

Capital of Suriname? Davis asked Max, jumping again, trying to gather momentum.

Of Suriname, said Max. Oh. I don't know.

You heard of it though, right? Small country in South America. Right there on the coast. Poor as fuck-all.

Max nodded. But he had not heard of it.

Paramaribo, Davis sung. *Paramaribooo.* I'm going to visit it when I graduate. I'm going to visit every country in the world, and then I'm coming right back to Alabama, so I can look at all these folks in the face and promise them that they're in the best place on earth. Ain't that right, Germany? Alabama the beautiful.

Max smiled. He pictured Davis walking through the streets of Hamburg, or on a bus like the confident Americans he'd seen. Davis would project the same poise, that buoyant self-assurance Max so wished he had. Davis would dash up the stairs that zigged through the city as if he'd done it a million times and knew exactly where they would take him.

Davis collapsed on the bed, out of breath from his jumping.

He turned his head toward Max. That cocky grin. The pit in his chin like a movie star. His corn-silk hair untangled.

Knox kicked open the door from the adjoining room.

I'm starved almost to death, he said.

Hush your mouth, said Cole. God'll hear you and test you, and we'll have to fast and go without dinner or something.

Strange, Max thought, how this God would punish them for their wanting.

They left the cabin and headed for a barn. Outside, Max's jaw knocked together. He wished for a better jacket. The mountains brought the cold. Max walked into the barn and his eyes fought to adjust. The only light was firelight. Torches lined the walkway from the door to an area in front that looked like a stage. Rope had been tied around piles of hay to hold them together. The piles became rows on which some boys already sat. The piles formed an ascending semicircle that faced the stage. Boys whom Max had never seen rested on the hay, chewed on the hay, stuck hay behind their ears. They must have arrived on another bus from another town. Everyone Max saw was young, except for a small group of adult men at the center of the ring who wore masks.

Max climbed through the pig smell of the barn to the top of the hay with the boys. They sat with their elbows on their knees. Max did not know what would happen. A banjo played, and a small choir of men sung in high voices. Beautiful voices, thought Max. A cottonmouth snake slid across the loose strands of straw at the bottom. Max knew it should scare him, should prove something to him, but it didn't. The snake swam through the ground like it was water.

Minutes passed while the men sung. Maybe an hour. Max grew

tired and the hay under him itched. He felt like sleep could enter him at any minute. He might sleep as he sat. Then the Judge appeared at the door and walked toward the front of the barn. Max's throat didn't feel right. His eyes widened. The Judge was like a magnet that pulled every gaze toward it. He tipped his cowboy hat to the crowd. He didn't wear a mask like the other men.

Max felt like the Judge was whispering just to him, at him. *Look*, the whisper said. *Just look. Just watch.* His black hat glowed holy as a halo. He held a book in his hands and started to sing. The song reached to the rafters of the barn. As if on cue the snake moved toward the men who had formed a circle around the Judge. The Judge reached down to pick up the snake. He held the snake's living body to the air and the head hissed. Then they danced together. The men around him picked up plastic buckets and lifted snakes out of them. They shook the snakes and danced behind the Judge.

That one's got poison in the teeth, said Lorne. But God is on his side.

The Judge walked with the snake held out before him. The snake straightened and stayed rigid in the air. Then the music stopped and so did the Judge. He dropped to his knees.

Hallelujah. God is good, he said.

Amen! said the men. A groan moved through the barn.

Something red came from the Judge's hands. It looked like blood, but it couldn't be blood. Max's heart beat faster. He wiped sweat from his palms onto his shorts. A snake's tail rattled. It sounded like a cymbal, the tinny high-hat on a drum. The Judge held his snake out in front of his chest. It hung from his huge hands. The snake tried to straighten out again. The Judge stood and moved around onstage, bending his knees up and down in a kind of dance, almost trembling. Then the Judge stopped dancing, and he began to tell them, to tell everyone, the story of love.

Max felt hot. So hot. Burning.

Drink this, said Lorne, as if he felt the heat, too.

He handed Max a tin cup, and Max swallowed a liquid that tasted like licorice but also like the back of a dirty hand. *Where did Lorne get the cup?* Max didn't ask. Max swallowed, licked his lips. Something sticky remained on them.

The Judge told of his bad past. Yes. He was lost once. So lost. Snorting pharmaceuticals lost. High on paint fumes lost. Cumming on the chest of cheerleaders bad. Something was missing. A great hole. A hole bigger than any girl or any cigarette or any cold bottle of beer or joyride through the sweet devil of midnight. Max's mind drifted toward Pan and for a moment he was sure that the hole inside of him might be Pan's exact size. When he lay next to Pan, stretched out on the blanket of his yard, his hole felt entirely full. Max wouldn't know where to put anything else, much less something as big as a god.

The boys beside Max rose to their feet. They rose to the tips of their toes as if they might fly away. Max felt delirious. The barn was hot as steam or hell or the place you go before you go to hell. Everyone poured sweat now and it collected in the dander above Max's upper lip and stung his eyes and he went dizzy. *Why dizzy?* He didn't know. He was hoisted up, and his arms slung around the strong shoulders beside him. Then Pan was in front, down near the Judge and Max called out to him. *Pan,* he said—but no sound came out. The Judge turned, and Pan was gone. Pan disappeared, or he was never there to begin with. Max didn't know which. Which witch. *Witch.*

Come down here, son, said the Judge. Come down here, Max. Bring him on down.

Max felt hands on his wings and on his spine, the dry sandpaper tongue of teenage boy palm. They pushed him forward toward the snake and toward the Judge's body where life was winning. No one needed to die just to be shown they could come back to life. Jesus already did that. And who did Pan think Max was? Max took off his shirt because God it was hot, and the Judge placed the snake onto the thick wads of flesh that were sculpted godlike on Max's chest. He was a warrior, and the snake was so cold and so good.

~~~~~

WHEN MAX woke up, the Judge was holding him like he was his baby. They were in the middle of the black lake. Max's thighs crested the water. It felt precious to be held like this. The Judge cradled Max to his chest and held him tight whispering for him to shush. Just shush. He rocked Max back and forth. Max concentrated on how the rocking felt. How it felt to be swayed, gently, carefully, by the arms of another man, held so that he might never fall. He let the water spin and twirl and churn below him, and he thought this was what it felt like right before you became born. The Judge dipped Max's head back into the water. Dunk. Another dunk. It felt refreshing. It felt so clean. Above the Judge's square jaw, a pair of pink lips frowned. His body walked waist deep through the black lake and in Max's eyes millions of stars burned out in the great big universe. Max saw the fire on the edge of the woods. He heard the boys praying. The fire leapt. The Judge whispered a line of words whose meaning fell outside of Max's comprehension.

Max saw the fire leap again. It leapt in a great orange dazzle toward heaven. It leapt with each *Father God* that tumbled from the boys' lips as they prayed loudly for him, for Max. The boys called out for their fathers. They stripped off their dirty flannels and undid the tired blue of their jeans. They prayed. They approached like pack animals— no, like a gathering of disciples—from their spots on the shore of the lake and walked right into the water. Their backs ached, and their wrists were sore and every one of them had tendinitis. Max knew their pain because it was his pain. He knew their pain in a way he could never know Pan's pain. He knew their pain because it was Max who'd bruised his knees and broken his fingers alongside them, just like it was they who had caused blood to burst from his nose.

The boys moved through the water as if the water, this lake, had the power to heal every one of them. And Max thought—*Well, I'm here, well, I'm here in the water with my hands, so maybe, just maybe, the healing will happen.* But for him to heal them, first they'd have to die, and Max was done with death. A comet carved its way through the night, and he decided it was a sign this was where he should be. He wondered if he could stuff something else in the Pan-shaped hole inside of him. He wondered if God could fit any hole. If he had the ability to shrink and expand to the proportion of his pain.

Max filled his mouth with water and let it flow from his nose and let urine go from his penis as he floated. He was done with healing. Finished. He was not a prophet. He was someone who had to be saved just like anyone else.

A mayfly drifted dead on the lake. Its paper-thin wings were drenched and broken. Max picked up the bug and held out his palm so he could watch it fly away back into the night, but nothing happened. No sweetness flooded into his mouth. Nothing moved the bug. It stayed crumpled and wrecked. He dropped it back into the water, where it drowned. Lorne floated up beside him. Lorne's eyes were wet, and his lips were blue. He let his eyes follow the entire length of Lorne's body, from bony feet to neck. He wanted to reach out and touch Lorne on the cheek. To slap him.

Lorne made a church steeple with his fingers and said, We've got to put an end to the evilness that lurks in our presence.

He said, We've got to kick the devil out of him or the devil's coming for us, too.

MAX HAD A HEADACHE FOR days after the lake. It haloed everything in a neon blue. He stumbled through school reaching for something to hold on to: a door, a wrist, a waist. He fell to the ground only to get up again. He limped when he walked. Water still sat in his ears. He wondered if the water had drowned his sin, extinguished his power like Billie did with the cigarette she snuffed out in her mouth. Max had gotten what he wanted. His curse was gone. How could he explain it? It was magic. If these boys weren't witches, then what was a witch?

Two nights after he'd returned from the lake, he cleared the dinner table and told his mother he would wash the dishes. He filled the sink with hot water and squirted a stream of soap into it. In plunged his hands. They felt lighter than they ever had, like he'd gotten a cast removed. He needed to relearn his mobility. He dropped a glass on the floor and watched it shatter. Its broken side bared jagged clear teeth at him. He had the desire to step his sockless foot onto the glass. He slammed his knuckles into the sink. An accident. He didn't know how to not bang his hand into something. Max looked at the back of it. Bruises darkened his pinkies and blended into the veins strung through his skin.

Baby, his mother said. The pull of her energy beside him at the counter. You okay? Did something happen? Did something happen at camp?

I'm fine, said Max. He tried to smile. Show teeth. Lift the corners of his mouth. He coughed and turned back to the sink.

With his powers gone, the headache, too, should have fled him. But it clung to the edges of everything. He burped. Up rose a dark orange feeling that sat raw in the throat. He feared that the lake had not drowned out his sin, but that his sin was now sealed inside him.

He did not feel free but trapped inside this body that couldn't do anything to save itself. His body, he felt, would die. The world would erode him, like it eroded everything. Maybe this is what being human felt like. The revelation blew through him and filled him with wind.

A body is not yours forever, Max thought. *It is lent to you and the earth will take it back.*

Max pictured all the bodies decomposing in the ground. In graveyards everywhere, bodies slept in different levels of fester and rot. He saw an ear sprouting from a garden, a corroded eye rolling across the brown back of a hill, an arm reaching out like a root under the base of a tree.

You're a waste.

He should have gone with Pan to the graveyard.

Hope drained into his feet. Pan had been right about him. Max hadn't used his power for anything good, and now it was gone. It had been taken from him. God had given him a chance to heal, and he had dashed it.

Max picked up a plate flecked with gravy, stained with the dark red of a raw steak. He scrubbed. Lorne's words rose to the surface of his thoughts, *We've got to kick the devil out of him.*

Is that what the Judge thought he'd done to Max, kick the devil out? If this was saved, Max didn't want it. He wanted to go back and climb from the Judge's arms and swim toward the fire instead.

MAYBE IF MAX WANTED IT bad enough, he could will the power back. Maybe he could reclaim it.

Magic is only real if you believe, Pan had said. *Magic only works if you believe.*

On a morning run, slow and sluggish and worse than any run he'd done, Max saw a run-over deer on the road. He laid his hands on the cold body to test himself. Flies roamed the open spaces of the deer's skin. Max held his hands to the deer's fur for a long time, stoked it, even kissed it, but the deer stayed dead. All that came was another headache. His mouth tasted like a handful of soil. Not sweetness as in life, but bitter as in death. That afternoon, he picked up a moth by its lifeless wing. Crushed coffee beans chalked up his tongue. No honey, no sugar. Max wanted to know why he had been imbued with power only to have it taken away. Why had he been chosen, and who had been the one to choose? A god or a devil and did it matter?

A poet does not make the poem, his Literature teacher in Germany had told his class. Poems exist in the world and on the back of the wind. A poem comes hurling through space. If the poet doesn't catch it, if a poet isn't listening close enough, the poem moves right through them and goes to someone else. Someone who will write it down.

I lost the poem, Max thought. *I didn't listen.*

IN FRONT OF HER OFFICE, the guidance counselor hung a clip-board with a sign-up sheet. Students could schedule an appointment to meet about college applications. Max scrawled his name in lean capital letters under someone named Mikey Sunman. The pencil in his hand kept slipping. His grip was still wrong. A blue cross grew from the bottom edge of the sign-up sheet. Max fought the urge to color the cross black.

College. Max had never considered college until now. He'd never considered much else but the moment he stood in or the moments from which he fled. The power had done that to him, he realized. His power pinned him to the present and to the past. The future had been a thing he ignored.

Max stood in the hall. In two years, he would be in college. Would he go somewhere in America? Would he return to Germany? His parents only planned to stay in Alabama for three years. Suddenly, that number sounded infinitesimal. A dot chewed out by the great jaw of the universe. Max wanted to stay, he realized. Maybe not in Alabama, but here. *In America.* Max pictured Pan at college somewhere in New England, a place he couldn't visualize, though he did conjure images of cardigans, fall leaves, fresh espresso. He thought of Billie in California drinking strawberry juice in the sun. Davis and Lorne would enroll at the University of Alabama. Max pictured himself with them, the easier road. He could meet a woman, fall in love, get married, have a child. *A child.* Max touched the open grate of a stranger's locker. *No.* A paper heart had been taped to the door. LUH U said the heart.

Max pictured himself in New England with Pan. He pictured them walking through campus drinking chai lattes. Pan was older, and his long hair was tied back in a bun. Max had a thick blond beard and an arm draped over Pan's shoulder. Pan might find a way to love him again. Max spread his bruised hands into the blank space in front of him. He held them up and studied them. They shook slightly, as if he was going through a withdrawal. He dropped his hands by his side and let them hang. He wondered if touching Pan with uncharmed palms would feel different. In his mind, he placed a finger to Pan's pulse. He might recoil and think, *The magic's gone.*

Pan did not appear in Physics. Hadn't been there for days. The seat beside Max was empty. Max checked his phone to see, but no messages were received. To know that Pan missed him could have been enough.

ON HIS WAY TO LUNCH, Max saw Glory and Wes at the end of the hall under a hunter green pendant that said God's Way. The pendant was suspended from the ceiling by thin metal rods. Max slipped behind a locker and watched them. They were out of earshot so he could not hear their conversation. Max grabbed onto a padlock that hung from a locker. The cold steel anchored him. Glory was animated, the one doing most of the talking, and Wes shook his head if he didn't want to listen. He seemed annoyed. When Wes tried to take a step back, Glory grabbed his wrist, and Wes let her hold on to him. She drew his face close and whispered something. Then Glory shoved him and laughed. Wes laughed, too, but they both still seemed upset.

Max wondered if Wes had ever been baptized. If he knew what happened at camp and if it was Glory who had held him back from going or if it had been his own decision not to go all along.

Glory turned in Max's direction, and he couldn't duck away in time.

She raised a hand.

Max, she called.

Wes waved. Sup, dude.

Max knew he was interrupting something private. He felt like an intruder. He wanted Glory to whisper into his ear whatever she'd said to Wes. He could tell they didn't want company. They glanced at each other. Sibling code that no one else could decipher. Max found himself walking toward them anyway.

Wes's eyes were red. Had he been crying? Max couldn't imagine Wes doing that.

Dude, I'm late for lunch.

Wes saluted them and walked away, leaving Max standing next to Glory. Her locker was open. The door cracked to reveal a clutter of paper and books. Taped to the wall inside was a painting of the cosmos. A swirl of candied constellations.

I'm sorry, Max said. Did Wes leave because I came?

Glory shrugged. She reached out and touched the cross on his necklace.

I would have told you not to go, she said. But Wes said you wouldn't have listened anyway.

She left her fingertips on his chest for a second too long. Max felt his teeth begin to kick against one another. What did Glory know?

MAX HAD HEARD THAT INTUITION was a muscle one could train to become stronger, like a bicep or an abdominal. He could develop the ability to answer questions before they were asked. He might learn to hand his mother the milk before she knew she wanted it. There were people who held knowledge in their mouths that addressed the hopes people kept only in their minds. For six nights, Max called Pan's phone, and every night, the phone rang and rang. No one answered. On the seventh night, Pan's mother picked up.

She cleared her throat like *you've done something wrong*, but her voice held a warm and sympathetic hand out toward him.

He isn't here, pumpkin. I'll tell him you tried to call.

Max's intuition purred beneath his rib. He felt Pan on the other side of the static.

THE BOYS ONLY WANTED TO TEST THEM.

Freak the witch out.

Chase the devil from their bones.

Clean out the sin.

That was what Davis said, frightened, yes, Max could hear he was frightened, when he answered Davis's call. His panic was as hard and real as the teeth rooted in Max's mouth. Max sat up in bed. Black middle of the night.

Just don't do anything else, Max said. Just do not move.

Come fast then, said Davis. We can't do nothing much longer.

The balloon in Max's chest expanded with each breath, pushed against the sides of him, made him feel like he could float away or lose touch with the ground under his toes. Just the night before, Pan was safe in his trailer.

He told us you could fix it, said Davis. What does he mean fix it? What does he mean?

Max took his parents' car keys from the loop by the front door. He'd never driven in Alabama, but his father had taught him how in Germany. Adrenaline led him down the front steps into the driveway. Adrenaline opened the car door. He drove out toward the field where he had first seen Pan run off with Lorne, where he tried to gather enough lust to desire Billie, where he had waded into the polluted pond and healed everything he could touch. His palms slipped from the wheel. They landed in his lap again and again. Sweaty, useless things. The tires yelled when he cusped the shoulder of the road. He had to swerve back to the center line.

Once in the field, the fence came into view. A body was propped up against it. There was Pan's mother's car—the burnt orange paint and the rust streaking up the side. The boys huddled around, hunched over, walked in circles that went nowhere. Max drove toward the scene, holding the slacken body in the headlight's eye. Max turned off the engine. He stepped out into the field. The boys held their phones like lanterns outstretched toward Max and then toward the body, and in the white light Max saw that it was not Pan, but Lorne roped to the wooden post. Lorne's face was no longer his face but a hot pulp of skin that had been pulled off in strings like the paint on the front door of the insane asylum. His lips were not lips but red strands that dripped down his chin. His ear was a folded, scary color that an ear should never be. His face was like every hue Max had ever seen the night contain.

A tin cup stood in the dirt beside him. It looked like the same cup Max drank from in the barn. He tasted the liquid when he looked at the cup. It washed through him as if he'd sipped from it again. Sharp and tinted and ready to take.

Lorne tried to pull his face off after he drank the poison, said Cole, voice trembling.

Lorne's face spilled the inside of him out. There was Pan standing off to the side. His white Walmart dress touched its hem to the mud. He held his own cheeks. He'd been crying and was still crying.

Pan. Max tried to focus on Lorne, but his attention drifted to Pan. Pan would not lift his eyes to Max. But Max felt Pan look without looking. The look was psychospiritual. The look said: *help.*

We found them together, Davis said. He was out of breath. Found them together, doing things, so we made them drink poison to get their sin out. To test if God was in them. And then Lorne went crazy.

Foundthemtogether.

Davis's voice caught in his throat. He coughed. Couldn't release the word.

Max placed his hands over his eyes. Pan thought Max could save Lorne. That's why he'd had Davis call him. Pan didn't know his powers had left him. Pan sat down in the mud and held his legs to his chest and rocked back and forth. Max felt snakes in his stomach. They swam in circles. The back of his hands looked up at him from the place on his knees where they steadied him. They gripped his thighs as he wrenched over to vomit and catch his breath and vomit. His vomit was pine needle green as if to say he, too, was of this world. Max, too, was the land. He stood up like a normal boy with no power at all.

Lorne did not see Max because Lorne was not there. He was unconscious, or he was gone. If Max were to turn and walk away, Lorne would never know. But Pan rocked and shook beside Lorne like a ghost who could not be killed. Pan would observe Max's failure. Pan's trust in Max had brought him there. He expected Max to move toward Lorne, take his broken face in his hands and heal him. If Max walked away now, Pan would never speak to him again. It would be the same as if he'd killed Lorne himself.

I'm broken, Max wanted to tell Pan. *I can't do it.*

Pan would tell him to try. Try to bring back Lorne, who dragged him across the roof in his dream. Bring back Lorne, who Pan loved like Max had loved Nils: wholly and completely like only a child knows how to love. *His first husband.* Price had collapsed on the ground and was supine gazing at the stars as if they could take him. A terrible scene, something Max wanted to wish himself away from. Cole leaned against a dogwood tree, held a wound on his neck, and hummed a song.

This, too, was the boys' destiny. Their arms knew how to dig holes that fit a body, how to remove the skin of a person still alive. How to loop a noose around a neck and hitch it up in a tree. They knew how to burn flesh, how to withhold water and food. They knew what part of their clothing would make the best whip, which part could make a weapon. Max felt it then, what Pan had told him about the energy, the lesions in the air, the blackening. He saw their jaws grinding. He saw the power of every bad thing that had been done before them on this land stand up inside of them and say: *yes.*

Lorne bit Cole, Davis said. He went crazy and tried to bite us all. We thought he could drink it and be fine. We thought God would save him. We thought Pan—

He couldn't finish his sentence, because Pan had been the one to swallow the poison and survive and no words could explain it.

A hole had been dug into the ground next to the fence. The hole was big enough for a burial. The red dirt let out its earthworms.

No one can know, said Davis, what's happened here.

Davis walked in a slow circle. The shovel he carried leaned against his shoulder. It was the shovel from the back of Pan's car, the shovel they would have used to use to dig up the graves. The shovel Pan held when Max watched him grow older right before his eyes under the sodium lights in the parking lot of the cemetery.

Max saw that it was not a rope, but a red football jersey that held Lorne to the fence. His arms were extended like the cross Max wore beneath his shirt. His wrists were bound tight. Max wondered if Lorne had ever wanted to hurt Pan or if he only wanted to love him, and the hurting had just happened. He wondered if Lorne had ever done a truly bad thing like leave a boy in a coffin buried alive or drag a boy to the edge of a roof and force himself inside. Max knelt at the foot of Lorne's freckled body, but he didn't touch him, because he was not sure he could do that, touch him, in front of everyone. If he did and Lorne woke up, what would they say? What would it mean? *The end of everything.* Would they descend on Max, too? A witch, in their presence, the devil among them? Would they force the poison to his lips? Could his body take it again?

Max felt Pan behind him. He felt Pan step closer. He didn't have to look to know it. Max stared at Lorne, at the dangled skin that used to be his face, and he prayed that Lorne moved without his hands. Then he prayed that his hands could move him. Max lifted up his palms and clasped them in front of his heart. He felt the boys gather behind him, ready to tear Lorne down from the post where they had bound him. He felt Pan's belief radiate and radiate. *Magic only works if you believe.* Max dug his knees into the rocks so that it hurt. *Good. Make it hurt.* He stared up at Lorne and said, *Come back*, and he didn't know, he still didn't know, if he would be able to make it so.

He reached out and felt heat. He placed a palm on Lorne's thigh, and he thought he sensed the body twitch, the leg kick. He heard bees, and he tasted wasps. The wasps meant a bad life. They meant tied to a fence by a father. His hands could do nothing. They fell from Lorne's thigh. Gravity pulled them off. Nothing moved through Max. Death rattled against his human body, the body with no alchemy or magic left. Life pushed against his skin, but it couldn't get in. Then Lorne's leg twitched, and Max placed his hands upon Lorne again. Max felt Pan's belief reach toward him. His belief circled him and Lorne. It moved on the margins as Max kept his hands against Lorne's twitching body. Max held Pan's belief inside of him. It rose up like a poem. He would catch the poem. When Max opened his mouth, he almost expected hornets to pour out.

ACKNOWLEDGMENTS

This book, my writing, exists because of the friendships, experiences, and works of art that have shaped me. I am grateful for the people I have encountered along this journey through literature and life, especially the following:

For my agent, Monika Woods, for believing in this novel from the beginning and for seeing what it could become. Thank you for the notes, the conversations, and the brilliance you shed onto each page.

For my editor, Gina Iaquinta, for reading each line with care and openness. This book is better, is more fully itself, because of your time. Thank you to Peter Miller, Nick Curley, and the whole team at Liveright for championing this book and for helping to shepherd it into the world.

Thank you to Tom Bissell, Charles D'Ambrosio, Rachel Kushner, Jon Raymond, Michelle Glazer, Renee Gladman, and to all of my teachers over the years. I am especially grateful to Leni Zumas, mentor and friend, for challenging me to make familiar things strange and for showing me how to listen to the sound of every sentence.

For the places and organizations that generously supported me and gave me precious time to write, think, and create: the MacDowell Colony, Caldera Arts, the Vermont Studio Center, Tin House, and the Fulbright Program. For the MFA Program at Portland State University. Thank you for investing in my process of creativity and artmaking.

For Maaike Muntinga, Jamie Carr, Kristin Dombek, Daniel Cecil, Jessica Walter, Mikkel Rosengaard, and Kevin Sampsell, for reading entire drafts of this book in earlier forms. For your patience, time, and brilliance. Thank you to Jeff Buckingham for your knowledge of high school science and to Chris Horton for the passages you read with care.

To my community of wise writers, of whom I am in awe, especially

T Kira Madden, Kimberly King Parsons, Kate Jayroe, Annabel Graham, Tomas Moniz, MJ Kaufman, Jane Lewty, Anna Arov, Jing-Jing Lee, Alma Mathijsen, Leah Dieterich, and all the others.

Thank you to the writers whose work has shaped me in profound ways. Especially Anne Carson, James Baldwin, Dorothy Allison, Alison Bechdel, Susan Sontag, Claudia Rankine, Clarice Lispector, Frank O'Hara, Roland Barthes, Audre Lorde, Maggie Nelson, Lynda Barry, Eileen Myles, Simone de Beauvoir, Michelle Tea, Alexander Chee, Garth Greenwell, and Melissa Febos. Thank you for writing my canon.

For Chelsea Bieker, my family and my fire. For sharing my dream of writing and having the same conversations with me over and over. For being the Duris to my Dennis. Thank you for being my unconditional, my constant.

To Matthew Zaccari, my Der. For the tarot cards you pulled on your bed in Brooklyn. For that night in Charleston, in my backyard, when you stood on the milk crate. You have the kindest heart of anyone I know. Thank you for giving me space inside it.

For Lisa Meersman and the most romantic of friendships. For embodying community and empathy. For holding space for every story, every moment, every laugh, and every gasp.

And for all of my dear friends, my chosen family, my community of queer people, thank you. To Emily Kingan and Zeyah Rogé, for letting me live in Narnia and showing me the truest kind of love. To Megan Watson, for pointing out the light where the trees meet the sky. To Katie Peterson, for holding space for me on the steps of Maybank so many years ago. To Timothy Pakron and your booming laugh that I can hear from your kitchen in New Orleans. To Sara Sutter, dearest Scorpio, who I would languish with any time under any summer sun. To Marc Tobia and David Nokovic and everyone who I haven't named but who I hold a candle for in my heart.

For my father, Jerry Hudson, who showed me how to fall in love with literature. For reading me *To Kill a Mockingbird* out loud from your chair in the living room. For writing stories with me in notebooks. For being Alabama.

Lastly, and most importantly, for my mother, Carmen Hudson, for your love of imagination. For your curiosity and quick laugh. For answering the phone whenever I call, wherever you are. For wanting me to build that treehouse. For believing that one day I would.

BOYS OF ALABAMA

Genevieve Hudson

READING GROUP GUIDE

BOYS OF ALABAMA

Genevieve Hudson

DISCUSSION QUESTIONS

1. Discuss your feelings and opinions about Max and how they changed over the course of the story. Did you like him? Were you "rooting for him"?

2. Max is an outsider, allowing the author to portray Alabama/America through his eyes. How did this affect your experience of the novel?

3. Why do you think the author titled this novel *Boys of Alabama?*

4. Do you see yourself in any of Max's thoughts, feelings, or experiences? How so?

5. Why do you think the author began the book with this prefatory quote by Clarice Lispector (*Hour of the Star*): "She believed in angels, and, because she believed, they existed"?

6. Describe Max's relationship with his mother versus his relationship with his father. How are these relationships different, and how do they evolve over the course of the novel?

7. The main characters are male, but occupy different points on the spectrum of sexuality and outness. Talk about this book through the prisms of gender and sexuality. How does the author write these characters so they feel real?

8. Did the book make you smile or laugh? When and how?

9. This book feels natural and real, even though its setting is very specific and unusual. At the same time, Max can resurrect animals and perform other supernatural acts. This duality invokes the genre of magical realism. How does this novel mix the magical with the realism?

10. Another genre this novel invokes is Southern Gothic. How does the book fit or not fit that genre?

11. What books, movies, or television series does this book remind you of and why?

12. Why and how is Max drawn to the Judge and his church?

13. "You of all people should know that there's more to this world than we can see," Pan tells Max (p. 155). What are the different forms of spirituality in the novel? Compare and contrast.

14. How did *Boys of Alabama* fit your views and impressions of the South and Alabama?